David Goodis's nihilistic portraits of the underbelly of urban society in the mid twentieth century, and his psychological studies of the lost, the lonely, the depraved, are widely considered to be on a par with those of Jim Thompson. His first crime novel, *Dark Passage* (1946), was the basis for the acclaimed film noir of the same title, starring Humphrey Bogart and Lauren Bacall. Other notable titles include *Down There* (filmed as *Shoot The Piano Player*), *Street Of The Lost*, *The Burglar*, *Moon in the Gutter*, and *Nightfall*.

Robert Polito is the author of *Savage Art: A Biography of Jim Thompson*, which received the National Book Critics Circle Award in biography, and the editor of *Crime Novels: American Noir of the 1930s and 1940s* and *Crime Novels: American Noir of the 1950s*. He directs the Graduate Writing Program at the New School in New York City.

STREET
OF NO
RETURN

Street of No Return

a novel by David Goodis

with a new introduction by Robert Polito

published by:
Millipede Press, Lakewood, Colorado

This is a Millipede Press Book
Published by Millipede Press
2565 Teller Court, Lakewood, Colorado 80214

First published in 1954 by Fawcett Publications, Inc.

ISBN 978-1-933618-22-7 (pbk.: alk. paper)
ISBN 978-1-933618-23-4 (hc.: alk. paper)

Printed in Canada on acid-free paper.
10   9   8   7   6   5   4   3   2   1

May 2007
www.millipedepress.com

–Contents–

–Introduction–

Among classic American noir novelists from Dashiell Hammett, James Cain, and Kenneth Fearing through Jim Thompson, Patricia Highsmith, and Chester Himes, David Goodis (1917-1967) appears to be the figure always most in need of reclamation, his books drifting out of print, his status shadowy, ever elusive. This predicament proves especially puzzling as his sly, resonant titles – *Dark Passage, Of Missing Persons, Street of the Lost, The Moon in the Gutter, Black Friday, Street of No Return, The Wounded and the Slain, Down There,* and *Fire in the Flesh* – distill into lyric epithets an entire iconic noir cityscape, and sentence-by-sentence, I would argue, Goodis is our most crafty and elegant crime stylist. Noir is characteristically a language of objects, places, and names, an idiom that in a few bluff words summons worlds. Listen to the opening sentence of Cain's *The Postman Always Rings Twice*: "They threw me off the hay truck about noon." Thompson's *The Killer Inside Me*: "I'd finished my pie and was having a second cup of coffee when I saw him." William Lindsay Gresham's *Nightmare Alley*: "Stan Carlisle stood well back from the entrance of the canvas enclosure, under the blaze of a naked light bulb, and watched the geek." But noir language just as distinctively proceeds by chipping away at the world and itself until there's only a vanishing distress signal from a void. Early on in *Dark Passage* (1946) Goodis advanced a vernacular prose of rococo repeated phrases that limn, then all but erase his characters, here, for instance, mournful Vincent Parry and his disappointed wife Gert:

> He began to remember the days of work, the day he had started there, how difficult it was at first, how hard he had tried, how he had taken a correspondence course in statistics shortly after his marriage, hoping he could get a grasp on statistics and ultimately step up to forty-five a week as a statistician. But the correspondence course gave him more questions than answers and finally he had to give it up. He remembered the night he wrote the letter telling them to stop sending the mimeographed sheets. He showed the letter to Gert and she told him he would never get anywhere. She went out that night. He remembered he hoped she would never come back and he was afraid she would never come back because there was something about her that got him at times and he wished there was something about him that got her. He knew there was nothing about him that got her and he wondered why she didn't pick herself up and walk out once and for all. She was always talking in terms of tall bony men with high cheekbones and hollow cheeks and very tall. He was bony and very thin and he had high cheekbones and hollow cheeks but he wasn't tall. He was really a miniature of what she really wanted. And because she couldn't get a permanent hold on the genuine she figured she might as well stay with the miniature.

Goodis would reprise these reiterative, claustrophobic

inflections for *Down There* (1956). But en route, by the time of *Street of No Return* (1954) and his other Gold Medal and Lion novels of the early 1950s, particularly *The Burglar* (1953) and *Black Friday* (1954), he stripped down his echo chamber style into spare, desolate phrases no less cunning or confining. Listen now as the three indistinguishable – at first – winos emerge out of Philadelphia's Tenderloin near the start of *Street of No Return*:

"We need a drink," one said. "We need a drink and that's all there is to it."

"Well, we won't get it sitting here."

"We won't get it standing up, either," the first one said. He was middle-aged and tall and very skinny and they called him Bones. He gazed dismally at the empty bottle between his legs and said, "It needs cash, and we got no cash. So it don't matter whether we sit or stand or move around. The fact remains we got no cash."

"You made that statement an hour ago," said the other man who had spoken. "I wish you'd quit making that statement."

"Well, it's true."

"I know it's true, but I wish you'd quit repeating it. What's the use of repeating it?"

"If we talk about it long enough," Bones said, "we might do something about it."

"We won't do anything," the other man said. "We'll just sit here and get more thirsty."

Bones frowned. Then he took a deep breath as though he were about to say something important. And then he said, "I wish we had another bottle."

"I wish to hell you'd shut up," the other man said. He was a short bulky bald man in his early forties and his name was Phillips. He had lived here on Skid Row for more than twenty years and had the red raw Tenderloin complexion that is unlike any other complexion and stamps the owner as strictly a flophouse resident.

"We gotta get a drink," Bones said. "We gotta find a way to get a drink."

"I'm trying to find a way to keep you quiet," Phillips said. "Maybe if I hit you on the head you'll be quiet."

"That's an idea," Bones said seriously. "At least if you knock me out I'll be better off. I won't know how much I need a drink." He leaned forward to offer his head as a target. "Go on, Phillips, knock me out."

Philips turned away from Bones and looked at the third man who sat there along the wall. Phillips said, "You do it, Whitey. You hit him."

"Whitey wouldn't do it," Bones said. "Whitey never hits anybody."

"You sure about that?" Phillips murmured. He saw that Whitey was not listening to the talk and he spoke to Bones as though Whitey weren't there.

If *Dark Passage* and *Down There* recall, say, Gertrude Stein, *Street of No Return* suggests Celine, or Beckett. In fact, Goodis' trio of tramps chatter and wait and go nowhere like exiles from a lost Beckett play with a bottle assuming the role of the slippery Godot. As so often in Goodis, oblique strategies, along the lines of Whitey's silence here, animate and stagger the narrative. During this same chapter he evokes a full-tilt race riot that Bones, Phillips, and Whitey overhear from some three dark blocks away, but do not see. Or later Whitey listens out of sight on a basement staircase as Gerardo, leader of the Puerto Rican gang around River Street, is pummeled by the "strong-arm specialists" Chop and Bertha, the scene a vivid mash of table talk, blows, howls, and pleas, but absolutely no visual cues about the participants at all.

Street of No Return focuses two interlocking stories —
Bones, Phillips, and Whitey's search for a drink, and then,
inside that story, Whitey's reluctant search into his own
obsessive and violent past. A famous band singer, with
something of the "small lean" physique and phosphorescent
swing-set appeal of early Frank Sinatra, before his love
for Celia, an ethereal dancer and prostitute, and a vicious
beating by the minions of her racketeer common law
husband, Sharkey, devastated his career, Whitey joins such
improbable but heartbreaking fallen Goodis virtuosos as
Eddie, the former Carnegie Hall pianist turned saloon
entertainer in *Down There,* and Hart, once a wealthy artist,
now appraising art for a heist outfit while he evades a murder
rap, in *Black Friday.*

Whitey (aka Eugene Lindell) is among the most idio-
syncratic and complex of Goodis' inventions. From the
outset, as he stares into his own reflection in an empty wine
jug — "The curved glass showed him a miniature of himself, a
little man lost in the emptiness of a drained bottle" — he seems
only numb, all his talk and actions performed "mechanically"
or "automatically." Goodis compares Whitey to a ruined
machine: "There was a dragging, weak clanking sound like
the useless noise of stripped gears, and he knew it came from
inside his chest. He had the feeling that all the flesh inside
was stripped and burned out." Whitey so wishes to be left
alone that he would rather turn himself over to the police
than respond to questions a new acquaintance, Jones Jarvis,
puts to him. "I'm tired of breathing," he says to Jarvis; and
then he says to himself, "No use continuing the masquerade...
The truth is buddy, you really don't give a damn, you'd just
as soon be out of it."

Yet this broken cipher recurrently charms himself out of
violent encounters, whether with Gerardo or Lieutenant
Pertnoy of the Clayton Street Police Station, and despite

insistent threats refuses to confess to a crime he didn't commit. At once fearless and incorrigible, he starts a small revolution in the cellblock, and thwarts a convoluted plot to incite a race riot on River Street. Goodis is especially deft at etching Whitey's monomania – his fixation on a fresh bottle, his tenacity at trailing Chop and Bertha after they resurface along Skid Row, his seven-year obsession with Celia. Jones Jarvis recalls hearing Gene Lindell, "the lad with the million-dollar voice," on the radio:

Singing from 'way up high on the moon an 'way down deep in the sea. High and low and high again, and it was a voice that made you high when you heard it, happy high and sad high, and you hadda close your eyes, you didn't wanna see a goddam thing, just sit there and listen to that singing. You knew you'd never heard a voice like that in all your born days. And then them bobby-soxers started yelling and screaming and you felt like doing the same. That voice did things to you, went into you so deep it made you get the feeling you hadda come out of yourself and fly up and away from where your feet were planted. So next day I walked into a music store and all the loot I saved was shoved across the counter. "Gene Liddell," I said. "Gimme his records." The clerk said, 'Sorry mister. We're all sold out.' A few days later I tried again, and this time he had just one in stock. I took it home and played it and played it, and for weeks I went on playing that record and the jitterbugs would come in and forget to chew their bubble gum, only thing they could do was stand there with their mouths open and get hit between their eyes with that voice. They'd forget to move their feet. They were jitterbugs but they couldn't jitter because that voice took hold of them and paralyzed them. That was what it did. It was that kind of voice.

Then Jarvis invokes Whitey's voice after Chop and Bertha worked him over:

> "Your voice," Jones said. "The way you can't talk above a whisper. As if you got a rupture in your throat. As it's all torn apart in there."
>
> Again Whitey looked at the floor. The grin was gone now and he didn't know what was on his face. He opened his mouth to say something and he tried to get the sound past his lips and nothing came out.

The "rupture" in Whitey's voice is just the most corporeal emblem for all the blocked, shattered lives in *Street of No Return*. Celia emerges as at least as vacant and lost as Whitey, and for all their frantic motion Chop, Bertha, and Sharkey sound as dead-ended as the original three winos. Sharkey mooning about Celia is not only Whitey's enemy, but also his double:

> "Look, I'll put it this way," Sharkey said, his smile very gentle, his voice soft and soothing. "My main interest in life is taking care of her. It's the only real enjoyment I get. I just wanna take care of her. If she was in a wheelchair I'd spend all my time wheeling her around. If she was flat on her back I'd stay in the room with her day and night. You get the picture."

The past and present of the novel will converge in the Philadelphia race riots, but *Street of No Return* arranges not so much a plot as a succession of astonishing, intermittently surreal spaces: the lights and noises of the Tenderloin against the black vacuum of Hellhole; the chaotic Police Station, full of "sounds he'd never heard in any station house, or even in the alcoholic wards of municipal hospitals"; the "network of winding alleys" that Gerardo guides Whitey through until they reach a rickety dwelling crammed with sleeping families and weapons; the spilled ash cans, smashed glass, and "asphalt ribboned with bloodstains." The boldest scenes mix familiar novelistic naturalism and a sort of pulpy surrealism — Whitey's genial dinner with Sharkey after the gangster catches him at the train station as he is about to depart with Celia; Jones Jarvis' peppy music fan palaver for the artist formerly known as Eugene Lindell; and the conversation in the back of a police car where Lieutenant Taggert calls Lieutenant Pertnoy "a freak" because "Once a week he gives a local whore ten dollars to tie his wrists and bind his eyes and put him in the closet for an hour." For *Street of No Return* Goodis devised a snaky diction, at once fantastic and matter-of-fact. Here objects tend to speak. A bottle, a blackjack, a window, a train, even Hellhole itself. "No sirree, the Hellhole said to Captain Kinnard of the Thirty-seventh District, this is our boy Whitey and we won't letcha have him...It wasn't anyone's voice and yet Whitey could almost hear it talking. He began to have the feeling a lot was going to happen before morning."

Although, as Whitey senses, "a lot was going to happen," and it does, *Street of No Return* tracks an elegant, convulsive circle, at once a resolution and an impasse, and of course he winds up back on the same corner with Bones and Phillips where he began. "Well? Shall we go," Vladimir asks Estragon at the conclusion of *Waiting for Godot*. "Yes, let's go," Estragon replies. But as Beckett's final stage direction reads, "They do not move."

Robert Polito

Street of No Return

-One-

There were three of them sitting on the pavement with their backs against the wall of the flophouse. It was a biting cold night in November and they sat there close together trying to get warm. The wet wind from the river came knifing through the street to cut their faces and get inside their bones, but they didn't seem to mind. They were discussing a problem that had nothing to do with the weather. In their minds it was a serious problem, and as they talked their eyes were solemn and tactical. They were trying to find a method of obtaining some alcohol.

"We need a drink," one said. "We need a drink and that's all there is to it."

"Well, we won't get it sitting here."

"We won't get it standing up, either," the first one said. He was middle-aged and tall and very skinny and they called him Bones. He gazed dismally at the empty bottle between his legs and said, "It needs cash, and we got no cash. So it don't matter whether we sit or stand or move around. The fact remains we got no cash."

"You made that statement an hour ago," said the other man who had spoken. "I wish you'd quit making that statement."

"Well, it's true."

"I know it's true, but I wish you'd quit repeating it. What's the use of repeating it?"

"If we talk about it long enough " Bones said, "we might do something about it."

"We won't do anything," the other man said. "We'll just sit here and get more thirsty."

Bones frowned. Then he took a deep breath as though he were about to say something important. And then he said, "I wish we had another bottle."

"I wish to hell you'd shut up," the other man said. He was a short bulky bald man in his early forties and his name was Phillips. He had lived here on Skid Row for more than twenty years and had the red raw Tenderloin complexion that is unlike any other complexion and stamps the owner as strictly a flophouse resident.

"We gotta get a drink," Bones said "We gotta find a way to get a drink."

"I'm trying to find a way to keep you quiet," Phillips said. "Maybe if I hit you on the head you'll be quiet."

"That's an idea," Bones said seriously. "At least if you knock me out I'll be better off. I won't know how much I need a drink." He leaned forward to offer his head as a target. "Go on, Phillips, knock me out."

Phillips turned away from Bones and looked at the third man who sat there along the wall. Phillips said, "You do it, Whitey. You hit him."

"Whitey wouldn't do it," Bones said. "Whitey never hits anybody."

"You sure about that?" Phillips murmured. He saw that Whitey was not listening to the talk and he spoke to Bones as though Whitey weren't there.

"I'll give odds on it," Bones said "This man here wouldn't hurt a living thing. Not even a cat that scratched him."

"If a cat scratched me I'd wring its neck," Phillips said.

"That's you," Bones said "Whitey ain't made that way. Whitey's on the gentle side."

"Gentle?" Phillips had a thoughtful look in his eyes as he went on studying Whitey. Then he said, "Maybe gentle ain't the word. Maybe the word is timid."

Bones shrugged. "Whatever you want to call it. That's the way he is." He spoke to the third man who sat there, not saying anything. "Ain't that so, Whitey?"

Whitey nodded vaguely.

"He ain't even listening," Phillips said.

"What?" Whitey blinked a few times. He smiled mildly and said, "What are you talking about?"

"Nothing," Phillips said. "Let it drop."

Whitey shrugged. He aimed the mild smile at the empty bottle. The curved glass showed him a miniature of himself, a little man lost in the emptiness of a drained bottle. Aside from what he saw in the bottle he was actually on the small side, five feet even and weighing 145. His eyes were gray and he had the kind of face that doesn't attract much attention one way or another. The only unusual thing was his hair. He was thirty-three years old and his hair was snow white.

Another thing not really unusual along Skid Row, was his voice. He always spoke in a semiwhisper, sort of strained and sometimes cracked, as though he had a case of chronic bronchitis. At times when he spoke there was a look of pain in his eyes and it seemed that the effort of producing sound was hurting his throat. But whenever they asked him about it he said there was nothing wrong with his throat. They'd insist there was something wrong and then he'd smile and say that his throat was dry, his throat was very dry and he could use a drink. Some of them would check on that and treat him to a drink and maybe two or more shots. But no matter how many shots he had, he went on speaking in the strained painful whisper.

He'd arrived on Skid Row seven years ago, coming out of nowhere like all the other two-legged shadows. He made the weary stumbling entrance to take his place in the soup lines outside the missions and the slow aimless parade up and down River Street. With nothing in his pockets and nothing in his eyes he joined the unchartered society of the homeless and the hopeless, to flop on any old mattress and eat whatever food he could scrounge and wear what rags he could pick up here and there. But the primary thing was the drinking, and was always a problem because there was always more thirst than cash to purchase drinks. In that regard he was identical with the others, and when they saw he was no different from themselves, they didn't bother to ask questions. He was accepted and included and completely ignored. There was an unspoken agreement that they'd leave him alone, they'd pay no attention when he got drunk and stumbled and fell and passed out. It applied to any condition he was in; they'd definitely leave him alone. That was all he wanted and that was why he liked it here on Skid Row.

The three of them sat there with Bones and Phillips discussing the alcohol issue and Whitey staring at the empty bottle. It was getting on toward midnight and the wind from the river was colder now, and much meaner. On both sides of River Street the taprooms and hash houses were crowded. In the hash houses there was a demand for hot soup. In the taprooms they hollered for double shots and gulped them down and hollered again. The bartenders hollered back and told them to be patient, a man had only two hands. The sounds of drinkers and bartenders were reaching the ears of Bones and Phillips and they were getting irritated and sad and then irritated again.

"Listen to it," Bones said.

"I'm listening," Phillips said. But as he said it the sounds he heard were not coming from the taprooms. These were new and abrupt noises from several blocks away. It was a clamor of shouts and screams, glass breaking and things crashing and footsteps running.

"They're at it again," Bones said.

"The hell with them." Phillips waved wearily in the direction of the violent noises.

"They buried two last week," Bones said.

The sounds were coming in waves, getting higher and higher, and at the top of it there was someone screeching. It was on the order of the noise an animal would make while getting crushed by a steam roller.

"It gets worse every day," Bones said.

Phillips made another weary gesture.

Bones said, "They've been at it for more than a month. You'd think they'd have it stopped by this time."

The screeching noise faded and then for some moments it was quiet down there three blocks away. But all at once there was a crash and more shouting and screaming and a raging flood of curses and then policemen's whistles and running feet.

Bones stood up to have a look. He was looking south along River Street but he couldn't see anything down there. Up here along Skid Row there were a lot of bright lights, varicolored and sprinkling the darkness with the allnight glow from eateries and cut-rate stores and pawnshops. But where Skid Row ended the bright lights ended, and down there south on River Street there were no lights at all, only the hulking shapes of four-story tenements and three-story warehouses, and here and there the masts and funnels of freighters docked in the river. Bones went on trying to see what was happening three blocks south and all he saw was the darkness. Finally he sat down again, and just as he did so there was a very loud scream from down there and then much more noise than before.

Now some of it was automobile noise, the roar of engines picking up speed, the whine of tires making sharp turns, then the high-octave scream of brakes performing sudden stops. But the human screams were louder than the automobiles; the yelling and crashing and thudding seemed to stifle the noise of the police cars.

It went on like that and the noise of the police cars was like frustrated growling, confused and fumbling, unable to cope with the louder noise.

Phillips snorted. "Them clowns."

"Who?" Bones asked.

"The cops," Phillips said. "The city's finest. The sturdy enforcers of law and order."

"They sound like they need help."

"They need brains, that's what they need. That's what's wrong with them, they got no brains."

Bones frowned indignantly. He assumed the look of a solid citizen defending the abilities of the police force. He said stiffly, "Quit jabbing needles in them. It ain't easy to be a cop in this district."

Just then there was a very loud crashing sound, as though one of the cars had collided with a brick wall. Or maybe it had run into another police car.

Phillips laughed sourly and disdainfully. "Listen to them," he said. "Now they're running around in circles and getting in each other's way."

"That sounded like a bad accident," Bones said.

Phillips snorted again. "They're always having accidents. They're always making mistakes. They're really brilliant, them policemen."

Bones folded his arms and gave Phillips a glaring look.

"It's easy to talk," he said. "Them cops are only doing the best they can."

24

"Yeah, I know." Phillips pointed toward the area of chaotic sound. "They're sure doing a wonderful job of it."

"I guess you could do better."

"Me?" Phillips looked thoughtful for a moment. "If I was a cop I'd stay the hell out of that neighborhood. They don't want cops down there. All they wanna do is raise hell and hammer away at each other. I'd let them do it to their hearts' content. I wouldn't give a damn if every last one of them wound up on a stretcher."

"It's no use talking to you," Bones said. "You just don't make good sense."

Phillips didn't bother to reply. He looked at Whitey to see if Whitey was interested in the conversation. Whitey's face showed no interest at all. He wasn't even listening to the hectic noises coming from three blocks south. Whitey sat there gazing at the empty bottle set between Bones's legs, and Phillips wondered seriously whether the small white-haired man was completely in touch with the world. He decided to find out, and he tapped Whitey's shoulder and said, "You hear the commotion? You know what's going on?"

Whitey nodded. But aside from that there was no reaction and he went on looking at the empty bottle.

"You know what it's all about?" Phillips persisted.

Whitey shrugged.

"They're fighting," Phillips said. "Can't you hear them fighting?"

Whitey shrugged again. "They're always having trouble down there."

"Not this kind of trouble," Phillips said. "This is different."

Bones nodded emphatically. "You can say that again," he said. "It used to be they'd settle for some black eyes and busted noses, and maybe some teeth knocked out. But now they're really at it. They're out for blood."

"They'll get tired of it," Whitey said. He sounded as though he weren't inclined to discuss the matter further. Again he set his gaze on the empty bottle.

Phillips shrugged inside himself and decided there was no use in trying to get an opinion from Whitey. And anyway, maybe Whitey had the right idea. Like that little country overseas that never got in a jam because it stuck to a policy of minding its own business. Except that Whitey took it a lot further than that. Whitey wouldn't even look, wouldn't even listen. Chances were that Whitey never gave a moment's thought to what was going on around him.

There was another burst of crashing and shouting and screaming from three blocks away and Bones said, "Listen to it. Good God, just listen to it."

Phillips didn't say anything.

"It's getting worse," Bones said. "The Lord only knows what's happening down there. It sounds like a slaughter-house."

Phillips opened his mouth to utter a comment and then changed his mind and locked his lips tightly to prevent himself from voicing any further opinions. The effort was rather difficult for him because he was a man who gave considerable thought to local issues and felt quite strongly about certain matters. But he realized he couldn't afford to feel too strongly; he suffered from a nervous stomach and at the clinic they'd told him it was important not to get excited. They said it was bad enough that he drank so much cheap wine and he shouldn't make things worse by getting excited.

But the noise from three blocks away was on the order of hammer blows banging at the skull of Phillips and he winced as though he could actually feel the impact. He had come to Skid Row to get away from the memory of hatred and violence in a little mining town where the miners went on strike and he'd scabbed. They had come to talk to him and he'd figured they

26

wanted to do more than just talk, and before it was ended there were three of them shot dead and a smoking rifle in his hand as he made a beeline for the woods. They were still looking for him in that part of the country, but that angle wasn't what bothered him. What bothered him was the memory.

The memory hit him and went in very deeply every time he heard the violence down there three blocks away. It was like a voice telling him that Skid Row wasn't really the hiding place it was supposed to be. It was a locale that constantly got played for a sucker. The Tenderloin tried its best to keep away from contact with the world but somehow or other the world always managed to make contact. The world tossed the bait and tossed it again and again, kept tossing it to get a nibble, and sooner or later the hook was taken and the line reeled in.

Phillips closed his eyes for a moment and listened to the sounds of the fighting in the street three blocks south of Skid Row. With his eyes shut very tightly he wished that Skid Row were soundproof.

He wanted to run down there and beg them to stop it. It was a silly notion and he smiled bitterly, knowing how silly it was. They called that area the Hellhole, and for more than one good reason. Along Skid Row the uninformed were firmly advised, "Don't walk too far south on River Street. Stay away from the Hellhole." In the past month it was more than just a matter of avoiding getting mugged or slugged or dragged into an alley. It was the idea of keeping away from the cobblestone battlefield where the combat was on an all-out basis. They were fighting with the whitehot fury that men display when they forget that they are men. In the Hellhole, these nights, they were having race riots.

Phillips had no idea how it had started. He knew that no one was sure about that. He remembered that around a year ago some Puerto Ricans had moved into the tenements down there and then more had come. And some more. And then they were saying there were too many Puerto Ricans moving in. The talk went on for a while but it was just talk and gradually it died down. Then all at once, five weeks ago, there was a riot. A few nights later there was another riot. Some people were hurt but there was no serious damage and for a week things were quiet and it looked as though the trouble had ended. But then they rioted again and it was mean ugly fighting and three men died. In the fourth riot there were two dead and one blinded with lye and several taken to the hospital, badly cut up. Tonight was the seventh riot and Phillips wasn't sure how many had died altogether but he knew the number was considerable. He told himself it was very bad and getting worse and he wondered how it would end. Or whether it would ever end.

He told himself to stop thinking about it. After all, it was a matter of geography and this was Skid Row and the Hellhole was three blocks away. He was here on Skid Row and the Hellhole was a million miles away. And so was yesterday, and so were all the memories of the little mining town.

The thing to do was play it Whitey's way and not let it touch him, let nothing touch him. He turned his head and looked at Whitey, knowing that Whitey's eyes would be aimed at the empty bottle and the only thought in Whitey's brain would be the need for another drink.

But Whitey wasn't looking at the bottle. Whitey sat there sort of stiffly, his mouth halfway open. He was staring at something on the other side of the street.

-Two-

Phillips frowned slightly. He studied the look of rapt attention on Whitey's face. Then he looked across the street to see what Whitey was staring at. He didn't see anything unusual over there. It was just some Tenderloin scufflers coming out of a hash house and a man walking south on River street and a woman walking north. The woman was nothing to look at. She was fat and shapeless and walked with the exaggerated wiggle of a very lonely female hoping for company.

Bones was saying, "We gotta find a way to get a drink. That's all it amounts to. We just gotta get a drink."

"That's right," Whitey said. But he didn't seem to realize he was saying it. The words came out mechanically. He sat there stiffly and went on staring at something on the other side of the street.

"What is it?" Phillips asked. "What're you looking at?"

Whitey didn't answer.

"The woman?" Phillips asked. "You looking at the woman?"

Whitey shook his head very slowly. Then, more slowly, he started to get up from the pavement. He was almost on his feet when he changed his mind and sat down again. He shrugged and turned his head and looked at the empty bottle. He grinned at the bottle as though it were telling him something funny. He spoke to the bottle, saying 'All right, I'll try it."

"Try what?" Phillips said.

"I'll try it and see what happens," Whitey said to the bottle. The grin on his face was vague and it went along with the dragging whisper coming from his lips.

"What is this?" Phillips said. He touched Whitey's shoulder. "What's wrong with you?"

Whitey didn't seem to hear. He went on grinning at the bottle and he said, "Sure, I might as well try it."

Then it was quiet and Phillips and Bones looked at each other. Bones shrugged as though to say there was no way to figure Whitey, and no use asking him what was on his mind.

Whitey stood up again. He put his hands in the pockets of his ragged overcoat and hunched his shoulders against the wind coming from the river. He approached the curb and then stopped to pick up a cigarette stub. The cigarette was less than half smoked and he started to put it in his pocket, then tossed the stub to Bones.

Bones reached inside his coat and found a safety match and lit the cigarette. He took a long drag and handed the cigarette to Phillips. They sat there on the pavement sharing the cigarette and watching Whitey as he crossed the street. They were waiting to see what he would do when he was on the other side. He looked very small and shabby as he crossed River Street and it didn't seem to matter who he was or where he was going or what he intended to do. But they watched him as though it were very important that they pay careful attention. They had the unaccountable feeling that he was something special to watch.

They saw him arriving on the other side of the street. On the sidewalk he stopped for a moment to pull up the collar of his overcoat. Then again his hands were in his pockets and he was walking. He was walking slowly, his white hair wind-blown, his legs moving off stride as he went along River Street in a sort of lazy shuffle.

"South," Phillips murmured. "He's headed south."

"That's going toward the Hellhole."

"No," Phillips said. "He wouldn't go there."

"Well, where's he going?"

Phillips didn't reply. He squinted through the glare of the Skid Row lights, watching the small white-haired figure going south on River and coming to the end of the block and still going south.

"He's damn sure going toward the Hellhole," Bones said.

Phillips took the cigarette from Bones's mouth and put it in his own. He sipped the smoke through his teeth and it came out slowly through his nose. He didn't taste it going in or feel it coming out. He listened for the sounds of street fighting from the Hellhole but now there was no sound down there. Only the darkness.

Something was shining far down there in the darkness and it was the white hair of the small man walking south on River Street.

"We oughta go after him," Bones said.

Phillips nodded slowly.

"Let's go," Bones said.

But neither of them moved. They sat there on the cold pavement with their backs against the wall of the flophouse. They watched the thatch of white hair getting smaller and smaller and finally it vanished altogether. They looked at each other and for some moments they didn't say anything.

Then Bones stared glumly at the empty bottle and said, "We need a drink. How we gonna get a drink?"

Whitey was on the east side of River Street three blocks away from Skid Row. He was walking very slowly and every now and then he stepped into a doorway and stayed there a few moments. Once he crossed to the west side of River and

31

stood beside an empty ash can, bent over it as though he were rummaging for something in the trash. But he wasn't looking inside the can. His head was turned slightly from the can and his eyes were focused on the man moving south on River.

It was the man he had seen walking past the hash house. The man was very short, around five-four, and extremely wide. The man's arms were unusually long, and came down past his knees. He moved somewhat like a chimpanzee, his head jutting forward and down, his arms swinging in -unison as he went along in a bowlegged stride. He wore a bright-green cap and a black-and-purple plaid lumber jacket. He was walking without haste but with a certain deliberateness, his hard-heeled shoes making emphatic sounds on the sidewalk.

There was no other sound. There were no other people on the street. In the tenements the windows were dark. There were countless mongrels and alley cats and sewer rats in this area but none were visible now. It seemed that all living things were hiding from each other. The silence in the Hellhole was colder than the wind slicing in from the river.

On the pavement and in the gutter there were certain souvenirs of what had happened here tonight. There were broken bottles and the splintered handles of baseball bats and a lot of red stains, still wet. There was the cracked pane of a store window and the smashed front door of a tenement, the door leaning far out on its hinges. There were strips of torn clothing and someone's hat ripped across the crown and wet red smears on it.

Whitey saw all of that but it had no effect on him, it had no place in his thoughts. He wasn't conscious of the fact that he was down here in the Hellhole. His full attention was centered on the man in front of him.

He saw the man turning off River to go east on a narrow side street. He quickened his pace just a little, came onto the side street, and saw the man stopped near a dimly lit lamppost, looking toward an alleyway. The man made a move toward the

32

alleyway, then stopped again. The man stood there as though trying to make up his mind whether to enter the alley. Some moments passed and then the man shrugged and continued on.

Whitey had ducked into a doorway and now he came out and resumed following the man. His pace was slackened again and he stayed close to the tenement walls, ready to use another doorway in case the man turned for a look. As he approached the lamppost he heard something that made him glance toward the alleyway. It was a quick glance and he couldn't see it distinctly and he kept on walking. He told himself to forget about the alleyway and what was happening there. Whatever it was, it had no connection with the man he was following. But then he heard it again and it seemed to reach inside him and beg him to stop.

He stopped. He listened to the sound coming from the alleyway. It was a gurgling, rattling noise. And then the faint voice saying, "Please. Please. Help me."

Whitey turned and walked quickly to the alleyway. He entered the alley and the glow from the lamppost showed him the brass buttons and the blue uniform. The policeman was sitting in the alley, his head down very low. His cap was off and his hair was mussed and the top of his head was all bloody.

The policeman looked up and saw Whitey and said, "Get an ambulance."

"I'll hafta phone."

"Use a call box. Call the station house. Ask for the Thirty-seventh District."

"Where's the nearest call box?"

The policeman opened his mouth to reply. The sound that came out was more gurgling and rattling. His head went down again and then he was falling over on his side. Whitey caught hold of him.

"The call box," Whitey said. "Tell me where it is."

The policeman gurgled very low in his throat.

"Tell me," Whitey said. "Try to tell me."

"It's on – " But the policeman couldn't take it further than that. His head was leaning against Whitey's chest and his hands clutched at Whitey's arms. Now he made no sound at all and his full weight was on Whitey. As Whitey knelt there holding him to keep him from falling, there was the sound of an auto and then the beam of a searchlight. Whitey turned his head and blinked in the glare of the light shooting into his face. He blinked again and saw the black-and-orange police car parked out there. The door opened and he saw the policemen getting out and running toward him.

They were young policemen and their faces were expressionless. One of them was grabbing for a revolver and having trouble pulling it from the holster. The other policeman grabbed Whitey's shoulder, couldn't get a good grip on the shoulder, and decided to hook his fingers around the back of Whitey's neck.

"Let go," Whitey said. "I'm not running."

"You telling me?" the policeman said. He tightened his hold on Whitey's neck.

"That hurts," Whitey said.

"Shut up." The policeman pulled Whitey to his feet. The other policeman had managed to get the revolver from the holster and was now trying to put it back in. Finally he got it in and then he knelt beside the injured policeman, who was now face down in the alley. He rolled the man over on his side and looked at the face. The eyes were half open and the mouth sagged at the corners. The color of the face was gray with streams of red running down the cheeks and dripping from the lips.

"It's Gannon."

"Bad?"

"Dead."

The policeman stood up. He looked down at the body and then he looked at Whitey.

-Three-

The station house of the Thirty-seventh District was on Clayton Street, six blocks west of the river and four blocks west of the Hellhole. It was a one-story brick structure that had been built some thirty years ago. At both sides of the front entrance there were frosted-glass lamps. In the glare of the lamplight Whitey stood between the two policemen. He was handcuffed but they weren't taking any chances with him. They were very young policemen and new to the force and this arrest was very important to them. One of them gripped Whitey's arm and the other had hold of his trousers. He looked very small standing there between the two tall policemen.

The entrance doors were wide open and Whitey could see it was very crowded in the station house. It was a noisy assemblage and some of them were shouting in Spanish. He saw a Puerto Rican woman pull away from the grip of a policeman and lunge at a yellow-haired man and her fingernails ripped the man's face. The man stepped back and hauled off and punched her in the breast. Three Puerto Rican men started toward the yellow-haired man and several policemen

35

moved in and for some moments there was considerable activity. One of the Puerto Ricans was completely out of control and Whitey saw the worried looks on the faces of the policemen as they tried to handle him. They couldn't handle him and two of them were knocked down. Then a very large man wearing the uniform of a police captain came walking toward the Puerto Rican and grabbed his wrist and then very quickly and precisely lifted him in a wrestler's crotch hold, lifted him high in the air, held him there for a long moment, then hurled him to the floor. There was a very loud thud and the Puerto Rican stayed there on the floor, face down and not moving. Another Puerto Rican shouted something and the Captain walked over to him and shot a fist into his mouth. The American-born prisoners shouted encouragement to the Captain and one of them was grinning and aiming a kick at the Puerto Rican who'd been hit in the mouth. The Captain took hold of the American and put a short left hook in his midsection, chopped a right to his head, then hooked him again to send him flying against the wall, and when he bounced away from the wall the Captain hit him once more to put him on the floor on his knees.

"Next?" the Captain said very quietly, looking around at the Puerto Ricans and the Americans. "Who's next?"

"You can't do this," one of the Americans said.

"Can't I?" The Captain moved slowly toward the American, who had a black eye and a cut on his face.

"All right, hit me," the American said. He pointed to his damaged face. "As if I ain't hurt enough. Go ahead and hurt me some more."

"Sure," the Captain said. "Sure, I'll be glad to." He said it sort of sadly, somewhat like a doctor telling a patient it was necessary to operate. Then quickly and neatly he threw a combination of punches and the American went down and rolled over and began to moan.

The Captain looked at the other Americans and the Puerto Ricans. "You want riots?" the Captain said. "I'll give you riots. I'll give you all you want."

"We want to be left alone," a Puerto Rican said in accented English. He pointed to the Americans. "They won't leave us alone."

"You're a goddamn liar," an American said. "You bastards started it. You started it and we're gonna finish it."

"No," the Captain said. "I'll finish it."

"I wish you would," the American said. He had a swollen jaw and under his nose there was dried blood. His face was pale and he was breathing hard. As he spoke to the Captain he stared at the Puerto Ricans and his eyes glittered. "I wish you'd use a machine gun. Mow them down. Dump them in the river."

"Shut your mouth," the Captain said.

"Dirty no-good spics," the American said. He breathed harder. "They're no good, I tell you. They're lousy in their hearts, every last one of them."

"You gonna shut up?" the Captain said.

"They're filthy. Filthy."

"And you?" said the Puerto Rican who had spoken. "You're not filthy?"

"We're Americans," the American said, his voice cracking with the strain of holding himself back from leaping at the Puerto Rican. "We were here before you."

"Yes," the Puerto Rican said. "And so were the sewer rats."

The Captain stood there between them. He looked from one to the other. His big hands were clenched and his big body bulged with power. But now he couldn't move. He couldn't open his mouth to say anything. He stood there in the middle and his eyes were dull and had the helpless look of someone caught in the jaws of a slowly closing trap.

The American went on shouting at the Puerto Rican and finally the Captain growled very low in his throat, reached out, and grabbed the American's hand by the fingers, twisting the fingers to bend them back from the knuckles.

"I told you to shut up," the Captain said. He went on twisting the man's fingers. The man's knees were bent and he was halfway to the floor, his eyes shut tightly. The Captain growled again and said, "You'll shut up if I hafta rip your tongue outta your mouth."

Then it was quiet in there and Whitey saw the Captain releasing the man's hand and walking back to the big high desk at the far side of the room. The Captain called out someone's name and a policeman took hold of a man's arm and brought him toward the desk. At that moment a man wearing a gray overcoat came out of a side room and crossed the floor to the front door, coming outside to face the two policemen who held Whitey.

"What are you standing here for?" the plainclothes man said. "Why don't you take him inside?"

"We were waiting, Lieutenant."

"Waiting for what?"

"For things to quiet down in there."

The plainclothes man smiled dimly. "That's good thinking, Bolton. That's the kind of thinking gets promotions."

"I don't know what you mean, Lieutenant."

"I mean your timing. You were timing it just right. Waiting until it was quiet and you'd have the Captain's undivided attention. Then make the grand entrance. Come in with the murderer."

The policemen didn't say anything. They knew he was having fun with them. This one had a habit of having fun with everyone. Usually they didn't mind and they kidded him back. But now it was an important arrest, it was a homicide and the victim was a policeman. Certainly it was no time for the Lieutenant to be having fun.

The Lieutenant stood there smiling at them. He hadn't

38

yet looked at Whitey. He was waiting for the policemen to say something. Behind him, inside the station house, another commotion had started, but he didn't turn to see what was happening in there.

Finally one of the policemen said, "We weren't timing it, Lieutenant. Only timing we did was according to the book. Used the radio and made the report. Waited there for the wagon to come and get the body. The wagon came and got it and now we're taking this man in. I don't see why we're getting criticized."

"You're not getting criticized," the Lieutenant said. His tone was mild and friendly and only slightly sarcastic as he went on: "I think you've done very nicely, Bolton. You too, Woodling."

The two policemen glanced at each other. They could feel the sarcasm and they wondered how to handle it.

The Lieutenant put his hands in the pockets of his overcoat and leaned back just a little on his heels. He said, "I'm sure you'll get a commendation from the Captain. He's gonna be very pleased with this arrest. It'll come as a pleasant surprise."

"Surprise?" Patrolman Bolton said. "I don't get that. Ain't he been told about the murder?"

"Not yet," the Lieutenant said.

"Why not?" Bolton was frowning. "We sent in the report thirty minutes ago."

The Lieutenant glanced at his wrist watch. "Twenty minutes," he corrected. Then he flipped his thumb backward to indicate the noisy action inside the station house. "The Captain's been very busy these past twenty minutes. I figured it was best not to bother him."

"Bother him?" Bolton came near shouting it. "For Christ's sake, Lieutenant —"

And Woodling was chiming in, "Listen, Lieutenant, this is serious."

The Lieutenant nodded very slowly and seriously. "I know,"

he said. And then for the first time he looked at Whitey. He gave a little sigh and said to Whitey, "You sure picked a fine time to do it."

"I didn't do it," Whitey said.

"Of course not," the Lieutenant said conversationally. Then he shifted his attention to the two policemen. "We'll have to wait a while before we tell the Captain." Again he glanced at his wrist watch and at the same moment his head was slightly turned, he seemed to be measuring the noise from inside the station house. He said, "I think we'll have to wait at least fifteen minutes."

"But why?" Bolton demanded.

The Lieutenant spoke slowly and patiently. "I'll tell you why. When a man has diarrhea you don't give him a laxative. You give him a chance to quiet down."

"But this —" Woodling started.

"Is dynamite," the Lieutenant finished for him. And then, not looking at anything in particular, sort of murmuring aloud to himself, "If I had my way, I wouldn't tell the Captain at all. He'd never get to hear about it. I think when he hears about it he's gonna get sick. Real sick. I only hope he don't burst a blood vessel."

The two policemen looked at their prisoner. Then they looked at each other. They didn't say anything.

The Lieutenant went on talking aloud to himself. "As if things haven't been bad enough. Getting worse all the time. And now we got this."

"Well," Woodling said, tightening his hold on Whitey's arm, "at least we got the man who did it."

The Lieutenant gave Woodling an older-brother look of fondness and gentle schooling. "You don't get the point. You're thinking too much in terms of the arrest. Try to forget the arrest. Think about the Captain."

The two policemen stood there frowning and blinking.

40

"The Captain," the Lieutenant said. He leaned toward them. He took his hands from his pockets and put them behind his back. "You get the drift of what I'm talking about?"

They went on frowning puzzledly.

"Listen," the Lieutenant said. "Listen to me. And it's very important that you listen carefully." He took a deep breath, and then his lips tightened and the words came out sort of hissing, like sound pumped from a hose. "From here on in," he said, "you'll be playing with a firecracker. Whatever you say to the Captain, think twice before you say it. And whatever you do, make sure it's not a mistake. He's in no condition to see you making mistakes, not even tiny ones. I'm telling you this so you'll remember it, and I want you to pass the word around."

Bolton blinked again. "Are things that bad?"

"Worse than bad," the Lieutenant said. He was about to say more when Woodling made a warning gesture, indicating that they shouldn't discuss this topic in front of the prisoner. For a moment the Lieutenant hesitated. Then he looked at the ragged little Skid Row bum, the white-haired blank-eyed nothing who stood there wearing handcuffs. He decided there were just three men present and he could go on with what he was saying.

He said, "This situation in the Hellhole. These riots. It's got out of control. Two nights ago I'm with the Captain when he gets a phone call from the Hall. The Commissioner. Wanted to know if we needed help. Said he was ready to send reinforcements. Add twenty men to this district, give us seven more cars. You know what that was? That was a slap in the teeth. That was the Commissioner telling the Captain to clean up the floor or give up the mop. In a nice way, of course. Very polite and friendly and all that."

Bolton spoke in a low murmur. "What did the Captain say?"

"He told the Commissioner to leave him alone. He said he

41

didn't need reinforcements, he could do this job without help from the Hall, and all he wanted was a promise that they wouldn't interfere. He said he'd been in charge of this district for nine years and he'd always been able to hold the wheel and if they'd only leave him alone he'd go on holding it.

"Now mind you," the Lieutenant went on, "that was only two nights ago. So what happens tonight? Another riot in the Hellhole, the worst yet. And something else. Something I knew was bound to happen sooner or later. We lose an officer."

It was quiet for some moments. Then both policemen turned their heads very slowly and they were looking down at the small white-haired man who stood between them. And Woodling said quietly to the prisoner, "You bastard, you. You miserable bastard."

Bolton jerked his head frontward as though he couldn't bear to look at the prisoner. He swallowed hard. "But—" he started, then blurted, "But my God, they can't blame the Captain for this."

"They will," the Lieutenant said.

"No." Bolton's voice was strained. "No. That ain't fair."

The Lieutenant shrugged. Then his face relaxed and the seriousness went out of his eyes. He was himself again and his voice went back to the easy, friendly, mildly sarcastic murmur. "Don't let it give you ulcers," he told the two youthful policemen. "You're too young to get ulcers."

"But this." Woodling spoke through his teeth, his thumb flicking to indicate the prisoner. "Who tells the Captain about this?"

"I'll tell him," the Lieutenant said. "I'll figure a way to break it to him." He bit his lip thoughtfully. "Tell you what. I'll take this man in through the side door. I wanna ask him some questions. Meantime, you go outside and wait."

The policemen released their holds on Whitey and entered

the station house. The Lieutenant looked at Whitey and said, "All right, come with me."

They walked down the steps and around the side of the station house. The Lieutenant had his hands in his overcoat pockets and moved along with his head down, his lips slightly pursed to whistle a tune in a minor key. It was a song from many years ago and he couldn't remember past the first few bars. He tried it a few times and couldn't get it. Whitey picked it up and hummed the rest of it. The Lieutenant glanced at Whitey and said, "Yeah, that's it. Pretty number."

"Yeah," Whitey said.

"What?"

"I said yeah."

"Can't you talk louder?" Whitey shook his head.

"Why not?" the Lieutenant asked. "What's wrong with your voice?"

Whitey didn't answer.

They were approaching the side entrance of the station house. The Lieutenant stopped and looked fully at Whitey and said, "You got bronchitis or something?"

"No," Whitey said. "I talk like this all the time."

"It sounds weird," the Lieutenant said. "As if you're whispering secrets."

Whitey shrugged. He didn't say anything.

The Lieutenant leaned in slightly to get a closer look at Whitey's face. A vague frown drifted across the Lieutenant's brow and he murmured, "I bet you're full of secrets."

Whitey shrugged again. "Who ain't?"

The Lieutenant mixed the frown with a smile. "You got a point there."

Then the Lieutenant was quiet and they went along the side of the station house. They came to the side door and the Lieutenant opened it and they went in. There was a narrow corridor and a door with a sign over it with the word "Captain"

43

and then another door with the sign "House Sergeant" and finally a door with the sign "Detectives." The door was partially open and the Lieutenant shoved it with his foot to open it all the way.

It was a medium-sized room with a floor that needed wax and walls that needed paint. There were some chairs and a few small tables and a roll-top desk. A tall man with a very closely waved and nicely cut pompadour of light-brown hair sat working at the desk. He glanced up at them, gave Whitey a quick once-over, and went back to work.

"Have a seat," the Lieutenant said to Whitey. He pointed toward a table that had a chair on either side. Then he took off his overcoat and put it on a hanger. On the wall next to the hanger there was a small mirror and the Lieutenant moved in close to it as though looking to see if he needed a shave. He stood there for some moments inspecting his face and adjusting his tie. He tightened the knot, loosened it, tightened it again to get the crease under the knot exactly in the middle. When he'd finished with that, he moved his head from side to side to see if he could use a haircut. Whitey began to have a feeling that it was sort of a gag and the Lieutenant was making fun of the neatly groomed man who sat at the rolltop desk.

Finally the man at the desk looked at the Lieutenant and said, "All right, cut it out."

The Lieutenant leaned in very close to the mirror and pretended to squeeze a blackhead from his chin.

"Very funny," the other man muttered. He bent lower over his work at the desk, his shoulders very broad and expanded past the sides of the chair. He wore an Oxford-gray suit of conservative but expensively tailored lines and his shoes were black Scotch grain and had the semiglossy British look. The Lieutenant had moved away from the mirror and was standing near the roll-top desk, looking down at the Scotch grain shoes.

44

"Where'd you get them?" the Lieutenant asked.

"Had them made," the other detective said.

"That's what I figured," the Lieutenant said.

The other detective sat up very straight and took a deep breath. "All right, Pertnoy. Lay off."

Lieutenant Pertnoy laughed lightly and patted the other detective's shoulder. "You're a fine man, Taggert. Really a fine man, and you always make a very nice appearance. We're all proud of you."

"Oh, drop it," the other said wearily. And then louder, almost hoarsely, "For Christ's sake, why don't you drop it? There's times you actually get on my nerves."

Lieutenant Pertnoy laughed again. "Don't get angry."

"I'm not," Lieutenant Taggert said. "But sometimes you go too far."

"I know," Pertnoy admitted. He said it with mock solemnity. "After all, there's a time and a place for everything."

Taggert swung around in the chair. He pointed to the mirror on the wall. "Let's understand something," he said very slowly and distinctly. "I put that mirror there. And I want it to stay there. And I don't want to be kidded about it. Is that absolutely clear?"

"Absolutely." It was an exaggerated imitation of the other's crisp official tone.

Taggert took another deep breath. He started to say something and then he noticed the ragged little white-haired man who sat at the table showing handcuffed wrists.

"What's that?" Taggert asked, gesturing toward Whitey.

"Nothing important," Pertnoy said.

"Why the cuffs? What's he done?"

Pertnoy smiled at Whitey. "Tell him what you did."

"I didn't do anything," Whitey said.

Pertnoy went on smiling. "You hear?" he said to Taggert. "The man says he didn't do anything. So it stands to reason he didn't do anything. It figures he don't need handcuffs." And then, to Whitey, "Want them off?"

Whitey nodded.

"All right," Pertnoy said. "You can talk better if you're comfortable. I'll take them off."

Pertnoy moved toward the table and took a key ring from his pocket. He selected a key and unlocked the handcuffs. Then the handcuffs were off and Pertnoy slid them toward the center of the table and said, "That better?"

"Yeah," Whitey said. "Thanks."

"Don't mention it," Pertnoy said. He walked across the room and stood near the roll-top desk. For some moments he stood there looking down at Taggert, who had resumed working with pencil and paper. Finally he tapped Taggert's shoulder and said, "Were you here when the report came in?"

Taggert didn't look up. "What report?"

"Nothing much," Pertnoy said. "I'll tell you later." Then, offhandedly, "Can you hold that work for a while? I want to talk to this man alone."

Taggert wrote a few more lines on the paper, folded the paper, and clipped it onto several other sheets. He put the papers in a large envelope and placed the envelope in one of the desk drawers. Then he stood up and walked out of the room.

Lieutenant Pertnoy glanced at his wrist watch. His lips moved only slightly as he said, "We got about five minutes." He looked at Whitey. "Let's see what we can do."

Whitey blinked a few times. He saw Lieutenant Pertnoy moving toward him. The Lieutenant moved very slowly and sort of lazily. For some moments he stood behind Whitey's chair, not saying anything. It was as though the Lieutenant had walked out of the room and Whitey was there alone. Then the Lieutenant moved again, circling the table and sitting down in the chair facing Whitey.

The Lieutenant sat almost directly under the ceiling light,

and now for the first time Whitey saw him clearly and was able to study him. Lieutenant Pertnoy looked to be in his middle thirties and had a glossy cap of pale blond hair parted far on the side and brushed flat across his head. He had a gray, sort of poolroom complexion, not really unhealthy, just sun-starved. There was something odd about his eyes. His eyes were a very pale gray and had the look of specially ground lenses. They gave the impression that he could see beyond whatever he was looking at. Whitey had the feeling that this man was cute with a cue stick or a deck of cards. The cuteness went along with the Lieutenant's slim and well-balanced physique, around five-ten and 150 pounds. He wore a gray flannel suit that needed pressing but wouldn't look right on him if it were pressed. It seemed to blend with his easy relaxed manner and his soft lazy smile.

The smile seemed to drift across the table, almost like a floating leaf in a gentle breeze. The Lieutenant was saying, "Tell me why you did it."

"I didn't do it," Whitey said.

"All right." The Lieutenant shifted in his chair, facing the wall on the other side of the room. "Let's take it slower. We'll talk about the weapon. What'd you hit him with?"

"I didn't hit him," Whitey said. "I didn't touch him."

Pertnoy smiled at the wall. He waved his hand lazily toward Whitey and said, "Look at your clothes. Look at the blood on you."

"I got that trying to help him. He was sitting there and I was holding him to keep him from falling."

Pertnoy gave a slow nod of assent. "That ain't bad. It might even stand up in court."

"Will it reach court?"

Pertnoy looked at Whitey and said, "What do you think?"

"I think you oughta go look for the man who did it."

"You mean you didn't do it?"

"That's what I been saying."

"Maybe you'll get tired saying it."

"Maybe." Whitey shrugged. "I'm getting tired now."

"Wanna break down?"

"And do what?"

"Cry a little," Pertnoy said. "Make some noise. Confess."

"No," Whitey said. "I'm not that tired."

"Come on." The Lieutenant's voice was very soft and kindly, like a doctor's voice. "Come on," the Lieutenant said, opening the table drawer and taking out a pencil and a pad of paper. "Come on."

"Nothing doing," Whitey said.

The pencil was poised. "Come on. You can spill it in just a few words. He's chasing you down the alley and you pick up a brick or something. You don't really mean to finish him. All you wanna do is knock him down so you can get away."

Whitey smiled sadly. "You putting words in my mouth?"

"I wanna put some words on this paper," Pertnoy said. He flicked another glance at his wristwatch. "We only got a couple of minutes."

Whitey stopped smiling. "Until what?"

"Until I break it to the Captain."

"Then what?"

"God knows," Pertnoy said. And then his expression changed. His face became serious. It was the same seriousness he'd displayed outside the front entrance of the station house when he'd told the two policemen about the Captain.

Whitey sat there blinking and not saying anything.

"Look," Pertnoy said. "It's like this. You give me a confession and I'll put you in a cell. Then you'll be safe."

"Safe?" Whitey blinked hard. "From what?"

"Don't you see?" The Lieutenant leaned forward sort of pleadingly. "From the Captain."

Whitey gazed past the gray face of Lieutenant Pertnoy. But

48

the wall of the room was also gray and it seemed to be moving toward him. "God," Whitey said to the wall. "Is that the way it is?"

"That's exactly the way it is," the Lieutenant said. He pointed his thumb over his shoulder to indicate something. It was the noise coming from the big room at the end of the corridor. It was the clashing mixture of shouts and curses in Spanish and English. There was a thud and another thud and then more shouting. "You hear that?" the Lieutenant said. "Listen to it. Just listen to it."

Whitey listened. He heard the cracking, squishy sound of someone getting hit very hard in the mouth. And then he heard the voice of the Captain saying, "Want more?" There was a hissing defiance in the voice replying, "Got any sisters?" Then a very cold quiet and then the Captain saying, "Sure. I got three." And there were three separate, precisely timed sounds, the sounds of knuckles smashing a face. After that it was just the vague noise of someone crumbling to the floor.

"You hear it?" Pertnoy said.

Whitey sat very low in the chair. He nodded slowly. He looked at Pertnoy's hand and saw the pencil poised above the pad of paper.

He heard Pertnoy saying, "You see what I mean?"

"Can't you stop him? Can't you do anything?"

"No," Pertnoy said. "We'd be crazy if we tried. There's no telling what he'd do. You heard what I told the blue boys. He's a sick man. He's getting sicker. I feel sorry for him, I swear I do. He's been trying his best to stop these riots, and the more he tries, the worse it gets. He's lost his grip on the neighborhood and he's losing his grip on himself. And now comes the pay-off. I gotta go in there and give him the news."

Whitey swallowed hard. He felt as if sawdust were going down his throat.

"I gotta give it to him," Pertnoy said. "I gotta tell him what

49

the Hellhole did to him tonight. How it hit back at him. How it hit him where it hurts most. One of his own men."

Whitey swallowed again and there was more sawdust going down. His voice was scarcely audible as he said, "Do I hafta be there when you tell him?"

"It's up to you," Pertnoy said. The seriousness went away and he was smiling again. "Can we do business?"

Whitey opened his mouth to reply. But there was too much sawdust and it choked him and he couldn't say anything.

"Come on," Pertnoy said. He touched the pencil point to the pad of paper. "Gimme some dictation."

"Can't," Whitey said. "Can't tell you I did something I didn't do."

Pertnoy glanced at the wrist watch. "Not much time," he said.

Whitey shut his eyes and kept them shut for a long moment. Then he looked at the Lieutenant and inclined his head just a little. He frowned slightly and worked a very dim smile along the edge of it. "Lemme ask you something," he said. "You conning me?"

Pertnoy gestured toward the noise coming from the big room. "Does that sound like I'm conning you?"

Whitey listened. He heard it thumping and thudding and sort of galloping toward him. He sat there wishing the chair had wheels and a motor and a reverse gearshift.

Again the Lieutenant glanced at the wrist watch. "I'm looking at the second hand," he said. "Twenty seconds."

"That's close," Whitey said.

"Damn close," the Lieutenant said. He kept his eyes focused on the dial of the wrist watch. "Fifteen seconds."

Whitey grinned. He wondered why he was able to grin. He heard himself saying, "The hell of it is, I got no hospital insurance."

"Maybe you'll need a hearse," the Lieutenant said. His lips

smiled as he said it but his eyes weren't smiling and there was no smile in his voice.

Whitey stopped grinning. "You think he'd go that far?"

"He might. Come on, buddy. It's ten seconds. Nine seconds."

Then it was very quiet in the room. There was only the tiny noise of the ticking of the watch.

"Five seconds," the Lieutenant said. He looked up. He kept the pencil on the paper, ready to write. The pencil was steady in his fingers, the point lightly touching the surface of the blank sheet.

"No?" the Lieutenant said.

"No." Whitey said it with a sigh.

"All right," the Lieutenant said. "No seconds. All gone." He stood up, motioning for Whitey to rise. "Come on, you're gonna meet the Captain."

-Four-

They were in the corridor walking slowly and going toward the noisy action in the big room. The Lieutenant was lighting a cigarette and holding it between his thumb and little finger, his eyes intent on the cigarette as though it were an oboe reed that must be handled delicately. He didn't exhale the smoke, it simply drifted from his lips of its own accord. It drifted sideways and floated past Whitey's eyes to form a wispy curtain. Whitey gazed through the curtain and saw the big room coming closer and it was blurry and he had the feeling it was unreal.

The feeling grew in him and he told himself all this was strictly on the fantastic side. The chaotic sounds of the big room were sounds he'd never heard in any station house, or even in the alcoholic wards of municipal hospitals. At least in the alcoholic wards there were white-garbed people in control of the situation, and despite all the hollering in the beds, there was an atmosphere of order and system. He'd been in more than one alcoholic ward, and certainly he'd been in many station houses, and he'd never seen anything that compared with this.

As the Lieutenant led him into the big room and he got a full front view of what was going on, he winced in wonder and disbelief. He stared at four men who were unconscious on the floor, and a few sitting there on the floor with bloody faces, and several sprawled on the benches along the walls, their heads down and the gore dripping from their chins. one man, a Puerto Rican, had his hands pressed to his throat and was making strangled groans. Another man, with Slavic features, stood holding his groin and shaking his head as though refusing to believe how hard he'd been hit there. A policeman stood beside him, showing him the night stick and letting him know it was ready for another smash. The policeman was breathing very hard and his mouth was wide open and he seemed to be having more distress than the man he'd hit. It was the same way with all the other policemen. Their faces were paler than the faces of the prisoners, their eyes showed more agony, more fear. They were staring at the Captain, who was talking to one of the men sitting on the floor.

"Get up," the Captain said.

The man sat there grinning at the Captain.

"You gonna get up?"

"No," the man said.

The Captain leaned down and took hold of the man's ankle, lifting the leg and twisting the ankle. The man grimaced but managed to hold some of the grin and showed his teeth to the Captain.

"You're gonna need crutches," the Captain said. He tightened his hold on the man's ankle and twisted harder.

"That's right," the man said. "Break it off."

"You think I won't?" the Captain said. His features were expressionless. He had his coat off and his shirt was torn, one sleeve ripped from wrist to shoulder with the blue fabric dangling in shreds. His face was shiny with sweat and his hair was mussed. He had pitch-black hair with some narrow ribbons of white in it and the white was like foam on a storm-tossed black sea. The Captain had blue eyes and his complexion was the color of medium-rare beef. He was built along the lines of Jeffries, about five-eleven and well over two hundred. There was no paunch and hardly any fat and most of his weight was above his navel. He looked to be around forty-five and it was altogether evident that he took very good care of himself and was in excellent physical condition. Yet somehow he gave the impression of a helpless creature going to pieces and slowly dying.

He went on twisting the man's ankle. Now the man's leg was bent at a weird angle, and the man let out an animal cry. And then one of the younger policemen said loudly, "Captain. For God's sake."

The Captain didn't hear. He was concentrating on the man's ankle.

"Captain" the young policeman said very loudly. "Captain Kinnard —"

It reached the Captain and he looked up. He blinked several times and shook his head like someone emerging from water. He let go of the man's ankle and looked up at the ceiling and there was a straining yearning in his eyes as though he wished fervently he could fly up there and go on through the roof and sail away.

Gradually the room became quiet. Whitey stood in the doorway with Lieutenant Pertnoy. He saw some of the policemen going to the aid of the men on the floor. He estimated there were some fifty people in the room. He counted eleven policemen and around twenty Puerto Ricans and the rest were Americans who looked to be of Slavic and Irish and Scandinavian descent. The policemen were moving in between the Puerto Ricans and the Americans, making sure there was plenty of space

54

between the two groups of arrested rioters, then shoving them back toward the benches along the walls. Finally the floor was cleared and all the benches were taken. The Captain had walked to the big high desk and now he sat there with his head turning very slowly, looking at the Puerto Ricans on one side of the room, the Americans on the other side, and back to the Puerto Ricans, then back to the Americans.

"Now then," the Captain said, but that was all he could say. He went on looking from one side to the other. He opened his mouth again and no sound came out. His mouth stayed open and then very slowly he lowered his head and looked down at the surface of the desk.

It was very quiet in the room.

Lieutenant Pertnoy turned to Whitey and said quietly, "You wanna tell him?"

"Tell him what?"

"What you did. What you did to one of his men."

Whitey didn't get it. He looked blankly at Pertnoy. He said, "Ain't it your job to tell him?"

"That's the point," Pertnoy said. "I wish it wasn't."

Whitey shrugged. He knew there was nothing more for him to say, nothing to think about, nothing to do to stop what was coming. He knew it was coming, he told himself it was coming sure as hell, and again he could feel the sawdust in his throat as he gazed toward the desk and saw the wide shoulders and thick-muscled arms and heavy hands of Captain Kinnard.

He heard Pertnoy saying, "Wanna sit down?"

"I'd rather lay down."

"You'll lay down," Pertnoy said.

Whitey sighed softly. He tried to shrug again, but now his shoulders felt too heavy. He told himself it was going to be a very long night for Whitey. Then, thinking deeply and seriously, he took it further than that. He reasoned it was quite possible that he'd never get out of here alive. He'd heard stories about it, the way it had happened in certain station houses when they brought in a cop-killer and maybe an hour later they'd take the man out through the back door with a sheet over his face. With no mention of it in the newspapers. Or maybe they'd tell the reporters that the man tried to get away. Then again, they might simply state the facts and admit that they'd hit the man just a little too hard. Whichever way they handled it, they never got blamed too much. Not when it came to cop-killers. The papers and the public were never sorry for cop-killers.

He stood there waiting for Pertnoy to walk him toward the big high desk. Then he was conscious of voices at his side. He turned and looked and it was Pertnoy talking to the tall and well-built and impeccably attired Detective Lieutenant Taggert.

"Who told you?" Pertnoy was saying.

"I got it from the house sergeant," Taggert said. He gave Pertnoy a narrow look and his mouth tightened just a little. "Why didn't you tell me? What's all this cover-up?"

Pertnoy made an offhand gesture. "No cover-up. I just figured it could wait."

"Wait? I don't get that." Taggert's eyes were narrower. "It isn't a snatched purse, it isn't a drunk-and-disorderly. It's a homicide. And the victim's a policeman from this district."

His head jerked sideways and for a moment he stared at Whitey. "Well," he said. "Well, now." Then he aimed the narrow look at Pertnoy and his voice was a needle jabbing gently. "You sure you know what you're doing?"

"I'm never sure," Pertnoy said. He smiled sort of wistfully. "I never give myself guarantees."

"Guess not," Taggert agreed, But his tone sent the needle in deeper. Then, still deeper, "The way you operate, there's no guarantee on anything. Or maybe you like it better that way. Sometimes I think you do it on purpose."

56

Pertnoy widened the smile. "Meaning what?"

"That it's more fun when it's thin ice. You're always out for fun, aren't you?"

Lieutenant Pertnoy shrugged and said, "It's a short life."

"Yeah," Taggert said. "Especially for cops. The cop who died tonight was forty-four years old."

Pertnoy didn't say anything,

"He was a twenty-year man with a perfect record," Lieutenant Taggert said, standing there tall and stalwart, solidly planted on his custom-made Scotch-grain shoes, his finely tailored Oxford gray correct in every detail, his fingernails immaculate, and his light-brown pompadour with every hair in place glimmering cleanly under the ceiling lights. He stood there exuding cleanliness and neatness and strength of mind and body. He said, "It's a serious loss. It's damn serious and it certainly doesn't call for fooling around."

"Fooling around?" Pertnoy smiled again. "Is that what I've been doing?"

Taggert's mouth was very tight. "All right, Pertnoy. I won't jockey with you. I want a direct answer and I think I'm entitled to it. Why'd you keep this thing quiet? Why haven't you told the Captain?"

Pertnoy looked across the room. Without words he was telling Taggert to look in the same direction. They both saw the Captain sitting at the big high desk on the platform three steps above the floor. The Captain was hunched low over some papers and he was trying to use a pencil. As they watched him, the pencil slipped from his hand, rolled across the desktop and off the edge, and dropped onto the floor. A policeman hurried forward, picked up the pencil, and handed it to the Captain. The Captain thanked him and started to write again, but somehow he couldn't move the pencil across the paper and finally he put it down and sat there staring at the paper.

"You see?" Pertnoy murmured.

Taggert didn't reply. He stood there watching the Captain. Then very slowly his head turned and he gazed along the rows of crowded benches, the Puerto Rican rioters on the other side of the room, the American rioters on this side, and the policemen standing stiff and tense and waiting for more to happen. They stood there lined up in the middle of the bloodstained floor, all of them holding night sticks and gripping them very tightly.

"You see?" Pertnoy said. "You get it now?"

Taggert gazed again at the Captain. For some moments Taggert didn't say anything, Then very quietly he said, "You want me to tell him?"

Pertnoy's smile became dim and dimmer and then faded altogether and he said, "Do you want to?"

"Well someone's got to tell him."

"All right," Pertnoy said. "You tell him."

Taggert took a deep breath. He turned and walked very slowly toward the big high desk. Whitey watched him as he approached the platform, saw him mounting the steps, heard the distinct clicking of his heels on the first step and the second and the third. There were other sounds in the room but Whitey didn't hear them. He was watching Lieutenant Taggert moving across the platform to the desk and bending over to whisper in the Captain's ear. The Captain's head was low and he was staring at the paper on the desk. Taggert went on whispering and Whitey saw the Captain gradually raising his head and sitting up very straight, rigid in a metallic sort of way, as though he were something activated by a lever. Then the Captain said something that Whitey couldn't hear and Taggert's reply was also inaudible but his arm was stretched out and his finger pointed at Whitey.

The Captain got up from the desk chair. He walked across the platform, moving like a sleepwalker except that his arms were stiff at his sides. He came down off the platform and there was nothing on his face but the flesh and yet it didn't seem like flesh, it was more like something made of ice and rock. He was headed on a diagonal going toward Whitey and it was like watching the slow approach of gaping jaws or a steam roller or anything at all that could manage and finish off whatever it touched.

Whitey stood there not breathing. He saw the Captain coming closer. Then closer. He saw the dead-white face of Captain Kinnard coming in very close, some ten feet away, then seven feet away, and he wondered if it made sense just to stand still and wait for it to happen. He decided it didn't make the least bit of sense and he edged away from Lieutenant Pertnoy, not thinking about Pertnoy or Pertnoy's gun or the guns of the policemen. He was thinking about the big hands of the Captain and telling himself to move and move fast.

He moved. He moved very fast. The only thought in his brain was the idea of fleeing from the big hands of the Captain. He was running, not knowing where he was going, not particularly caring, just so long as it took him away from the Captain. He heard someone shouting, "Get him!" and then another voice, and he saw the policemen coming toward him.

In the same moment he heard a lot of shouting in Spanish from the other side of the room. He caught a flash of the Puerto Ricans leaping up from the benches and hurling themselves toward the opened door that led to the street. The policemen stopped and stared and for a split second they didn't seem to know what to do. In that instant the American rioters got the exit notion and jumped up and started looking for exits. A moment later the room was boiling with men running in all directions, bumping into each other, fighting to break free of each other to reach the doors and windows, the policemen grabbing at them and trying to hold on, or else using the night sticks to break it up that way, but there was no breaking it up, there was no stopping it, not even when Lieutenant Taggert

59

reached for his shoulder holster and drew his revolver and fired a warning shot. He fired another shot at the ceiling and then decided to really use the gun. He fired at one of the Puerto Ricans and the man went down with a bullet in the kneecap.

That should have stopped it. But all it did was increase the action, the prisoners accelerating their efforts to get through the doorways and windows. Lieutenant Taggert fired again and a big Ukrainian-American was hit in the abdomen and now some of the policemen had drawn their guns and were shooting. One of them hit a Puerto Rican in the shoulder. Another put a bullet through the thigh of an Irish-American who was caught in a traffic jam at the front door. Then another policeman took aim at the crowd trying to get through the front door and changed his mind and aimed his gun for a longer-range shot, pointing the gun toward the large window behind the desk platform on the far side of the room. The window was open and Whitey was climbing through.

The policeman shot and missed and fired again and the .35 slug punctured the window sill an inch away from Whitey's ribs. Whitey threw a sad-eyed, scared-rabbit glance backward at the seething room and saw all of it in a flashing instant that showed convulsive, tumultuous activity. It was a very busy room. The noise was terribly loud, a cracking-up noise that sounded like the end of everything. In the same instant that he glimpsed the frenzied action, Whitey saw the two men who were not taking part in the action, just standing on the side lines and watching it. The two men were Lieutenant Pertnoy and Captain Kinnard.

The Lieutenant stood in the corridor doorway and he had his hands in his trousers pockets. One side of his mouth was curved up, but it wasn't a smile; it was sort of quizzical, like the expression of a man looking at a board and studying a mathematical equation. A few feet away from the Lieutenant the bulky shoulders of Captain Kinnard were limp and the

60

Captain's arms hung loosely and he was shaking his head very slowly. His eyes were half closed and his mouth sagged. He was slumped there against the wall like a fighter on the ropes getting hit and hit again and not allowed to fall.

Whitey saw all of that but couldn't see more of it because now there was another shot and the bullet split the glass of the raised window above his head. He decided he wasn't traveling fast enough, and instead of climbing through the window and then climbing down, he dived through, going headfirst and then twisting in the air, twisting hard to bring his legs down. He landed on his side on the gravel driveway some ten feet below the window. He rested there with his eyes closed, wondering whether he had a broken hip. He felt it and it wasn't broken and he told himself to get up. He got up and started to walk. At first he walked slowly and with a limp. Then he limped faster. The injured hip gave him a lot of pain, but it was more flesh burn than bone hurt, and maybe if he didn't think about the pain he wouldn't need to limp. He stopped thinking about the pain and stopped limping and started to run.

He ran. He picked up speed and told himself he needed more and then he was really sprinting.

—Five—

It was three minutes later and they were chasing him down an alley off Clayton Street. Then it was five minutes later and he was in another alley four blocks east of Clayton. He was moving east and coming out of the alley and running across River Street. They came running after him and he went twenty yards going south on River, then ducked into a very narrow alley and headed east again in the thick blackness of the Hellhole, going toward the river and telling himself it might work out all right if he could reach the river. Along the water front there were a lot of places where he could hide. And maybe later he could sneak onto one of the ships. But that was for later. Much later. Right now the river was a long way off. And the law was very near. And he was very tired.

He heard them coming down the alley and he hopped a fence, getting over it before their flashlights could find him. Then across the back yard and over another fence. Then a third fence, and a fourth, with the back yards very small and piles of wood stacked here and there for fuel in the wooden shacks, just enough space for the firewood and the garbage can and the outside toilet. It was a matter of running zigzag to get to the next fence. He knew the next fence would be the last because now he was really all in. He got there and climbed over the fence and fell on his back. There was a dragging, weak clanking sound like the useless noise of stripped gears, and he knew it came from inside his chest. He had the feeling that all the flesh inside him was stripped and burned out. But it was nice to rest there flat on his back. They'd be coming soon and maybe when they saw what shape he was in they'd take him to a hospital instead of returning him to the station house. That would be a break. He closed his eyes and dragged the wonderful air into his lungs and waited for them to come.

But they didn't come. Several minutes passed and they didn't come. There was no sound and no reflection of flashlights. He reasoned they were still headed east, they probably figured it wouldn't be these back yards and their man was trying for the river. That meant their search would be concentrated along the water front. He decided they'd be busy there for the rest of the night and he might as well go to sleep here. His arm curled under his head and he closed his eyes.

The wind from the river was very cold but he was too tired to feel it. It took him less than a minute to fall asleep. An hour later he opened his eyes and a light hit him in the face. It was a flickering light and it had nothing to do with the back yard. He told himself he was still asleep. But then he opened his eyes again and realized he was really awake and this wasn't the back yard.

It was the interior of the wooden shack. He was resting under some blankets on a narrow cot against the wall. The other furniture was a three-legged stool and a two-legged table with the other two sides supported on wooden fruit boxes. The flickering light came from a candle in a small holder on the table. Along the walls there were rows of gallon jugs containing colorless liquid. On the table there was a bottle half filled with the colorless liquid, and alongside the bottle there was an empty water glass. There was only one door in the room and Whitey knew that what he'd thought was the back yard was really the front yard. So this place had no back yard; in the back it was just another alley and then more wooden shacks. He knew it because now he was fully awake and able to think fairly clearly, able to judge the distance he'd covered from the station house to here. This was strictly seven-dollars-a-month territory. This was the Afro-American section of the Hellhole.

The door opened and a colored man came in. The colored man was as dark as the emery strip of a match book. He was around five-nine and couldn't have weighed more than 115 at the most. There was no hair on his head and there weren't many wrinkles on his face and it was impossible to tell how old he was. He wore rimless spectacles and a woman's fur coat made of squirrel.

Whitey was sitting up in the cot and looking at the woman's fur coat.

"Don't get the wrong notion," the colored man said. He fingered the squirrel collar. "I just wear this to keep warm. I'm an old man and I can't take cold weather. Gotta have this fur on me to keep the chill away."

The colored man had several chunks of firewood tucked under his arm and he moved slowly across the room and put the wood in a small old-fashioned furnace that had a crooked handmade outlet going up through the ceiling. For some moments the colored man was busy with the furnace and then he closed the lid and walked to the three-legged stool and sat down. He had his back to Whitey and all he did was sit there, not moving, not saying anything.

It went on like that for the better part of a minute. There was a certain deliberateness in the way the colored man sat there motionless with his back to the man in the cot. It was as though the colored man were experimenting with the man in the cot, waiting to see what the man would do while he had his back turned.

Whitey caught the drift of it. "You don't hafta test me," he said. "I'm straight."

"Yiz?" the colored man said. He still had his back turned. "How do I know?"

"You musta thought so, or you wouldn't have brought me in here."

"I brought you in cause you were out there freezing. You were half froze when I dragged you in. Just as stiff as a carrot in an icebox."

Whitey didn't say anything. He was thinking about the colored man's accent. There was some South in it, but not much. It was mostly New England. Some of the words were clipped and the edges polished and it was like the highly cultured voice of someone on a lecture platform. Other words were spoken in the nasal twang of a Vermont farm hand. Then at longer spaced intervals there'd be a word or two from way down deep in Mississippi. It was as though the colored man weren't quite sure where he'd come from. Or maybe he was continually reminding himself of all the places he'd seen, all the accents he'd heard. Whitey had the feeling that the colored man was very old and had been to a lot of places.

"I hadda go out to use the toilet," the colored man said. "I saw you out there flat on the ground and I didn't like that, I didn't like that at all."

"Did it scare you?" Whitey said.

"No," the colored man said. "I never get scared." He was quiet for a long moment. And then, very slowly, "But sometimes I get curious."

Whitey waited for the colored man to turn on the stool and face him. The colored man didn't move from his position facing the table.

65

"You wanna leave now?" the colored man said.

"I'd like to stay here for a while. That is, if you'll let me."

"I'm thinking about it," the colored man said. There was another long pause. And then, again very slowly, "You wanna help me decide?"

"If I can."

"I guess you can." The colored man turned on the stool and looked at Whitey and said, "All you gotta do is tell me the truth."

"All right."

"You sure it's all right? You sure it won't hurt you to tell the truth?"

"It might," Whitey said.

"But you're willing to take a chance!"

Whitey shrugged. "I got no choice."

"That ain't the way I see it. I'm prone to think you might try to bluff me."

"No, I wouldn't do that."

"You mean you couldn't do that." The colored man took off his rimless spectacles and leaned forward just a little, his eyes glinting bright yellow, like topaz. There was a certain see-all, know-all power coming from the topaz eyes and shooting into Whitey's head. And the colored man said, "I want you to know it in front. No use trying to bluff me. Ain't a living ass in this world can bluff Jones Jarvis."

Whitey nodded in agreement. It was a slow nod and he meant it. He had the feeling that the colored man was not bragging or exaggerating, but merely stating a fact.

"Jones Jarvis," the colored man said. "Once when I had a phone they'd get it wrong in the book and list me under Jones. Did that year after year and finally I got tired telling them to change it. Got rid of the phone. Man has a right to have his name printed correct. It's Jones first and then Jarvis. The name is Jones Jarvis."

66

"Jones Jarvis," Whitey said.

"That's right. That's absolutely correct. I like everything to be correct. Exactly in line. It's gotta be that way or there ain't no use talking. So now I want to hear your name."

"They call me Whitey."

"You see, now? You're pulling away from it, you're not telling me correct. I want your real name."

Whitey winced slightly. He told himself it was seven years since he'd used his real name. All the reasons why he'd stopped using it came back to him and hammered at his head and he winced harder. In the instant that his eyes were closed he saw the short and very wide and very long-armed man with the bright-green cap and black-and-purple plaid lumber jacket. Just for that instant and that was all. And then his eyes were open and he was looking at Jones Jarvis. He heard himself saying, "My name is Eugene Lindell."

The colored man sat motionless for some moments and then very slowly raised his head and looked up at the ceiling. "I know that name," he said.

Whitey didn't say anything.

The colored man went on squinting up at the ceiling. "I'm sure I know that name" he said. "I'll be a son of a bitch if I ain't heard that name before."

Then it was quiet and Whitey waited and wondered whether the colored man would remember. The colored man was trying hard to remember, snapping his fingers as though he thought the sound of it would bring back the memory.

Finally the colored man looked at Whitey and said, "Tell me something. We ever meet before?"

"No," Whitey said.

The topaz eyes were narrow. "You sure about that?" Whitey nodded.

"Well, anyway," the colored man said, "I know that name. I swear I've heard it someplace. Or let's see now, maybe I read

67

about it someplace." He was looking past Whitey. He raised a wrinkled finger to his chin. "Let's see," he murmured aloud to himself. "Let's see if we can hit this."

"It ain't important," Whitey said. Something in the way he said it caused Jones Jarvis to look at him, and he added offhandedly, "At least, it ain't important now."

The topaz eyes narrowed again. "Was it important then?"

Whitey looked at the floor.

"Want me to skip it?" the colored man said.

Whitey went on looking at the floor. He nodded very slowly.

"All right," Jones Jarvis said. "We'll skip it. Whatever happened to you long ago ain't none of my business. Only questions I'm privileged to ask are about tonight. I wanna know what you were doing on my property."

"Hiding," Whitey said.

"From who?"

"Police."

"I figured that," Jones said. And then, for the first time, he showed a smile. "Can always tell when a man is hot, even when he's freezing. I took one look and you were hot, really hot."

Whitey pulled his legs from under the blanket and lowered them over the side of the bed. He smiled back at Jones and said, "I'm still hot. I'm hot as hell."

"Don't I know it?" Jones said. "I'm taking your temperature right now. Using two thermometers." And he pointed to his own eyes. Then, leaning back a little, with the squirrel coat unbuttoned to show the toothpick build attired in pale-green flannel pajamas, crossing one skinny leg over the other and clasping his knees, he said conversationally, "Tell me about it."

"It happened about an hour ago" Whitey said. "Or maybe ninety minutes. I'm not really sure."

"Let's check that," Jones said. "I always like to be sure of the time." He reached into a pocket of the squirrel coat and took out a large pocket watch and looked at the dial. "It's one-twenty-six A.M.," he murmured. "That help you any?"

Whitey knew he was still under close scrutiny and technical appraisal. He realized that one wrong answer would lose him this hiding place that he needed very badly. The topaz eyes told him to get his answers exactly correct.

He said, "Closest I can come is a little after midnight. Let's say twelve-ten." He smiled openly and truthfully, "That's really the best I can do."

"All right," Jones said. He put the watch back in his pocket. "Where were you at twelve-ten?"

"On a side street not far from here."

"How far?"

"I'd say a coupla blocks."

"What were you doing?" Jones asked.

"Taking a walk."

"Is that all?"

"No," Whitey said. But he couldn't take it past that. He knew he couldn't make mention of the man he'd been following, the man who wore a bright-green cap and a black-and-purple plaid lumber jacket. If he started talking about it he'd be going away from tonight, going in reverse, going back seven years, and it would get very involved. It would be like opening a tomb in his mind and seeing a part of himself that had suffered and died and wanted to stay dead and buried.

Yet somehow he could feel it straining to come alive again, as he'd felt it earlier tonight when he'd seen the very short, very wide man who wore the bright-green cap. He could feel the tugging, the grinding, the burning of a deep pain that tightened his mouth and showed in his eyes.

And the pain was there in his cracked-whisper voice as he said, "I won't say what I was doing on that street. It's got nothing to do with why I'm hiding from the law."

Jones Jarvis was quiet for some moments. He was studying the pain-racked eyes of the small white-haired man. When Jones finally spoke, his voice was very soft and almost tender. Jones said, "All right, Eugene. We'll let it ride."

"But I want you to believe me. I'm giving it to you straight."

"Yes," Jones said. "That's the impression I get. Even though it's kind of blurry at the edges."

"It'll have to stay that way. I can't trim it down any closer."

"I guess you can't," Jones said. "But all the same, you got me sidetracked. You tell me it was past midnight and you're out for a stroll. In the Hellhole. You're just taking a stroll down here in the Hellhole. Where no man in his right mind walks alone after midnight. Unless he's looking to get hurt. Or do some hurting."

"I said I can't tell you —"

"All right, Eugene, all right." Jones smiled soothingly. "Let's leave it at that. Go on, take it from there."

Whitey took it from there and told the rest of it just as it had happened. He said it matter-of-factly, looking levelly at the old man, who sat there on the three-leg stool looking at him and into him and nodding slowly at intervals. When it was finished, he leaned back on the cot, resting on his elbows, waiting for the old man either to accept the story or to start looking for loopholes in it.

Jones Jarvis did not indicate whether he was buying it or doubting it or wondering how to take it. It seemed that Jones was thinking about something else. Now his eyes were aimed past Whitey, like lenses fixed for a wider-range focus.

Finally Jones shook his head very slowly and said, "I feel sorry for the Captain."

"It he ever gets hold of me," Whitey said, "I'll feel damn sorry for myself."

"He's really got his hands full," Jones said.

Whitey shrugged. "I don't care what he's got in his hands. Just so long as it ain't me."

But Jones was thinking above that and far beyond that. "I've lived in this neighborhood a good many years," he said. "It's always been exactly what they call it, a hellhole. But lately it's been worse than that. Like a furnace that can't hold the fire and all the flames are shooting out. It puts a certain smell in the air. Sometimes I walk outside at night and I can smell it. The smell of men hating each other. The rotten stink of race riot."

Whitey was only half listening. He was concentrating on the necessity of remaining hidden from the law. He wondered whether the old man would allow him to stay here for a day or two.

But the old man was thinking about the race riots and saying, "It's a pity. It's a terrible pity. I wonder what started it."

Whitey looked around at the four walls of the small wooden shack. The boards were loose and splintered and in places the wood was decaying. But somehow the walls seemed very secure and there was the comfortable feeling of safety. It was nice to sit here on the cot with the four walls around him and he hoped he'd be permitted to stay for a while.

Then he heard the old man saying, "What do you think started it?"

He looked at the old man. "Started what?"

"These riots. These race riots."

"Damned if I know," Whitey said without interest. And then, shrugging, "Anyway, it don't concern me."

"No?"

"Why should it? I got no ax to grind."

Jones Jarvis took off the rimless spectacles. His naked eyes, narrowed and glinting, drilled into the face of the small white-haired man and he said, "You sure?"

"Absolutely," Whitey answered. It was an emphatic word

and he tried to say it with emphasis. Rut it didn't come out that way. It came out rather weakly.

He heard the old man saying, "Every man has an ax to grind. Whether he knows it or not."

Whitey didn't say anything.

"I've been on this earth a long time," Jones Jarvis said. "I'm eighty-six. That makes me too old to grind the ax. But the Lord knows I did it when I was younger. Did it with all the strength in my body. And don't think I wasn't scared when I did it. So scared I wanted to turn and run and hide in the woods. Much safer that way. Much healthier. But there's some things more important to a man than his health. So I stayed there and saw them coming to grab me and I didn't move and when they got in real close I looked them straight in the eye. I talked back to them and said I hadn't touched that white girl and I gave them the facts to prove it. They moved in closer and I pulled the blade from my pocket and showed it to them. And I told them to come on, come on, come and get me. They stood there and saw that blade in my hand. Then one of them said, "You swear to it, Jones? You swear you didn't do it? On your mother's life?" I looked at this man who had the rope in his hand all ready for me and I said, "How'd you like to kiss my black ass?' So then all they did was turn and walk away. I waited until they were gone, then made for the woods, and later that day I hopped a freight going north. But it wasn't no scared weasel running away. It was a man. It was a man going on a trip."

Whitey was looking at the floor. He was frowning slightly and his mouth scarcely moved as he said, "All right, you've made your point. You're a man. And I'm just a scared weasel."

"You really believe that? You want it that way?"

"Sure," Whitey said. He looked up. "Sure. Why not?" Again it sounded weak and he told himself he didn't care how weak it sounded. He put a very weak grin on his lips and he said

72

loosely and lazily, "I lost my spinal column a good many years ago. There ain't no surgery can put it back. Even if there was, I wouldn't want it. I like it better this way. More comfortable."

"No," Jones said. "You're telling a fib and you know it."

Whitey widened the grin. He said joshingly, "How can you tell?"

"Never mind," Jones said. "I can tell, that's all. It shows."

"What shows?" The grin began to fade. He pointed to his shaggy mop of prematurely white hair. "This?"

"That's part of it," Jones murmured. "And your eyes. And the way your mouth sets. And something else." He leaned forward and let the pause come in and drift for a long moment, and then he said, "Your voice."

"Huh?"

"Your voice," Jones said. "The way you can't talk above a whisper. As if you got a rupture in your throat. As if it's all torn apart in there."

Again Whitey looked at the floor. The grin was gone now and he didn't know what was on his face. He opened his mouth to say something and he tried to get the sound past his lips and nothing came out.

"Or maybe it ain't the throat," the old man said. "Maybe it's the heart."

"It's the throat," Whitey said.

"Maybe it's both."

Whitey lowered his head and put his hand to his eyes and pressed hard. He was trying to deepen the blackness of the dark screen that ought to be very black because it was only his closed eyelids, but something was projected on it and he was forced to look and see. It was a memory he didn't want to see and his hand pressed harder against his closed eyes. On the screen it showed clearly and vividly, and he thought: Now, that's queer, it oughta be foggy. After all, it's an old-time film, it's seven years old.

He heard Jones Jarvis saying, "I'm prone to think that maybe it's both. Ruined throat. Broken heart."

"Let it ride," Whitey mumbled. He still had his hand pressed hard to his eyes. "For Christ's sake, let it ride."

"Eugene Lindell," the old man said.

"No."

"Eugene Lindell." And then the loud crisp sound of snapping fingers. And the old man saying, "Now I get it. It's been coming slowly and now it's really hit me and I got it. Eugene Lindell."

"Please don't."

But the old man had it started. And he had to go on with it. And he said aloud to himself, "First time I heard that name I was listening to the radio. The announcer said, 'And now the lad with the million-dollar voice. Here he is, folks, Gene Lindell, singing—'"

"Stop it," Whitey choked.

"Singing—"

"Will you stop it?"

"Singing from 'way up high on the moon and 'way down deep in the sea. High and low and high again, and it was a voice that made you high when you heard it, happy high and sad high, and you hadda close your eyes, you didn't wanna see a goddamn thing, just sit there and listen to that singing. You knew you'd never heard a voice like that in all your born days. And then them bobby-soxers started yelling and screaming and you felt like doing the same. That voice did things to you, went into you so deep it made you get the feeling you hadda come out of yourself and fly up and away from where your feet were planted. So next day I walked into a music store and all the loot I'd saved that week was shoved across the counter. 'Gene Lindell,' I said. 'Gimme his records.' The clerk said, 'Sorry, mister. We're sold out.' A few days later I tried again, and this time he had just one in stock. I took it home and played it and played it, and for weeks I went on playing that record and the jitterbugs would come in and forget to chew their bubble gum, only thing they could do was stand there with their mouths open and get hit between the eyes with that voice. They'd forget to move their feet. They were jitterbugs but they couldn't jitter because that voice took hold of them and paralyzed them. That was what it did. It was that kind of voice."

Whitey was sitting bent very low on the edge of the cot. He had both hands covering his face. It seemed he was trying to shut himself away from the living world.

But he could hear the old man saying, "You had it, Gene. You really had it."

He took his hands away from his face. He looked at the old man and smiled pleadingly, pathetically. His cracked-whisper voice was scarcely audible. "Why don't you stop it? What do you want from me?"

"Just a simple answer," Jones Jarvis said. He had leaned back and now he leaned forward again. "Tell me," he said. "How did you lose it? What happened to you?"

The smile widened and stiffened and then he had it aimed past the old man, his eyes glazed and fixed on nothing in particular. It all added up to a sort of crazy grimace.

"Won't you tell me?" the old man asked very softly and gently. And then, plaintively, "I think I got a right to know. After all, I was one of your fans."

Whitey sat there and tried to look at the old man. But he couldn't look. And he couldn't get the grimace off his face. He was trying very hard but he couldn't do anything but just sit there and stare at nothing.

Jones watched him for some moments. Then Jones's expression became clinical and he said, "Maybe you could use a drink."

Whitey tried to nod. But he couldn't move his head. It felt very heavy and sort of crushed, as though steel clamps were attached to his temples and pressing against his brain.

75

Jones got up from the three-legged stool and moved toward the row of gallon jugs filled with colorless liquid. He picked up a jug, took it to the table, and began pouring the liquid into the half-filled bottle. He poured until the bottle was completely full. Then he put the jug back in its place among the others. He set it down very carefully, moved some of the other jugs to get them exactly in line along the wall, then nodded approvingly like a show-window expert satisfied with the display.

"It's high-grade merchandise," Jones said, as though he were talking to a potential customer. But his tone was sort of forced. He was trying to get Whitey's mind away from Whitey. He made a stiff-armed gesture, pointing to the gallon jugs, and went on: "I manufacture it myself. Know everything that goes in it, and I guarantee it's a hundred per cent pure, it's really high-grade. Just alcohol and water, but the way it's mixed is what gives it the charge. So it ain't no ordinary shake-up. It's a first class brand of goathead. Real fine goathead. The finest goddamn goathead ever made in any cellar."

He glanced at Whitey, hoping for a comment or any reaction at all. But there was nothing. Whitey just sat there with his glazed eyes staring fixedly at empty space, the wide-smile grimace now wider and crazier, way out there in left field, very far away from Jones Jarvis and the goathead and everything.

The old man gave it another try. He pointed to a hinged arrangement on the floor that indicated a floor door and he said, "That goes down to the cellar. All day long I'm down there making it, mixing it, tasting it so's I'll be sure it's just right. Sometimes it tastes so good I forget to come upstairs. Wake up a day later and wonder what the hell happened. But never sick. With Jones Jarvis' goathead it just ain't possible to get sick. That junk they sell in the stores can make a man sick as hell, he'll pay two, three, three-and-a-half a pint and wind up paying five to get his stomach pumped out. But that won't happen when he drinks my brand. No matter how much he drinks, he'll never get sick. And it sells for only six bits a pint.

"That's value, man, that's real value," he went on, trying very hard to get Whitey's mind away from Whitey. "Them big whisky people oughta be ashamed of themselves, charging what they do for that stuff they advertise. They give it a fancy name and a fancy label, with pretty pictures in the magazines, a big-shot businessman sitting there in the big fine room with all the books and a couple of high-priced hunting dogs and he's holding the glass and saying it's real good whisky and he drinks it and you oughta drink it too. What he should do is come here and buy a bottle of Jones Jarvis' goathead. He'd never touch that other junk again. He'd –"

Whitey was getting up from the cot. As he lifted himself to his feet, the wide-smile grimace began to fade from his face. His eyes gradually lost the glazed staring-at-nothing look and the stiffness was gone from his lips. It was a slow change and he went through it quietly and calmly, and finally he stood there completely relaxed.

Then he moved toward the door.

"Where you going?" Jones said.

"Out."

"But where?"

"Station house."

The old man moved quickly to insert himself between Whitey and the door. "No," the old man said. "Don't do that."

Whitey smiled mildly and politely and waited for the old man to get away from the door.

"Listen, " the old man said. "Listen, Gene –"

"Yes?" he murmured very politely.

"Stay here," the old man said. "Stay here and have a drink."

"No, thanks. Thanks very much."

"Come on, have a drink," the old man said. He gestured

toward the filled bottle on the table. "There it is. Right there. Waiting for you."

"No," he said. "But thanks anyway. Thanks a lot."

"You mean you don't drink?" the old man asked. His eyes tried to pull Whitey's eyes away from the door. He was trying to make it a conversation about drinking.

"Yes," Whitey said. "I drink. I do a lot of drinking. I drink all the time."

"Sure you do." Jones Jarvis smiled companionably, as one drinker to another. "Come on, let's have a shot."

Whitey smiled back and shook his head very slowly.

"Come on, Gene. It'll do you good. You know you want a drink."

"No," Whitey said, wanting a drink very badly, his mouth and throat and belly begging for the colorless liquid in the bottle on the table just a few steps away.

"Just one," the old man said. He moved quickly to the table, pulled the cap off the bottle, and brought the bottle to Whitey. "I want you to taste this goathead."

"No," Whitey said. He was looking past the old man, at the door. "I'm going back to the station house."

The old man stood there between Whitey and the door. For some moments he looked at Whitey's face. Then he looked down at the bottle of goathead. He lifted the bottle to his mouth and took a quick swallow. As it went down and burned and hit like a blockbuster hitting the target, his body vibrated and his old man's head snapped forward and back and forward again. "Goddamn, " he said, speaking to the bottle. "You're bad, man. You're a bad sonofabitch."

Whitey reached past the old man and put his hand on the doorknob.

"Don't," the old man said. His hand came down very gently on Whitey's arm. "Please, Gene. Please don't."

"Why not?" He kept his hand closed on the doorknob. He was looking at the door and saying, "What else is there to do?"

"Stay here."

"And wait for them to find me?" He smiled sadly, resignedly. "They're gonna find me sooner or later."

"Not if you hide. Not if you wait for a chance to run."

"They'd get me anyway," he said. "They're bound to get me, no matter what I do. When they're looking for a cop-killer, they never stop looking."

"But you're not a cop-killer," Jones said. His hand tightened on Whitey's arm. "Use your brains, man. Don't let yourself go haywire. You know you didn't do it. You gotta remember you didn't do it. If you go back to that station house, it's just like signing a confession. Like walking into the butcher shop and putting yourself on the meat block."

The sadness went out of the smile and it became a dry grin. Whitey was thinking of the Captain. In his mind he saw the Captain attired in a bloodstained butcher's apron. He saw the cleaver raised and coming down, but somehow he didn't care, maybe it was all for the best. What the hell, he should have been out of it a long time ago. No use continuing the masquerade. He said to himself: The truth is, buddy, you really don't give a damn, you'd just as soon be out of it.

He heard Jones Jarvis saying, "Or maybe you just don't care."

Whitey winced. He looked at the old man's topaz eyes, peering inside his brain.

Jones said, "You gotta care. You gotta drill it into yourself you got something to live for."

"Like what?" he asked in the cracked whisper that always reminded him it was a matter of no hope, no soap, nothing at all.

But the old man was still in there trying. And saying, "Like looking for an answer. No matter what the question is, there's always an answer."

"Sure," he agreed, grinning again. "In this case, it's strictly zero."

"It's never zero," the old man said. "Not while you're able to breathe."

"I'm tired of breathing." As he said it, it sounded funny to him, and he widened the grin.

"It's a goddamn shame," the old man said. He loosened his grip on Whitey's arm. He looked down at the bottle in his hand, then gazed down past the bottle to focus on the splintered shabby boards of the floor. He spoke to the floor, saying, "My fault. It's all my fault. I couldn't keep my big mouth shut. I couldn't leave it where it was, with him sitting there on the cot, man named Whitey just sitting there cooling himself and getting comfortable. I hadda open up my goddamn mouth and talk about Gene Lindell, the singer."

Whitey held onto the grin. "Don't let it bother you, Jones."

Jones went on talking to the floor. It was as though Whitey had already walked out of the shack. "Now he's going back to that station house and the Captain'll tear him to shreds. Really go to work on him, that's for sure. And it's my fault. It's all my fault."

"It ain't no such thing," Whitey said. He put his hand on the old man's shoulder. "It's just the way things are stacked up, that's all. You mustn't feel bad about it. Maybe all they'll do is throw me in a cell."

"I wouldn't bet on that," the old man said. He lifted his gaze from the floor and looked at Whitey. "Not even with fifty-to-one odds. Or make it a hundred-to-one and I still wouldn't take it. That Thirty-seventh Precinct is a madhouse. It's these race riots, getting worse and worse, and now the riots really score and a cop from the Thirty-seventh gets put in the cemetery. And that does it, man, that really does it. That flips the Captain's lid, and I'm prone to say right now he's just about ready for a strait jacket."

Whitey shrugged. "Maybe he's wearing it already."

"No," the old man said. "They don't put strait jackets on police captains." And then abruptly and somewhat frantically he gripped Whitey's wrists. "Don't go back there, Gene. Please. Don't go back."

Whitey shrugged again. It was a slow shrug and it told the old man that Eugene Lindell was headed for the station house. The old man's hands went limp and fell away from Whitey's wrists. Whitey turned the doorknob and opened the door and walked out of the shack.

−Six−

It was like walking inside an overturned barrel that revolved slowly and wouldn't let him get anywhere. There were no window lights and no lampposts, as though all electric bulbs were conspiring to put him in the dark and get him lost. It was the same with the sky. There was no moon at all. It was hiding behind thick clouds that wouldn't allow the glow to come through. The sky was starless and pitch-black.

The only light that showed was the yellow face of the City Hall clock, very high up there about a mile and a half to the north of the Hellhole. The hands pointed to one-forty-five. But he wasn't interested in the time element. He wished that the lit-up lace of the City Hall clock could throw a stronger light so he could see where he was going.

He was really lost. There were too many intersecting alleys and narrow, twisting streets to confuse him and take him into more alleys. He was trying to find River Street, so that he could get his bearings and go on from there to Clayton and then to the station house. But in the darkness his sense of direction was confused. And the maze of alleys was like a circular stairway going down and putting him deeper and deeper into the Hellhole.

One wrong turn had done it. When he'd walked out of the wooden shack he'd gone left instead of right, and after that it was right turn instead of left, then south instead of north, east instead of west. He might have used the City Hall clock as a point of reference, except that it wasn't there all the time. It played tricks on him and vanished behind the tenement rooftops. Then it showed again and he'd use it for a while until there'd be a dead-end street or alley and he'd have to go back and start all over. Finally the clock was hidden altogether and he couldn't see anything but black sky and black walls and the dark alleys that were taking him nowhere.

It went on like that and it got him annoyed. Then very much annoyed. Then it struck him sort of funny. As though the Hellhole were using him to joke around with the law. The Hellhole was getting clever and cute with the Thirty-seventh District. Like saying to the Captain: This stupid bastard wants to give himself up, but you don't get him that easy. We'll let him outta here when we're good and ready.

Whitey laughed without sound. It was really as though the Hellhole were pulling the Captain's leg. Or sticking in another needle. Ever so gently. To let the Captain know that law enforcement was not welcome in this neighborhood, that all honest cops were enemies and the dark alleys were friendly to all renegades. With extra hospitality for copkillers. No sirree, the Hellhole said to Captain Kinnard of the Thirty-seventh District, this is our boy Whitey and we won't letcha have him. Not yet, anyway. But don't worry, Captain, don't get your bowels in an uproar, it ain't even two o'clock and maybe you'll have him before morning.

It wasn't anyone's voice and yet Whitey could almost hear it talking. He began to have the feeling that a lot was going to happen before morning.

The feeling grew in him and he tried to make it go away but it stayed there and went on growing. He was walking slowly down a very narrow alley and seeing the darkness ahead, just the darkness, nothing else. Or maybe there was something down there that he could see but didn't want to see. Maybe he was trying not to look at it. He blinked hard and told himself it wasn't really there.

Then he blinked again and focused hard and he knew it was there.

He saw the faint glow pouring thinly from a kitchen window, floating out across the alley and showing the color and the shape of the moving figure.

Bright green. That was the cap. Black and purple. That was the plaid lumber jacket. The shape was very short and very wide, with extremely long arms.

Hello, Whitey said without sound. Hello again.

He stood motionless and saw the short wide man standing there in the back yard under the dimly lit kitchen window. The distance between himself and the man was some forty yards and he couldn't see clearly what the man was doing. It seemed that the man wasn't doing anything. Then Whitey noticed the tiny moving form at the man's feet. It was a gray kitten lapping at the contents of a saucer.

The glow from the window showed the short wide man stooping over to pet the kitten. The kitten went on with its meal and the man knelt beside it and seemed to be talking to it. Presently the kitten was finished with the meal and the man picked it up with one hand, fondled it with the other, held its furry face to his cheek to let it know it had a friend in this world. The kitten accepted the petting and Whitey could hear the sound of its contented meow. The man put it down and gently patted its head. It meowed again, wanting more petting. The man turned away and moved across the back yard under the

84

glow from the kitchen window, opening the kitchen door and entering the house.

Whitey moved automatically. He wasn't sure what he was thinking as he walked down the alley toward the lighted window. He tried to tell himself it didn't make sense to move in this direction, just as it hadn't made sense to follow the man when he'd seen him earlier tonight on Skid Row. It just didn't make sense at all.

It had no connection with now. It was strictly a matter of past history. Something from 'way back there, seven years ago. There was no good reason for going back. And every damn good reason to stay away from it, not let it take him back.

Check it, he said to himself. Stop walking and check it and forget about it. Let it rest where it is. For Christ's sake, bury it, will you?

But the lighted window said no. The lighted window was a magnet, pulling him closer. He moved on down the alley, his feet walking forward and his brain swimming backward through a sea of time. It was a dark sea, much darker than the alley. The tide was slow and there were no waves, just tiny ripples that murmured very softly. Telling him all about yesterday. Telling him that yesterday could never really be discarded, it was always a part of now. There was just no way to get rid of it. No way to push it aside or throw it into an ash can, or dig a hole and bury it. For all buried memories were nothing more than slow-motion boomerangs, taking their own sweet time to come back. This one had taken seven years.

He went on down the alley and came to a loose-nailed fence with most of the posts missing. He gazed across the small back yard, seeing through the kitchen window a still-life painting of some empty plates and cups stacked on a sink. The background was faded gray wallpaper, torn here and there, some of the plaster showing. Then some life crept into the painting, but it wasn't much, just one of the smaller residents of the Hellhole, a water roach moving slowly along the edge of the sink.

He stood there waiting for more life to appear in the kitchen. Nothing appeared and there was no sound from inside the house. It was a small two-story wooden house, very old and with a don't-care look about it. Typical Hellhole real estate. On either side it was separated from the adjoining dwellings by not more than a few inches of empty air. In addition to the kitchen window there was the back door and one dark window on the second floor and then there was a very small cellar window with no glass in it, and he thought: They're not living very high these days. Looks like business ain't been so good.

Just then someone came into the kitchen. It was the short wide man. He had taken off the bright green cap and the lumber jacket and he stood there at the sink pouring himself a glass of water. He filled the glass to the brim, jerked it to his mouth, and drained it in one long gulp. Then he put down the glass, turned slowly so that Whitey saw him in profile, and began a meditative scratching along the top of his head.

His head was completely bald. It glistened white and there were seams in it from stitched scars and it was like a polished volleyball. He had very small ears and the one that showed was somewhat mashed. His nose was badly mashed, almost completely disorganized, so that it was hardly a nose at all. His lips were very thick and the lower lip was puffed at the corner. Also, his jaw was out of line, as though it had been fractured more than once. It was hard to tell his age, but Whitey knew he was at least fifty.

Whitey stood some fifteen feet away from the kitchen window, his hands resting on the back-yard fence, his eyes focused on the man in the kitchen, his lips saying without sound, Hello, Chop.

And then someone else appeared in there. A big woman. She was very big. Really huge. Around fiveeleven and weighing

86

over three hundred. Built like a tree trunk, no shape at all except the straight-up-and-down of no breasts, no belly, no rear. She was in her middle thirties and looked about the same as she'd looked seven years ago. Same bobbed hair with the neck shaved high and the mud-brown hair cut very close to the sides of her head. Same tiny eyes pushed into the fat meat of her face like tiny pins in a cushion. Same creases on her thick neck and along the sides of her big hooked nose. Same great big ugly girl named Bertha.

Hello, Whitey said without sound. Hello, Bertha.

He watched the two of them in there in the kitchen. They were talking. The window was closed and he couldn't hear what they were saying. He saw Chop taking another drink of water, then moving to the side to make room for Bertha at the sink. Bertha turned on the faucet and started to wash the dishes. She washed them without soap and used her hand for a dishrag. Chop walked out of the kitchen and Bertha continued to wash the dishes. She paused for a moment to light a cigarette, and while she was lighting it another face appeared in profile in the window.

It was a man wearing a bathrobe and smoking a cigar. The man was in his middle forties, sort of flabby and out of condition but not really unattractive. He was a six-footer and weighed around 190, and if it hadn't been for the paunch it would have been a fairly nice build. He had all his hair and it was a thick crop, dark brown, parted on the side and flowing back in long loose waves. His features were pleasantly shaped and balanced and wholesomely masculine. The cigar looked very appropriate in his mouth. His appearance summed up was that of a medium-successful businessman.

Whitey looked at the six-footer in there in the kitchen. Without sound Whitey said, Hello, Sharkey.

Then his hands were tighter on the top of the wooden fence. He was waiting for another face to appear in the window. He told himself he'd seen three of them and that made it three fourths of what he'd come here to see. Or maybe the three he'd seen were nothing more than preliminaries leading to the windup. If that fourth face showed, it would really be the windup. And he'd paid a lot for his ringside seat. He'd paid plenty. The ticket of admission was a stack of calendars. Seven calendars.

He went on waiting for the fourth face to appear in the window. And he said to himself: All you want is a look-see, that's all, you just wanna get a glimpse of her.

Just a glimpse. Just a chance to look at her again after all these years. He thought: What a chance, buddy, what a chance to let it hit you between the eyes and cut through you and eat your heart out. If you had one grain of brains you'd get the hell away from here.

But he stayed there at the fence, grabbing at the chance, just as he'd grabbed at it when he'd seen Chop walking past the hash house on Skid Row; when he'd followed Chop down River Street, with his thoughts not on Chop, but only on Chop's destination, the long-shot bet that wherever it was, whatever it was, she might be there and he could peer through a window and get a look at her.

And while he waited, all other factors drifted away. He forgot where he was. The locale didn't matter in the least. Instead of a kitchen window in a Hellhole dwelling it might be any old window in any Old Main Line mansion. Or Irish castle. Or Chinese pagoda. It might be the eyepiece of a telescope aimed at the moon. He stood there focusing with his eyes burning hard like dry ice getting harder. With his mind pulled away from all current events involving the Skid Row bum named Whitey, the captain named Kinnard, the detective lieutenants named Pertnoy and Taggert, the old man named Jones Jarvis, who'd come out with the cosmic conclusion. "Every man has an ax to grind."

But cosmic conclusions and current events had no connection with the kitchen window. In the blackness of the night it was the only thing that showed, the only thing that mattered. It was the chance to get a glimpse of her.

He went on waiting. The window showed Sharkey smoking his cigar and having a quiet discussion with Bertha. Then Sharkey walked out of the kitchen and Bertha resumed washing the dishes. She worked very slowly, and once she stopped to light another cigarette, then stopped again to scratch herself under her arms. Some minutes later she was finished with the dishes and finished with the cigarette. She threw the stub in the sink and reached up toward the wall switch.

No, Whitey said without sound. Don't put that light out.

But Bertha was walking out of the kitchen and her thick finger flicked the switch. So then it was just an unlighted window that showed black nothing.

Well, Whitey thought. That's it. The show's over. But you didn't see what you came to see and you oughta get your money back. Or get a rain check and come back tomorrow night.

But he knew there'd be no rain check for tomorrow night. By then he'd be in the grip of the law and locked up in a little room with barred windows. Or in a bed in a white room with his face all bandaged, a pulpy mess resulting from the two big fists of Captain Kinnard. Or maybe the Captain's fists would take it all the way, and Pertnoy's mention of a trip to the morgue would be no exaggeration.

At any rate, there'd be no show tomorrow night. No second chance to visit this house and take a look through the kitchen window and get a glimpse of her.

His brain came back to current events. This man here was just a Skid Row bum named Whitey, just a punching bag for the slugger named Kid Fate. So what the hell, he thought, it's easier to take the slugging than to wait and think about it.

He told himself to start walking and find his way back to the station house.

He let his hands slide off the fence. He started to turn away and took one step going away and came to a rigid halt.

The kitchen window was lighted again.

He looked. He saw her.

He saw a woman in her late twenties. She was about five-four and very slim, almost skinny except for the sinuous lines that twisted and coiled, flowing warm-thin-syrupy under gray-green velvet that matched the color of her eyes. Her hair was a shade lighter than bronze and she had it brushed straight back, covering her ears. Her features were thin and her skin was pale and she was certainly not pretty. But it was an exciting face. It was terribly exciting because it radiated something that a man couldn't see with his eyes but could definitely feel in his bloodstream.

Hello, he said without sound. Hello, Celia.

He stood there sinking into yesterday, going down deeper and deeper and finally arriving 'way down there at the very beginning...

The beginning was the orphanage, the day he'd won first prize in the singing contest. Someone told someone about how this kid could sing. Then that someone told him. Eventually some papers were signed and his legal guardian was a third-rate orchestra leader who paid him thirty-five a week. He was seventeen at the time and had the idea he was a very lucky boy, getting all that money for merely doing what he enjoyed doing most of all. No matter what songs they gave him to sing, he sang with gladness and fervor and a certain rapture that really melted them. It finally melted the orchestra leader, who told him he was too good for this league and belonged up there in the big time. The orchestra leader gave up the orchestra and became the personal manager of Gene Lindell.

When Gene Lindell was twenty-three, he was making around four hundred a week.

A few years later Gene Lindell was making close to a thousand a week and they were saying he'd soon hit the gold mine, the dazzling bonanza of naming his own price. Of course, the big thing was his voice, but his looks had a lot to do with it, the females really went for his looks. They went for his small lean frame, which was somehow more of a nerve-tingler than the muscle-bound chunks of aggressive male, the dime-a-dozen baritones with too much oil in their hair and in their smiles. There was no oil in Gene's pale-gold hair, and his smile was as pure and natural as a sunny morning. It was the kind of smile that told them he was the genuine material, everything coming from the heart. So they couldn't just say he was "cute" or "nifty" or "keen." They really couldn't say anything; all they could do was sigh and want to touch him and tenderly take his head to their bosoms, to mother him. There were thousands upon thousands of them wanting to do that, and some of them put it in writing in their fan letters. There were some who took it further than sending a fan letter, and managed to make physical contact, and these included certain ladies from the Broadway stage, from café society and horsey-set society, from the model agencies and small-town beauty contests. And there were a few who were really expert in their line, veteran professionals from high-priced call houses, the hundred-dollar-a-session ladies who never gave it for free, but when Gene pulled out his wallet they wouldn't hear of such a thing. You wonderful boy, they said, and walked out very happy, as though he'd just given them a gift they'd never forget.

But with all of these ladies it was only once, it was never more than a night of having fun. He didn't need to fluff them off next morning when they asked for another date; they seemed to realize he wasn't in the market for anything serious. Or if he was, they couldn't provide it, because this was no ordinary male and it would take something very special to really reach him in there deep.

When it finally reached him it went in very deep and took hold of him and spun him around and made him dizzy. And it was very odd, the way it happened, it was almost silly. At first he couldn't believe it. He tried to tell himself it was impossible. But the only thing impossible was getting away from it. There was no way to get away from it.

He'd been invited to a stag party given by a big name in the entertainment field. He didn't like these smokers because he didn't go in for filth and he told his manager he wasn't going. His manager said it was important that he attend, you can't brush off these big shots, in this game it's all a matter of getting in solid with the right people. So finally he gave in and went to the smoker and it was a lavish affair with the best of food and drink and the comedians knocking themselves out. Gradually the evening became dirty and they showed certain motion pictures imported from France. It was weird stuff and it became very weird and presently it was the kind of cinema that made Gene somewhat sick in the stomach. But he couldn't walk out. It would be more embarrassing to walk out than to sit there and watch it.

They finished the movies and the stage was lit up and the girls came on. The man sitting next to him said, "Now you're gonna see something." He tried not to see it, tried to look down at his coffee cup and finally managed to focus on the cup and keep his eyes aimed there, away from the ugliness taking place on the stage. The all-male audience shrieked encouragement to the all-female cast that came out in pairs, then in trios, finally in quartets performing stunts that made the onlookers shriek louder. But all at once there was no shrieking, no sound at all, not even from the musicians up front. He wondered what was happening, and he looked up.

He saw her walking across the stage. That was all she was doing. Just walking.

She wore a gray-green long-sleeved high-necked dress of velvet. He saw the gray-green eyes and the bronze hair, saw them very clearly because he had a special-guest seat at the front-row table.

He heard the master of ceremonies announcing from the wing, "This – is – Celia."

Then the music started, and she began to dance. The music was very soft, on the languid side, and the dance was a slow mixture of something from Burma and something from Arabia and something far away from any place on earth.

It wasn't a strip tease. All her clothes stayed on, and there was nothing vulgar or even suggestive in the motions of her body. It went high above that, far beyond that, it was a performance that had no connection with matters of the flesh.

The audience didn't make a sound.

He wasn't conscious of the soundless audience. He wasn't conscious of anything except a certain feeling he'd never had before, a feeling he couldn't begin to analyze because his brain was unable to function. He was dizzy and getting dizzier.

She finished the dance and walked off the stage. He heard some applause, a vague sound that didn't mean anything because they didn't understand what they were applauding. Certainly it wasn't the kind of applause that called for an encore. They wouldn't be able to take an encore. She'd done enough to them already. They hadn't come here to be immobilized, to be made to feel like worms crawling at the feet of something they didn't dare to touch or think of touching. They stirred restlessly, anxious to forget what they had seen, impatient for the next number, wanting it to be very raw and smutty and ugly to get them back to earth again.

Two girls came onto the stage. One of them wore masculine

attire and the other was entirely naked. Gene didn't see them. He was up from the table and going somewhere and not knowing where but knowing he had to get there. He was in a corridor, then another corridor, then seeing Celia walking out of a dressing room and toward the stage door. He said hello and she stopped and looked at him.

He smiled and said, "I hope you don't mind."

She frowned slightly. "Mind what?"

So then he came closer and said, "I wanted to see you again. Just had to get another look at you."

She let go of the frown and smiled dimly. "Well, that's all right," she said. "That happens sometimes." She leaned her head to the side and said, "Aren't you Gene Lindell?" He nodded, and wondered what to say next, and heard her saying, "It won't be easy, Gene. You better not start."

It was a fair warning aimed at herself as well as at him. It was a warning they both ignored. There was really nothing they could do about it. They went out through the stage door and minutes later they were in a cab and the driver was saying, "Where to?"

Gene was looking at her and saying, "Just drive."

The cab moved slowly through downtown traffic. Gene went on looking at her. The cab got past the heavy traffic and headed toward the big municipal park. Gene tried to speak and he couldn't speak and he heard her saying, "We shouldn't have started. Now I think it's too late." The cab was moving along the wide avenue of the parkway, going deeper into the black quiet of the park, and she was saying, "It's like this. There's a man. He's crazy jealous."

"I bet," he said.

"Look," she said. "What're we gonna do?"

"I don't know."

"Oh, God," she said. "Good God."

"Is it that bad?"

94

She looked at him. "You know how bad it is."

"Yeah," he said. "I know."

She gazed past him, out through the cab window, at the black lacework of trees and shrubs sliding backward, going very fast. "Tell you what," she said. "Better take me home. Let's forget it, huh?"

"No" he said. "I can't."

"I'll tell the driver," she said. She leaned forward to give the driver her home address. Her mouth opened and nothing came out of her mouth. She fell back in the seat and shook her head slowly and mumbled to herself, "It's no use."

The cab was moving very slowly on a narrow road that bordered a winding creek.

"It's getting worse" she said. "I can feel it getting worse."

"I'm sorry," he said.

"You are? Then do something about it." Her voice was low and quivering. "For heaven's sake, do something."

"I don't know what to do."

"You're just gonna sit there? Not even gonna touch me?"

"If I touch you," he said, "I'll really go nuts."

"You're nuts already. We're both nuts." She took a deep straining breath, as though fighting for air. "I've heard them tell about things like this, the way it happens so fast, but I never believed it."

"Me neither," he said.

"All right, Gene." Her voice changed, rising an octave to a medium pitch, level and cool and trying to stay that way as she said, "Let's get it over with. We'll find a room somewhere."

"No."

"We gotta do it that way. This way it's miserable, it's grief."

"And that way?"

"Well, that's fun, that's having a good time."

"I'm not looking for a good time."

"I wish you were," she said, and her voice dropped again. "I wish that's all it amounted to. Maybe if we went to a room and got it over with — "

"Celia," he said.

"Yes."

"Listen, Celia — "

"Yes? Yes?"

"I — " He saw the driver glancing backward and he said sharply, "Watch the road, will you? You wanna put us in the creek?"

Celia gave a little laugh. "The creek," she said. "We're in the creek already. Up the creek."

"No," he said. "It'll be all right. It's got to be all right. We'll think of something."

"Will we? I got my doubts. I got very serious doubts about that. The way I see it, mister, we're miles and miles up the creek and it's gonna be rough getting back."

"I don't want to get back. I want it to be like this."

"You see?" She laughed again, brokenly, almost despairingly. "That's what I mean. You can't stop it and I can't stop it and it's really awful now."

"Yes, " he admitted. "It sure is."

She took another deep breath, braced herself for an effort, then leaned forward again and managed to give the driver an address. Twenty minutes later they arrived at the address, a row house in a somewhat shabby neighborhood. He opened the door and she got out. He started to follow her and she shook her head. He sat there in the cab looking at her and she looked past him, past the walls of the houses on the other side of the street as she told him her telephone number.

On the following day he phoned and a man answered. He pretended he'd called a wrong number. A few hours later he called again. This time it was Celia and he knew the man was there because she said it was the wrong number. Late in the afternoon he tried again and she was there alone. She gave him the address of a taproom downtown and said she'd be there around midnight.

It was a sad-looking place on the fringe of Skid Row, mostly ten-cent-beer customers. He arrived at eleven-fifty and took a booth and ordered ginger ale. It had to be ginger ale because he never used alcohol. He sat there drinking the ginger ale but not tasting it, waiting for her to show. Twenty minutes passed, and forty minutes. He had the glass to his lips when he saw her coming in and the ginger ale in his mouth was liquid fire going down. The sight of her was really combustible.

At the same time it was softly cool, like floating in a pool of lily water. The sum of it was dizziness, and as she sat down in the booth facing him, he had no idea this was a booth in a taproom; he had the notion it was some place very high above the clouds.

They sat there talking. She ordered double straights of gin with a water chaser. She did most of the talking and she was trying to tell him why they couldn't go on with this.

For one thing, she said, he'd get his name loused up if he got involved with her. There was a big career in show business ahead of him, she said, and already he was in the public eye, he couldn't afford to muddy his reputation. It would really be mud, she explained, because she was a bum from 'way back and she had a jail record for prostitution and all her life she'd been mixed up with small-time pimps and small-time thugs and ex-cons. Her first husband had been a second-story man shot and killed by a house owner, and that made her a widow when she was seventeen. Then came the prostitution and a ninety-day stretch and then more prostitution and a longer stretch. So then she was finished with the prostitution and tried to play it clean and got married again. This second one was a truck driver who seemed all right in the beginning but it turned out he was really an expert hijacker specializing in liquor jobs. They finally busted him to make him a three-time loser and send him up for fifteen to thirty. It was too long for him and one day in the prison laundry he drank from a bottle of bleach and died giggling. While she was wearing black she met the one she had now. It was a common-law arrangement and his name was Sharkey.

"This Sharkey," she said, "he ain't so bad. At least, he tries his best to make me comfortable. Another thing, he don't shove me around like the others did. First man I ever lived with who never gave me a black eye. So that's something, anyway. But all the same, I ain't kidding myself about Sharkey. I know he's meaner than the others. Much meaner. It hasn't come out yet, but I know it's there. It sorta shows when he smiles real soft and tells me how much he trusts me. As if to say that if I ever disappoint him, he won't be able to take it and he'll do something crazy. That kind of meanness. That's the worst kind. Soft and quiet on the outside, and on the inside really crazy.

"These stag-party jobs I do," she went on, "if Sharkey was making a dollar he wouldn't let me do it. But it brings in an average of a C note a week and we really need the cash, Sharkey's accustomed to living high and he don't know how to budget. He used to be a big man in the rackets and he got in bad with the bosses, not bad enough to get himself bumped, but enough to be told he wasn't needed any more. Since then he's been mooching around and looking for an angle and every once in a while he gets hold of something. Like a bootleg setup. Or numbers. Or girls. But it never amounts to anything, it always gets messed up before it can build. I've tried to tell him it's no use, all these operations are strictly syndicate and an independent don't stand a chance. So then he smiles real soft and says nice and sweet, 'You do your dancing, Celia, let me run the business.' And that always gives me a laugh. The business. Some business! He hasn't made a dime in two years."

She shrugged, "I don't know. Maybe if he didn't have

me, he could concentrate and promote something and make himself some decent money. He's got the brains for it. I mean something legitimate like handling talent or selling used cars. On that order. But no, he's got me and he wants me to have the best and his hands are itching for important money. The damn fool, last month he went out and borrowed three hundred dollars from God knows who, just to buy me a birthday present. Sooner or later I'll hafta pawn it so he can pay the guy he borrowed it from. Well, that ain't nothing new. That always happens when I get a present from Sharkey."

She shrugged again. "I don't know, maybe one of these days he'll find that angle he's looking for. He says it's around somewhere, all he's gotta do is find it. Lately he's been getting too anxious and sorta jumpy and I'm afraid he's headed for some genuine aggravation. He's hooked up with a couple of strong-arm specialists, a husband-and-wife team that make a business of putting people in the hospital. Or maybe putting them away altogether. Anyway, it makes me nervous, because they're living in the house with us and in the morning when I'm in bed I hear them in the next room, the three of them, Sharkey and Chop and Bertha, having their daily conference. I can't ever hear what they're saying, but I think I know what it's leading up to. When it's a strong-arm routine, it's either extortion or protection racket or a collection agency for clients who want blood instead of money. I don't know why I'm telling you all this. It's got nothing to do with you and me."

"Look," he said. "If it concerns you, it concerns me."

She smiled down at the empty shot glass. "You hear that?" she murmured to the glass.

"Listen, Celia —"

"I know what you're going to say." She looked at him, looked deep into him. "I know everything you want to tell me."

"But listen —"

"No," she said. "It won't work. There's no way you can take

me away from him. He just won't let you do it. If you try, he's gonna hurt you. He's gonna hurt you bad."

"I don't care."

"I know you don't. But you would if you could use your brains. That's what I'm trying to do. That's why I'm drinking so much gin. To steady myself and think straight. At least one of us has to think straight."

"Want another drink?"

"Yeah," she said. "Better buy me a pint. Then maybe I can think real straight. Maybe I'll be able to walk out on you."

"No," he said. "You won't be able to do that."

"I'm gonna try." She pointed across the room, at the bartender. "Go on, tell the man to sell you a bottle. I'm gonna give this a real try."

He bought a pint of gin. And she tried. She tried very hard. At one point she said, "Well, here's where I get off," but somehow she couldn't leave the booth. Then later she managed to get up from the booth and gazed past him and said, "Nice to have met you, and so forth," and turned away and started toward the door. She made it halfway to the door and came back to the booth and said slowly and solemnly, "You bastard, you." She sat down and lifted the half-empty bottle to her mouth and took a long quivering gulp. She went on with the drinking, taking it fast and then much too fast and finally she passed out.

When she was able to sit up he phoned for a cab. She said she didn't want to leave, she wanted to drink some more. She said it would be nice if she could really knock herself out and stay that way for a week, so then she wouldn't be able to see him. Maybe that would do it, she said, with her eyes saying that nothing could do it, nothing could keep her away from him.

He put her in the cab and they arranged for the same time, same place tomorrow night.

So then it was tomorrow night. It was a succession of

tomorrow nights in the booth in the taproom with ginger ale for him and gin for her. Sitting there facing each other and not touching each other, and it was three weeks of that, just that, just sitting there together until closing time, when he'd put her in a cab and watch the cab going away.

Then on Tuesday of the fourth week she said she couldn't take this much longer and if they didn't find themselves a room somewhere, she'd have convulsions or something.

He didn't say anything, but when the cab arrived to take her home, he climbed in with her. He said to the driver, "Take us somewhere."

The driver took them to a cheap hotel that paid certain cabbies a small commission.

In the bed with her it was dark but somehow blazing like the core of a shooting star. It was going 'way out past all space and all time.

"Lemme tell you something," she said afterward. "I gotta spoil it now. I gotta get dressed and scram outta here."

"No."

"But I gotta," she breathed into his mouth. "It's risky enough already. I don't wanna make it worse."

"All right," he said.

"Please." She touched his arm. "Don't get sore."

"I'm not sore," he said. He was sitting up in the bed. He spoke thickly, falteringly. "Its just that I hate to see you leave."

"I know," she said. "I hate it too."

Then in the darkness of the room she was out of the bed. He heard the rustling of fabric as she began to put on her clothes. The sound was difficult to take. She was getting dressed to walk out of here and it was really very difficult to take.

"Celia—"

"Yes?"

"Let's go away."

"What?" she said. "What's that?"

"We'll go away." His voice throbbed. "It's the only thing we can do."

"But — "

"Look," he cut in quickly. "I know it's wrong. It's giving him a raw deal, it's sorta like larceny. But that's aside from the issue. We just gotta do it, that's all."

For a long moment she didn't speak. And then, very quietly, "What do you want me to do?"

"Write him a note. Pack some things. We'll fix a time and you'll meet me at the train station."

There was another long quiet. He waited, not breathing, and then he heard her saying, "All right. When?"

They arranged the hour. It would be late afternoon. She finished dressing and there was no further talk and then she walked out of the room and he tried to go to sleep. But he couldn't sleep and already he was counting the minutes until he'd see her again. On a small table near the bed there was a lamp and he switched it on and glanced at his wrist watch. The dial said four-forty. He'd be meeting her at the station in approximately twelve hours. He thought, Twelve times sixty makes it seven hundred and twenty minutes, that's a long time.

He lit a cigarette and tried to think in practical terms of what must be done in the next twelve hours. It would be a busy twelve hours because he'd have to cancel several bookings. He was listed for nightclub engagements and guest appearances on several radio shows and a large recording company had him scheduled for some platters. All these bookings were very important, especially the radio and the recordings. His manager would start hopping around and yelling that they couldn't afford these cancellations, there was too much money involved, and another factor, a bigger factor, he hadn't yet reached big-name status and he wasn't sufficiently important to walk out on these contracts.

102

But, he said to himself, you're sufficiently mad about her to walk out on contracts and manager and everything, if it comes to that. You don't really care if it comes to that. You don't care about anything except her.

As it turned out, the cancellations were handled smoothly and there were no negative reactions. He told his manager that he was very tired and needed a rest and had to go away for at least a month. His manager nodded understandingly and patted him on the shoulder and said, "You got the right idea, Gene. Your health comes first. So what's it gonna be? Florida?"

He said he wasn't sure. He told his manager that he'd send a postcard just to keep in touch. But there mustn't be any publicity, he was really very tired and he just wanted to get away from people for a while. His manager promised to keep it quiet. His manager said, "Leave everything to me. Just have yourself a nice vacation and get plenty of sun. And for crissake stay out of drafts, don't come back with a sore throat."

They smiled and shook hands. The cab was waiting and he climbed in and set his suitcase on the floor. He settled back in the seat and the cab went into gear and moved away from the curb. He looked through the window and saw his manager waving good-by. He waved back and then the cab turned a corner and began to work its way through the heavy downtown traffic.

At the railroad station he was in the waiting room and the big clock said five-fifty. He wondered what was keeping her. Then the clock said six-ten and he wondered if he should make a phone call. When the clock said six-twenty he got up from the bench and moved toward a phone booth.

He was in the phone booth, putting the coin in the slot, then starting to dial, and then for some unaccountable reason his finger wouldn't move the dial. It happened in the instant before he turned and looked and saw the man outside the booth.

The man was smiling at him. The man was a six-footer

wearing a dark-brown beaver and a camel's-hair overcoat and smoking a cigar. The man had pleasant features and he was smiling softly and good-naturedly.

He'd never seen this man before, but without thinking about it, or trying to think, he knew it was Sharkey.

He opened the door of the booth and said, "Well? What is it?"

"Can we talk?"

"Sure," He stepped out of the booth. Well, he thought, here it comes. He told himself to take it calm and cool. Or at least try. His voice was steady as he said, "I guess it's better this way. She tell you about it?"

"No," Sharkey said. He widened the smile just a little. "I hadda find out for myself."

He gazed past Sharkey and he saw some people getting up from the benches and walking out of the waiting room. They were headed toward the stairway leading up to the platform. In a few minutes they'd be getting aboard the six-thirty southbound express. He thought of the two empty seats and it gave him an empty feeling inside.

Then he looked at Sharkey. "All right," he said. "I'm listening."

Sharkey took a slow easy pull at the cigar. The smoke seeped from the corners of his lips. He said, "Coupla weeks ago. I got to thinking about it. She was staying out too late. A few times I checked with the stag parties and they said she'd left the place hours ago.

"I didn't ask her about it," Sharkey went on. "I just waited for her to tell me. Well, you know how it is, you get tired of waiting. So one night I followed her."

It was quiet for some moments and Sharkey pulled easily at the cigar, sort of guiding the smoke as it came out of his mouth. The smoke drifted lazily between them.

Then Sharkey said, "Next night I followed her again. And

every night from then on." He shook his head slowly. "It wasn't fun, believe me. I was hoping it would end so I could check it off and forget about it. But every night there she is, meeting you in the taproom. And there I am, sitting in a rented car parked across the street.

"So you see it cost me money. Six bucks a night for the car. And a nickel for the newspaper to hold in front of my face."

"Why'd you do it that way? Why didn't you come into the taproom?"

Sharkey shrugged. "It would have been an argument. I don't like arguments. It always gives me indigestion."

From the platform upstairs there was the sound of the train coming in.

He heard Sharkey saying, "Well, that's the way it was. I'd be sitting there in the car and then I'd see you putting her in the cab. And the cab going away and you standing on the corner. Then I'd put the car in gear and step on the gas to get home before she did."

The sound of the train was louder, coming closer, and then there was the squealing sound of the train drawing to a stop at the platform.

And Sharkey was saying, "Every night the same routine. Until last night. When you got in the cab with her. And I knew I had to follow the cab.

"I swear I didn't want to follow that cab. I knew where it would go. Some cheap hotel with a clerk who doesn't ask questions. So that's the way it was. I'm in the car and it's parked near the hotel and I'm waiting an hour and then another hour and more hours. Finally she comes out and gets in a cab. When she comes home, I'm in bed. Today I told her I'd be away on business. I watch the house and I see her walking out with a hatbox and a suitcase. So then it's another cab and I'm in the rented car and there's a couple people with me."

"Chop and Bertha?"

"Yeah." Sharkey's eyebrows went up just a trifle. "She tell you about them?"

He nodded.

"Well," Sharkey said, taking another easy pull at the cigar, "It figures. I guess she told you everything."

Then from upstairs along the platform there was the sound of the train moving away and gathering steam.

"We stopped her when she got out of the cab," Sharkey said. He laughed softly, amiably. "She's some girl, that Celia. She didn't even blink. I told her to get in the car with Chop and Bertha and she said, 'O.K., Boss.' She always calls me Boss."

The train was going away. He tried to tell himself there'd be another train. He begged himself to believe there'd soon be another train and they'd be on it. But the sound of the departing train was a good-by sound, like music fading out, saying, No more, no more.

"They took her home," Sharkey said. "I knew you'd be here in the waiting room and it was time for you and me to talk."

He looked at the cigar in Sharkey's mouth. It was coming apart and he knew it was a cheap cigar. Then he looked at the camel's-hair coat that must have cost over a hundred when it was new but now it was very old and wouldn't bring fifteen in a secondhand store. The same applied to the brown beaver. The band was tattered and the crown was dull from loss of fibers. Without seeing inside Sharkey's wallet, he knew it contained one-dollar bills or maybe none at all. For some vague reason he felt like treating Sharkey to something. He heard himself saying, "I'm gonna have dinner. Join me?"

"All right," Sharkey said.

They walked into the station restaurant and took a table. There was a wine list and Sharkey ordered double bourbon straight and a water chaser. The bourbon was a bonded brand costing eighty cents a shot. Then Sharkey ordered a four-fifty T-bone.

He said, "Make it two," and the waitress wrote it down and walked away from the table. He looked at Sharkey and said, "I'd have a drink with you, except I don't drink."

"It's better not to," Sharkey said. "I don't use it much myself. Not on an empty stomach, anyway. It don't pay to drink too much on an empty stomach."

"I wonder why they do it," he said.

"Do what?"

"Drink themselves half crazy."

"You mean," Sharkey murmured, "the way she does?"

He didn't say anything. He wasn't looking at Sharkey.

"I'll tell you," Sharkey said. "She don't get crazy from it. Fact is, it does her a lot of good. She needs it."

"Why?" And now he looked directly at Sharkey. "Why does she need it?"

"Problems," Sharkey said.

"You think she'll do a lot of drinking now?"

Sharkey put his large hands flat on the tablecloth and looked down at his thick fingers. "What do you think?"

"I think she'll do an awful lot of drinking."

"For a while, anyway," Sharkey said. He went on looking down at his fingers. "Let's say a few days. A week at the most."

"Longer than a week" he said. "You know it'll be longer than a week."

"Maybe." Sharkey nodded slowly. "Maybe an entire month. Maybe six months." He looked up, showing the soft easy smile. "Maybe she'll stay drunk for a year."

"And then into next year. And the next."

"Well," Sharkey said, "that's up to her." He leaned back and hooked his arm over the back of the chair. "Tell ya the truth, I don't care if she stays drunk the rest of her life. Just so long as she stays with me."

"What if she gets sick?"

"I'll take care of her."

"What I mean is, really sick. I mean — "

"Look, I'll put it this way," Sharkey said, his smile very gentle, his voice soft and soothing. "My main interest in life is taking care of her. It's the only real enjoyment I get. I just wanna take care of her. If she was in a wheel chair I'd spend all my time wheeling her around. If she was flat on her back I'd stay in the room with her day and night. You get the general idea?"

"Yes," he said. "I get it."

Sharkey took the mangled cigar from his mouth and put it in the ash tray. He sighed softly and said, "It's a queer thing. I used to be a cake of ice when it came to women. I mean, they were all right to play with, but aside from that I wasn't in the market. Sure, I got married a couple of times, but only so's I'd have it ready for me when I came home. In each case it wasn't any deeper than the mattress. The first one turns out to be a nympho and I pay her off and send her to Nevada. The next number is all right in the beginning, but then she develops a weakness for rumba teachers and I hafta throw her out. Then this one comes along and I take one look and it's like falling off a cliff with nothing underneath, just falling and falling. All the time falling."

The double bourbon arrived and Sharkey shot it down and ordered another. Then he had a third, and he was on the fourth when he laughed apologetically and said, "Look at me, the man who says he don't drink on an empty stomach."

"Go on and drink. Drink all you want."

Sharkey went on laughing lightly. "You wanna get me drunk?"

"No, it isn't that."

"I think I know what it is," Sharkey said. "You feel that you owe me the drinks, the steak dinner. Sure, that's what it is, you just feel that you owe me something."

"Maybe," he said, and he was staring past Sharkey. "I'm not really sure."

"Well, anyway," Sharkey smiled, "I'll have another drink."

Sharkey was on the seventh double bourbon when the waitress brought the T-bones. The steaks were large and prime and he watched Sharkey tackling the plate with considerable appetite. His own appetite was less than zero and he tried a few bites and couldn't go on with it. He pushed his plate aside and lit a cigarette, and it was quiet at the table except for the sound of Sharkey's knife and fork working methodically on the T-bone, Sharkey with seven double bourbons in him but not the least bit drunk, doing a thorough job on the steak and French fries, doing it medium fast and with reasonable etiquette and finally lifting the napkin to his lips and saying, "Goddamn, that was good."

He smiled sadly. "I'm glad you enjoyed it."

"What about yours? Something wrong with yours?"

"No," he said. "I'm just not hungry."

Sharkey nodded slowly and understandingly and somewhat sympathetically. The waitress came to the table and asked if they would like dessert. Sharkey told her to bring a pot of coffee and another double bourbon. Then Sharkey grinned at him and said, "It ain't often I get a treat like this. I might as well take advantage of it."

He didn't say anything. He went on smiling sadly.

"Another thing," Sharkey said. "Maybe I'll get my name in the columns. I'm having dinner with a celebrity."

"I'm not a celebrity."

"Well, maybe not yet. But you're getting there. You're really getting there. I heard you on the radio last week. The disc jockey played three of your records, one right after another. They never do that except with the solid talent."

It was a genuine compliment and he started to murmur thanks. But it wouldn't come out. His hands gripped the edge of the table and he said, "Listen, Sharkey – "

And Sharkey went on quickly: "You're a cinch to hit the top brackets. I can tell. It's like at the races when I look at a horse and I just know it's gotta come in. So it's — "

"Listen," he said, not loudly but aiming it, shooting it. And then, sending in the clincher, "I want her."

Then it was quiet. Sharkey was looking down at the table. He had a technical expression in his eyes, like a dealer studying all the cards face up.

"I want her." Now it was louder. And it quivered. "I can't give her up. Just can't do without her."

Sharkey went on looking at the table. His lips scarcely moved as he said, "You know something? I think we're in trouble."

Then quietly again, and feeling very friendly toward Sharkey but wishing Sharkey didn't exist, he said, "I'm gonna take her."

"Goddamn." As if the cards on the table showed a sorry mess. "We're in real trouble."

"I've gotta have her and I'm gonna have her, that's all."

Sharkey looked up. The technical expression went out of his eyes and the only thing in his eyes was sadness. It was sincere sadness and his voice was gloomy as he said, "It's a goddamn shame."

"Well, anyway, now you know. You know what I'm gonna do."

"Yeah," Sharkey said "I know. I wish you hadn't told me."

The rest of it was rapid and blurred and there was no thought, no plan, no logic in the pattern of getting up and leaving Sharkey sitting there at the table. He lunged toward the waitress and jammed a twenty-dollar bill into her hand. He ran out of the restaurant, leaving his hat and coat on the hanger, his suitcase forgotten, everything forgotten in the rush to get out of there and get into a cab. The only symbols in his brain were the four numbers of the address where she lived with Sharkey and Chop and Bertha, and what he had to do was erase those numbers, take her out of there, take her far away and make sure they'd never carry her back.

As he entered the cab and gave the address to the driver, he didn't feel the winter cold, he didn't notice the evening blackness, and of course he paid no attention to the telephone wires stretched high above the street, glimmering silver against the darkness. If he had focused on the wires, if he'd been able to think clearly and with a reasonable amount of arithmetic, he would have known what was happening up there at this very instant. He would have known that the wires were carrying Sharkey's voice from a phone booth to the address where the cab was headed.

When he arrived there, they were waiting for him, ready for him. The short wide man opened the door for him and he walked in and then the short wide man moved in close behind him and swung a blackjack and knocked him unconscious. The big woman who weighed more than three hundred was smiling down at him and then she picked him up from the floor and carried him as if he were a child. Or as if she were a child carrying a rag doll. The smile on her face was childlike, and while she carried him down the cellar stairs she purred, "You pretty little boy. You're so cute."

He heard the voice but he didn't know what it was saying. He had a feeling of being carried but there was no way to look and make sure. It seemed there was a thick spike planted in his skull, cutting off all communication between one side of him and the other.

At intervals he could hear her saying, "Really cute."

And then the voice of the short wide man: "Why don'tcha kiss him? Go on, kiss him."

She laughed and said, "Should I? Well, maybe I will, while I got the chance."

He wasn't sure that the big woman was kissing him, he

couldn't feel anything on his face except the pressure of some gushy substance, tons of it, as if a carload of jelly had fallen on him.

Then for a long time there was nothing.

When he heard the voices again, Sharkey's voice was included and Sharkey was saying, "Make sure he don't come back."

"You mean finish him?" It was the woman.

"No," Sharkey said. "That's out. Don't do that."

"Why not?" It was Chop. "It's easier that way. All we gotta do is—"

"Please keep quiet and listen to me." The soft gentle voice of Sharkey. "All I want is a guarantee that he don't come back."

"That's gonna be complicated," the woman said.

"It's complicated already," Sharkey said. "It's so goddamn complicated it's making me sick."

"I think we oughta finish him," Chop said. "We could do it right here in the cellar."

"Hell, no," the woman said. "I been working all day cleaning up this place. I don't want it messed up."

"It wouldn't be no mess," Chop told her. "What we do is put him in the furnace."

"Not in one piece" she said. "He wouldn't fit. We'd have to cut him up and that needs a meat cleaver. It means I'll hafta use a scrubbing brush for at least an hour. It's eight-fifteen now and I wanna be upstairs when Bob Hope comes on."

"He ain't on tonight," Chop said. "It's tomorrow night."

"Don't tell me," she said. "I know when he comes on."

"I'm telling you it's tomorrow night."

The woman spoke loudly. "You stupid sonofabitch, you don't even know what day it is."

"Don't shout at me, Bertha. You don't hafta shout at me."

"I wouldn't hafta shout if you weren't so stupid."

"That's another thing I don't like," Chop said. "I don't like when you call me stupid."

"I'll call you stupid whenever you're stupid. All right?"

"Now look, Bertha—"

"Drop it," Sharkey cut in. His voice was low and thoughtful. "Here's what I want you to do. You'll carry him outta here. Put him in the car and take him away from town."

"In the country?" Chop asked.

"Yes" Sharkey said patiently. "Someplace in the country. Say like twenty, thirty miles out of town."

"Like in the woods?" Chop asked.

"No." It was Bertha again. "We'll find a place where there's a crowd. So they can stand and watch while we do it. We'll sell tickets."

"Lay off me," Chop mumbled.

"Please," Sharkey said. "Please, the two of you. Keep quiet and listen carefully. You'll get him off on a side road someplace. Now check this, I want it clearly understood you're not to finish him. All you do is convince him. He's gotta be convinced. You see what I mean?"

"You mean really convinced?" Chop asked.

"Yes," Sharkey said.

"Goddamnit," the woman said. "Thirty miles out in the country. Now I'm gonna miss Bob Hope."

They carried him out of the house and put him in the rented car. Some twenty minutes later he started to regain consciousness. Then it was forty minutes and he was able to focus and realize what was happening. He was sitting in the back of the car with Bertha. He saw Chop sitting up front behind the wheel. The car was moving very fast on a bumpy road. They were passing through open countryside and there were some lighted windows here and there, but not many. Then minutes later it was another road, much narrower, and more trees and higher grass and no lighted windows.

He sat up straighter. He reached slowly for the door handle and Bertha saw him doing it. She grabbed a handful of his hair and her other hand was a big fist banging him hard on the cheek just under the eye. He went on trying for the door and she hit him again in the same place. He wondered if his cheekbone were broken. It really felt broken. While he thought about it he kept going for the door handle and Bertha kept pulling his hair and hitting him in the face. The car slowed down and Chop said, "What's the matter back there?"

"Keep driving," Bertha said.

"What's he doing?"

"He's trying to open the door," Bertha said. She used her fist again.

"You want the blackjack?" Chop asked.

"No," Bertha said. "I don't need the blackjack. You just keep driving. I'll take care of this."

She smashed her fist into the battered cheek, then aimed for the mouth and shot the right hand short and straight and he felt the teeth coming out of his gums. He could feel the two teeth rolling along his tongue. He spat them out and tried to turn his head to look at Bertha but he couldn't move his head because she was still pulling his hair. His scalp hurt worse than his cheek and his mouth, and he thought: It can't be a woman, it's like something made of iron.

Just then she hit him again and it was really like getting hit with a sledge hammer. She had all of her weight behind the blow and he took the full force of over three hundred pounds of hard-packed beef. It knocked several more teeth out of his mouth and it broke his jaw. He started to pass out and tried to hold on and managed to hold on. He collected everything he had and put it in his left arm and swung his left arm but it didn't go anywhere. It was just a feeble gesture that tagged empty air.

"Well, whaddya know," Bertha said. "He tried to hit me."

"Quit batting him around," Chop said. "You keep it up like

114

that, you're gonna finish him. Sharkey gave instructions not to finish him."

"I won't finish him," Bertha said. "But I'm sorta disappointed. I thought he was a gentleman. A gentleman don't raise his hand to a lady."

"What's he doing now?"

"He ain't doing anything."

"Then leave him alone."

"Sure," she said. "I'll leave him alone. Just one more lick to keep him quiet."

She sent her fist to his head and it crashed against his temple and again he was unconscious.

When he came to, the car had stopped and they were dragging him out of the car. He was spitting blood and teeth and shreds of flesh from his torn mouth. They lifted him to his feet and walked him away from the car. It was a muddy clearing that sloped downward from some trees. A few times he slipped in the mud and they picked him up and tightened their hold on him to keep him from falling again. They walked him some fifty yards going down to where the clearing ended against a wall of thick trees. Then they turned him around so that he faced them, his back pressing against the jagged bark of a tree.

They had him placed so that he stood in the glow of the car's headlights. The car was about sixty yards away but the bright beam was on and it hit him hard in the eyes. He blinked. He tried to look away from the headlights. The headlights seemed to reach out like burning fingers going into his eyes and he blinked again.

"All right" Chop said. "Let's get started."

Chop was wearing a lumber jacket zipped up to his collar. He zipped it halfway down to loosen it. Then he loosened the sleeves and rolled them up just a little. He reached to the rear pocket of his trousers and took out the blackjack.

"Wait," Bertha said. "I wanna talk to him."

"Talk?" Chop looked at her. "Whatcha gonna talk about?"

"I want him to know why."

"He knows why."

"I wanna make sure he knows," Bertha said.

She moved toward him where he stood slumped against the tree. Her massive bulk blotted out the glare of the headlights and he was thankful for that. But then her face came closer and he saw the big hooked nose and the tiny eyes. It wasn't an easy face to look at. He preferred the burning force of the headlights.

She said, "You get the idea?"

He didn't say anything. It wasn't because he refused to answer. His mouth and jaw hurt terribly and would hurt worse if he tried to talk.

"Answer me," Bertha said.

He told himself to give her an answer. But somehow he couldn't open his mouth. She stepped back and hauled off and punched him in the stomach. He went to his knees. She picked him up and pushed him back against the tree.

"You're gonna answer me," she said.

Chop moved in. "Lemme handle him."

"No," she said. "I'm doing this. He's gonna answer."

"For Crissake," Chop said. "How can he talk if he can't move his jaw?"

"He can move it. He's just stubborn, that's all. Stubborn and cute. Real cute."

He saw she was going to hit him again. He tried to fall away from it but her arm was faster and he took it again in the stomach. And then again. She was in real close, and he sagged against her. She hooked one arm around him and used the other arm to keep banging him in the stomach.

It went on like that for some moments. When she stopped punching him it was as though the punches were still coming and forcing his stomach out through his spine and into the tree.

She had him pressed hard against the tree and it seemed as if the tree were eating away at his stomach.

"Now listen," Bertha said. "Listen careful and try to understand. That girl belongs to Sharkey."

He shook his head.

"No?" Bertha said. "You won't agree on that?"

"No," he managed to say.

Bertha took a deep breath. She looked at Chop. She said, "You hear? He ain't convinced."

"I'll convince him" Chop said.

"No, I'll do it. I know just what it needs. Gimme the blackjack."

"Now be careful," Chop said, handing her the blackjack. "Remember what Sharkey told us."

"Don't worry." She hefted the blackjack, holding it in her right hand, then slapping it gently against the palm of her left hand.

"Well, all right," Chop said. "But just be sure you don't finish him."

She took another deep breath. He saw her raising the blackjack. There was no way to get away from the blackjack and he didn't bother to try. The leather-covered cudgel came in from the side and hit him in the ribs. There was the sound of bones breaking and his mouth opened automatically and he let out a dry dragging sob.

"Convinced?" Bertha said.

He sobbed again. "No."

"All right," Bertha said. "We'll break a couple more. Let's see what that does."

The blackjack came in very hard. He could feel more bones breaking and he heard himself sobbing. He said to himself: What's the matter with you? Why don't you give in?

"Convinced now?" Bertha said.

"No."

She hit him again, a roundhouse swing that sent the blackjack crashing into his hip joint.

"Now?" she said.

"No."

She stepped back, looking him up and down, like a craftsman examining a partially completed work. Her tongue was out and wetting her lower lip and then she swung again and the blackjack hammered the injured hip joint.

"Well?" she said. "Well?"

He shook his head.

Bertha aimed the blackjack at his hip joint again. Chop walked in and touched her arm and said, "That ain't the place to hit him. You gotta hit him where it does real damage."

"Like where?"

"There," Chop said, his finger pointing. "Try it there."

Bertha stepped back again. She took careful aim, her arm going back very slowly. He stood there waiting to take it. He didn't know what was holding him up, maybe it was the tree, or maybe he was just curious and wanted to find out how much he could take. Whatever it was, it caused him to smile.

Bertha saw the smile. She saw it showing through the blood and the wreckage of his face. She frowned and slowly lowered the blackjack and said to him, "You know what? I think you're crazy."

"Sure he's crazy," Chop said. "He's gotta be crazy to take it and want more."

"Why?" Bertha wanted to know. She moved toward him, and said objectively, "What's the matter with you? What makes you so crazy?"

He gazed past Bertha, past Chop, past the trees and the darkness and everything. He heard himself saying, "Celia."

Then it was quiet. Bertha and Chop looked at each other.

His eyes came back to them and he smiled again and said, "I know you don't get it. Maybe I don't get it, either."

118

"It don't make sense" Bertha said.

"I know." He shrugged and went on smiling.

"Now look," Bertha said. She had a two-handed hold on the blackjack, gripping it at both ends. "I'm gonna give it one more try. I'm gonna tell you what you'll get if you don't give in. You're gonna get ruined, sonny. It's gonna be the throat."

She reached out and her finger gently nudged his throat. "There," she said. "Right there. So you'll wind up with a busted phonograph. And that would really be the payoff, wouldn't it? Sharkey told us you're a famous singer, night clubs and radio and your records selling by the carloads. It figures you don't wanna lose all that."

He stared at the blackjack. It looked very efficient. It was definitely a capable tool in the hands of a professional.

"He looks sorta convinced," Chop said.

"I'll know when he tells me." She put her face close to the bloody, broken face and said, "Come on. Tell me. You gonna stay away from her? You swear on your life you'll stay away from her?"

He said to himself: All right now, Gene, enough is enough, you've taken too much already, you'll hafta give in, you'll hafta say it like they want you to say it.

The blackjack was waiting.

He said to the blackjack, "Well, you almost did it. But not quite."

"What's that?" Bertha said.

"It's no sale."

"That final?"

"Final."

And then he heard Chop saying, "My God." Saying it very slowly in an awed voice, and adding, "What these dumb bastards will do for a jane."

As he heard it, he saw the blackjack coming. It came like something alive, a gleaming black demon going for his throat.

It smashed into his throat and he felt the destruction boiling in there, he could almost see the foaming bubbles of purple matter getting split apart.

The blackjack hit him again. And then again. Bertha swung it the fourth time but her aim was too high and the blackjack caught him on the side of the skull.

He went down, falling flat and then going out and way out. And in the instant before he went over the edge, he thought: Well, anyway, that's all for now.

Then it was late the next morning and some country boys played hookey from school and went out hunting for rabbits. At first they thought he was dead. But then he rolled his bulging eyes. He had to tell them with his eyes because he didn't have a voice.

He was in the hospital for nine weeks. There were times when they didn't think he'd make it. Too much traumatic shock, they said, and then of course there was the internal bleeding, the brain concussion, the complications resulting from an excess of broken bones. But the worst damage was in the throat. They said it was a "comminuted fracture of the larynx" and they told him it was urgent that he shouldn't try to talk.

When he was able to sit up, they gave him a pencil and a pad of paper so he could make his wants known to the nurses. One day the law came and wanted to know what happened and he wrote on the pad, "Can't remember."

"Come on," the law said. "Tell us who did it."

He shook his head. He pointed to what he'd written on the pad.

Next day the law tried again. But he wouldn't give them anything. He didn't want the law brought into it. He told himself he wasn't sore at anybody. The only thing he wanted was to see her again. He was certain that any day now, any hour, she'd be visiting the hospital. It had been a front-page story, so of course she knew all about it. And now that he was allowed to have visitors, she'd certainly be coming. With the pencil and paper he asked the nurses, "Did Celia phone?" They said no. He kept asking and they kept saying no. So then it began to hit him. Not even a phone call. Not even an inquiry as to how he was doing.

He'd sit there in the bed looking at the other visitors. His manager. Or the radio people. Or the nightclub people. They gabbed and chattered and he had no idea what they were saying. He'd stare past the blurred curtain of their faces and he'd think, Why? Why didn't she come to me? Why?

But he went on waiting. And hoping. Waking up each morning to start a day of looking at the white door and begging it to open and let her come in. Or handing the written question to the nurses. "Did she phone?" With his eyes pleading for a yes, and their faces sort of gloomy as they gave him a no.

Then it was the ninth week and one night he opened his eyes and looked up at the black ceiling. He had a feeling it was trying to tell him something. He didn't want to be told and he tried to go back to sleep. But he went on looking at the ceiling. And it seemed to be lowering, it was coming toward him, a huge black convincer, the business end of a blackjack so big that it blotted out everything else.

He spoke to it, saying without sound, All right, Mac. You win. I'm convinced.

As he said it, he could feel his spinal column turning to jelly. But it didn't bother him. In a way it was almost pleasant, really soothing and sort of cozy. On his face there was a lazy smile, just a trifle on the slap-happy side, and it stayed there as he fell asleep.

It was there in the morning when he heard the doctor saying, "You're going home today."

The smile widened. But not because he was glad to hear the news. It was just his way of saying, So what?

"I want to see you in a few days," the doctor said. He was a very expensive throat specialist who'd been called in by the manager. He said, "You've made excellent progress and I'm reasonably sure you'll soon regain your voice."

So what? So who cares?

The doctor went on: "Of course, we mustn't be overly optimistic. I'll put it this way: It's a fairly good prognosis. About fifty-fifty. In all these cases the healing process is rather slow. There's a gradual thickening and induration of the vocal cords, resulting in subsequent ability to produce sound. A certain amount of hoarseness, and quite naturally the volume is decreased. What I'm getting at, Mr Lindell, it's all a matter of hoping for the best. I mean – your singing career – "

He wasn't listening.

And although he kept his appointment with the doctor, and kept all the appointments in the weeks and months that followed, he paid very little attention to the healing campaign. He went to the doctor's office because there was no other place to go. It was costing a lot of money, but of course that didn't matter, for the simple reason that nothing mattered. His manager took him around to keep him in contact with the right names, the well-fed faces in the elegant offices of big-time show business, and they were very nice to him, very kind, very encouraging. They said he'd soon be up there again, making a sensational comeback. His reply was the lazy smile that said, Thanks a lot, but it's strictly from nowhere, I just don't give a damn.

They began to see that he didn't give a damn and gradually they lost interest in him. It took a longer time for the manager to lose interest, but when it happened it was definite. The manager said bluntly, "Look, Gene. I've tried. God knows I've tried. But I can't help a man who don't wanna be helped. It's plain as day that you don't really care."

A shrug. And the lazy smile.

"Well, I'm sorry, Gene. Fact is I got other clients need my attention. I'm afraid we gotta call it quits."

A slow nod. The lazy smile. The limp hand extended. His manager took it and patted him on the shoulder regretfully.

"Good luck, Gene."

As he walked out of the manager's office he passed a wall mirror and it showed him that his hair was turning white. But of course that didn't matter, either.

It was on the fourth floor, but he didn't take the elevator going down. For some reason the stairway seemed like a better idea. He walked down the stairs very slowly, enjoying the feeling of going down one step at a time, lower and lower, nice and easy, no effort at all.

One step at a time. He stopped going to the doctor. He started gambling. He was able to announce his bets in a very weak whisper. Then it became a louder whisper as the larynx continued to heal. And finally it was a cracked hoarse whisper that spoke every night at the dice tables or the card tables, with the lazy smile always there, the hair getting whiter, the eyes getting duller. And the cards and dice eating into his bank account, bringing it down from sixteen thousand to fourteen to eleven to eight and always going down. Some nights he'd get way ahead but he'd sit there and make stupid bets and manage to lose it all, and then more. One night it was five-card stud and he bet several thousand on his two pair against a very evident three queens. As he walked out with an empty wallet, he heard their comments drifting through the hall.

"Can't figure that one. He plays like he wants to lose."

"Sure. I've seen a lotta them that way. It's a certain condition they get in."

"Whaddya mean? What condition?"

"Like suicide. Doing it slow."

"Slow-motion suicide." And then, with a chuckle, "That's a new one."

"All right, ante up. Let's raise it a hundred."

He went back the next night and dropped another roll. It went on that way, and on one occasion he dropped forty-seven hundred dollars. The following day he walked into the bank and took out what was left. It amounted to a little over seven hundred. That afternoon he decided it was time to start with alcohol. He'd never tried alcohol, and he was curious as to what it would do.

It did plenty. It took him a few thousand feet above the rooftops, then dropped him with a thud, and the windup was an alley with a couple of muggers rolling him for every cent.

So then it had to be employment. He got a job washing dishes. But he wasn't thinking in terms of rent money or food money. He liked the idea of alcohol; it was a very pleasant beverage. He began spending most of his weekly earnings on whisky. As the months passed he needed more whisky, and more, and still more.

Going down. One step at a time.

He was fired from so many jobs that he lost count. He was picked up for drunkenness and tossed into cells where other booze hounds were sleeping it off. It reached the point that it always reaches when there isn't sufficient cash for whisky. He started to drink wine.

And from there it was only a few steps down to Skid Row.

On Skid Row it was a bed for fifty cents a night or any old floor where he happened to fall. Or else it was a free mattress in the alcoholic ward of whichever hospital had available space. No matter where it was, he'd be waking up at five-thirty and wanting more wine.

Twenty-nine cents for a bottle of muscatel. It was the outstanding value in the universe. There was no better way of killing time.

But sometimes he didn't have the twenty-nine cents, or any sum near it, and when that happened he'd go for anything that was offered. It might be homemade rotgut or something made from dandelions or ruined plums handed out free at the water-front fruit market. It might be the liquid flame that they sold in Chinatown for a dime a jar. They made it from rice and it was colorless and had no smell, but going down the throat it was relentless and when it hit the belly it was merciless. And then of course there was the canned heat, strained through a dirty rag or a chunk of stale bread. And the bay rum. And on one very thirsty night, a really difficult night, there was a long delightful drink from a bottle of shoe polish.

Through winter and summer and winter again.

Through all the gray Novembers of getting up early to distribute circulars door to door. It had to be that kind of job. It didn't take much thinking. It paid two dollars a day, and sometimes three dollars when the weather was bad and the pavements were icy. On some mornings the sign was out, "No Work Today" and if the sign stayed there for three days in succession it was a financial catastrophe; it meant a long cold wait in the soup lines.

And sometimes he'd go lower than the soup lines, much lower than that, lower than any graph could indicate.

He'd stand in a shadowed doorway with his palm out.

"Got a nickel, buddy?"

The cold stare. "What for?"

He'd always reply with the wary smile. "I'm kinda thirsty."

"Well, at least you're honest about it."

"That's right, mister." With the coin dropping into his palm. "It's the best policy."

But at other moments it was the worst policy and they'd look at him with disdain and disgust and walk away.

Or else they'd take the trouble to say, "Why don't you wise up?"

Or "Nothing doing. I don't give people money to poison themselves."

Or the sour voice of a blasphemer saying, "Tell you what. You go ask Jesus. He'll never fail you."

Then another Samaritan and another nickel. And finally, with fifteen cents in his hand, he'd go looking for Bones and Phillips. They'd pool their resources and make a beeline for the nearest joint that sold the bottled ecstasy.

It was the only ecstasy they sought.

But every now and then the other kind would come his way, a Tenderloin slut just slumping along and looking for company. It would be like a meeting of two mongrels in the street no preliminaries necessary. Her bleary eyes would say, I need it tonight, I need it something awful.

He'd look at the shapeless chunk of female wreckage. No matter who she was, she'd be shapeless. If she didn't weigh much, she'd be a string bean. If she carried a lot of poundage, her body would resemble a barrel. The women of Skid Row had lost their figures long ago, along with their hopes and their yearnings. But the juice was still there, and every now and then it churned and bubbled and they had to announce their gender.

His eyes would say, All right, Lola.

Lola, Scotch-Portuguese-Cherokee. Or it would be Sally, of Polish-Peruvian ancestry. Or chinless Lucy, descended from Wales and Norway and certain ports on the shores of Arabia. And others whose prebirth histories went back to various ports along various shores. From anyplace at all where long dead sailors and drifters had met the long dead great-great-grandmothers. So now the result was the walking debris, walking with Whitey toward the dusty hovel where the stuffing was spilling from the mattress.

At any rate, he'd think, it's a mattress, it's better than a cold floor.

Then in the dark it would happen as it happens with the animals. Nothing to say, nothing to think about, just doing it

126

because one was male and the other was female. And it was preferable to being alone.

Yet somehow it was ecstasy, a sort of rummage-sale brand, but ecstasy nonetheless. For one spasmodic moment it took him away from River Street and sent him sailing up into cloudland. And even though the clouds were gray, it was nice to be so high above the Skid Row roofs. He'd hear a sigh, and that was nice, too.

Later she'd say, "You wanna sleep here?"

"Might as well."

"All right. Good night, Whitey."

"Good night."

He'd fall asleep very fast. It was easy to fall asleep because there was nothing to occupy the mind. But at five-thirty in the morning he'd be wide awake and telling himself he needed a drink.

Why?

Then automatically it would come, the lazy smile. And he'd say to himself: Quit asking, bud. You know why.

It never went further than that. He'd get up from the mattress and walk out. He'd hit the street and join the early-morning parade that moved in no special direction, the dreary assemblage of stumble bums going this way and that way and getting nowhere.

From November to November. And on and on through all the gray Novembers.

Seven Novembers.

He stood there in the alley and his thoughts returned to now. He gazed across the back yard and through the kitchen window and saw the gray-green eyes and the bronze hair, the face and the body, the living cause of it all.

He wasn't sure what he was thinking or feeling. Whatever it was, there was too much of it, a mixture of uncertain contradictions that choked the channels of his brain. His mental mechanism was like a flooded carburetor.

But finally he managed a single thought, pushing it through the maze to make it objective and practical, saying to himself: All right, you've had it, you've seen her, and now it's time to get moving.

He told his legs to move, to backtrack down the alley and resume the march that would take him back to the station house.

And that'll do it, he thought. That'll really finish it, make it final and complete, so the Thirty-seventh District is the end of the road, it's the cashier's desk where you'll get the payoff, the last installment of what you've earned.

You've really earned it, he thought. You've played a losing game and actually enjoyed the idea of losing, almost like them freaks who get their kicks when they're banged around. You've heard tell about that type, the ones who pay the girls to burn them with lit matches, or put on high-heeled shoes and step on their faces. That kind of weird business. And it's always the same question. What makes them that way? But you never took the trouble to figure the answer. What the hell, it was their private worry, it didn't concern you.

Not much it didn't. So now you're getting to see. You're in that same bracket, buddy. You're one of them less-than-nothings who like the taste of being hurt. That makes you lower than the mice and the roaches. At least they try to save their skins, they got a normal outlook. But you, you're just a clown that ain't funny. And that's a sad picture, that's the saddest picture of all. Like on the outside it's the stupid crazy smile and inside it's a gloomy place where all they play is the blues.

He frowned. It was a solemn frown and he was saying to himself: It's high time you made some changes.

Like what? he asked himself.

128

He was searching for an answer and not looking at the kitchen window. His eyes aimed downward through the fence posts and all he saw was the rutted black earth of the back yard. The only sound was the purring of the kitten on the doorstep. Then another sound flowed in and at first he didn't hear it. The sound was cautious and very slow and creeping, coming down the narrow alley, coming toward him, stalking him, the way leopards stalk their supper. They were only a few feet away when he heard them and he looked up and sideways and saw the coffee-colored faces of two Puerto Ricans.

One of them carried a knife. It was a large ripple-edged bread knife. The other Puerto Rican was armed with a beer bottle that had its neck broken off.

He wasn't looking at the knife or the jagged-edged bottle. He was watching their eyes. Their eyes were dull, showing no emotion, only purpose, and he knew they were moving in to kill him.

-Seven-

He told himself he wasn't quite ready to be killed. His brain snatched at ideas and found one that seemed plausible. The lazy smile came onto his lips and he said, "Got a cigarette?"

It stopped them for just a moment. They looked at each other. The one with the knife was medium-sized and in his early twenties. He wore a bandage around his forehead and it was bloodstained and there was a wide gash of dried blood under his nose, slanting down past the corner of his mouth. The other Puerto Rican was about five-three and very skinny. He looked to be in his middle thirties and there were ribbons of baldness showing through his slicked-down jet-black hair. His left eye was puffed and almost closed and under it the cheekbone was swollen and shiny purple.

"Please," Whitey said. "I need a cigarette."

Again it stopped them. They didn't know what to make of it. The taller one came in very close to Whitey held the knife up in front of his eyes and said, "You see thees? You know what thees is for?"

Whitey went on smiling past the blade. "You ain't even got a cigarette?"

"You keed me? You make fun?"

"I'm dying for a smoke," Whitey said.

"You dying, period," the little one said. He spoke with a less pronounced accent than the other Puerto Rican. "You gonna die right now, you know that?"

"Die?" Whitey told himself to blink a few times. "What for?"

"For damn good reason," the little one said. "You hate Puerto Ricans, we hate you. You want us dead, we want you dead."

"Me?" Whitey pointed to himself. "You mean me?"

"Yes, you," the little one said. "You're one of them."

"One of what? Whatcha talking about?"

"Hoodlum gang," the taller one said. "*Americano* sonsabeeches. Make trouble for us. Start riots. So what eet is, we fight you. We fight you to the end. You hear?"

Whitey shrugged. "I ain't fighting nobody. Crissake, I'm in trouble enough as it gets."

"Trouble?" The little one moved in closer. His eyes narrowed. "What you mean? What trouble?"

"Police," Whitey said. "They're looking for me." He shrugged again. "They claim I killed a policeman."

"Yes?" The little one looked Whitey up and down. "You did that, eh? That makes me interested, you know? I think I know you from someplace." He nudged the broken bottle against Whitey's chest. "Keep talking."

"They took me to the station house," Whitey said. "I — "

"Wait," the little one interrupted. "What station house?"

"Thirty-seventh District."

"On Clayton Street? Captain Kinnard?"

"Yes," Whitey said.

The little one turned to the other Puerto Rican and said something in Spanish. Then he faced Whitey and his eyes were very narrow. "Tell me. When this happen?"

"Tonight," Whitey said.

Again the little one looked at his partner and spoke in Spanish. He spoke rapidly and somewhat excitedly and then he turned back to Whitey and said, "All right, we check this. We check it real careful. What happens at the station house?"

"It was jammed," Whitey said. "They'd brought in a flock of prisoners and everything was all bolixed up. I saw the Captain giving them the treatment and it was bad, it was plenty bad. What I mean, he was really doing damage, he was like a wild man. So I figured it was no place for anyone charged with killing a cop. I took a long chance and busted loose. The idea caught on and there was one hell of a commotion. Everyone was running for the doors and windows and — "

"All right," the little one said. He was smiling thinly. "It checks O.K. I wanted to be sure it was you."

"You were there?" Whitey asked.

"Yes," the little one said. "And him too." He pointed to the other Puerto Rican, who nodded, grinning. "We get nice greetings from the Captain. Very nice greetings." He indicated his puffed-up eye and bruised cheek. The taller Puerto Rican fingered the bloody gash running from nose to chin. They both grinned widely as they stood there displaying their injuries, and the little one said, "This Captain Kinnard, he hits very hard."

Whitey nodded. "I saw the way he hits."

"And that's why you run, eh? You don't want him to hit you?"

"That's it," Whitey said. "That's the general idea."

The little one laughed. "You do smart thing to run. Is no make sense to stay there and get hit. You don't run, you get hurt. So you run. You run away from station house." He laughed louder; it really tickled him. "Very smart," he said. "Much brains."

"It didn't take much thinking." Whitey said. "It was all down here," and he pointed to his legs.

"Yes," the little one said. "You tell them to move, they move."

132

He laughed again. "I remember you now. Little white-haired bum who stands with detective on other side of room. Then the Captain, he comes walking slow, and you see him coming closer and you say to your feet, Come on, boys, move. So then you take off, you start to walk, and then you walk faster, and then you run. So we get same idea. We run too. We go out the door and down the street and the cops make chase but we get away."

"We damn sure get away," the taller Puerto Rican said, and he laughed loudly. "The cops, they look so funny. They jump up and down, they don't know what to do."

The little one was suddenly serious. He gave Whitey a sideward look and said, "You know something, man? I think you did us a good favor. If not for you, we no get away."

"Well," Whitey said, "I'm glad you made it, anyway."

"You mean this? You are really glad?"

"Sure," Whitey said. "It ain't a healthy place, that station house. I like to see people staying healthy."

"What people?" The little one's eyes were narrow again.

"All people," Whitey said.

"Even the Puerto Ricans?"

"Of course," Whitey said. "Why not?"

"You don't hate Puerto Ricans?"

"I don't hate anybody."

"You sure about that?"

"Absolutely," Whitey said. "Why should I hate the Puerto Ricans?"

"Listen to me, mister. Listen careful, now. There is many Americans no like Puerto Ricans. Why they not like us? They say we dirty, we rotten. They say we steal and make trouble and jump on their women. They call us rats and snakes and all names like that. And then they come in gangs, they use clubs and split our heads wide open, we get our teeth knocked out, we get broken arms and legs, and some of us get killed. You think we gonna take that? You think we are damn fools?"

"I don't think anything" Whitey said. "It ain't for me to say who's right and who's wrong."

"You mean you are not interested? You don't care?"

Whitey smiled dimly. "You want the truth, don't you?"

"It better be the truth."

"All right." Whitey said. "Here's the way it is. If I said I cared, I'd be a goddamn liar. I don't give a damn what goes on here in the Hellhole. What happens in this neighborhood ain't none of my business."

"You don't live here?"

"No."

"Then where? Where you from?"

"Tenderloin."

"That is what I thought," the little one said. "You look like Tenderloin bum. In the eyes it shows, that look, that don't-give-a-damn look. But something else I see. Something under that look. It is what?"

Whitey didn't say anything.

"It is what?" the little one repeated. "You give it to me straight, mister. What you doing here?"

"Like I told you," Whitey said, "I'm running from the heat. I'm looking for a place to hide."

The little one was quiet for some moments. Then he turned to the other Puerto Rican and said something in Spanish. They commenced a rapid conversation in Spanish and it went on like that for the better part of a minute. Finally the little one looked at Whitey and said, "You sure you tell the truth?"

Whitey nodded.

"I don't know" the little one said. He looked down at the broken bottle in his hand, his eyes centered on the jagged edge. "I am not so sure."

"Add it up," Whitey said. "You saw it with your own eyes. You saw me running out of the station house. So it figures I'm hot and I'm looking for a hideout."

There was another flow of quiet. The light pouring from

the kitchen window came slanting down across the back yard to make a pool of vague yellow glow in the narrow alley. It showed the thoughtful, doubtful frown on the face of the little Puerto Rican. The taller Puerto Rican was not frowning, not appearing thoughtful or dubious or in any way affected by the issue. His face was blank and his eyes were focused on Whitey's belly, the knife in his hand pointed at the same spot. His attitude was purely functional, like a poultry-market laborer getting set to kill a chicken.

Then the taller Puerto Rican said something in Spanish and took a slow step forward. The little one blocked him with an outswept arm and said, "No."

"*Sí,*" the taller one said. He was very anxious to start using the knife.

"No," the little one said. He pushed his partner backward. He looked at Whitey and spoke quietly and slowly. "I tell you something, man. You lucky for now. But maybe only for now. We take you to boss and hear what he says."

"Boss?" Whitey asked.

"Sure, we got boss." The little one smiled thinly. "This riot thing is big fight, man. Is like real war. You know how is with soldiers? The soldiers, they need leader. We got leader."

The little one made a gesture telling Whitey to turn and start walking. Whitey turned, and in doing so he caught a glimpse of the kitchen window. It was dark now and it had no importance, no meaning at all. It was just like all the other dark windows, and he thought: Well, anyway, it was interesting while it lasted.

Then he was walking slowly, with the Puerto Ricans walking behind him. The alley was very narrow and they had to move along in single file. For a moment he played with the idea of running. But he knew they could run just as fast, or faster. He felt sort of sorry for them, not pity really, just sorry they were having such a rough time.

-Eight-

At the end of the alley there was a narrow cobble-stoned street and they crossed it and went down another alley that had no paving and was mostly mud and stones. All the dwellings were wood, or sheet-metal roofed with tar paper. In the back yards there were a lot of cats and some dogs and he could hear them busily engaged in looking for food or romance or argument. There was no loud barking or meowing, just the scuffling and the scurrying, the convulsive squirming and the sound of furry bodies rolling around. At intervals he saw large rats darting between the fence posts. The rats were very large. He told himself he'd never seen them that big. He saw two of them leaping down from a fence and going after a cat. The cat was not yet full grown and it wasn't quite sure what it should do. As it hesitated, the rats pounced on it, but then a larger cat lunged in and the rats scampered away.

The alley extended for three blocks and gave way to a vacant lot heaped with rubbish and garbage and animal excrement. They moved along the edge of the lot, going east toward the river, and now he could see the lights along the water front, the lamps in the warehouses, and here and there the lighted portholes of freighters and tankers. With the little Puerto Rican giving directions, they skirted a lumber yard and another vacant lot and a wide area filled with scrap metal, going north now and entering a network of winding alleys that sloped downward and then up and then down again. The dwellings there were very old, with the wooden walls splintered and some of them partially caved in, and there were large gaps where there wasn't any wall at all. The wind whistled shrilly coming in from the river and racing through the gaps in the walls. Most of the dwellings were two-story structures, and he wondered what was keeping them upright. They looked very weak and flimsy, sort of leaning over and just about ready to go.

He felt a hand on his shoulder and he stopped and heard the little one saying, "In here."

It was one of the two-story houses. It didn't have a doorstep and there was no glass in the first story windows. The windows were stuffed with cardboard and newspapers to keep the wind out. Along the base of the front wall there were jagged holes where rats had gnawed through the wood. The wood looked easy for the teeth of the rats; it had long ago lost its hardness and resistance, it was more like the pulpy fungus-mushy substance of rotted trees.

The taller Puerto Rican stood close to Whitey while the little one stepped up to the door. The little one hit the heel of his palm against the wood, hit three times and waited, hit again and waited, and then hit very hard with the back of his hand, the wood creaking and groaning from the impact of his knuckles.

From inside the house there was a query in Spanish.

"*Soy yo, Luis,*" the little one said. "*Luis y Carlos.*"

"*Como?*"

"*Luis.*" The little one spoke louder. "*Luis, digo!*"

"*Qué pasa?*"

"Goddamnit," the little one said, then he shouted something in Spanish. After that, in English, "Come on, you dumb bastard, open the door."

The door opened. The man in the doorway was very old and wore a torn overcoat and tattered gloves and had a muffler wrapped tightly over his chin. He was shivering and his thin lips were more bluegray than red. He made an impatient and somewhat frantic gesture, telling them to come inside so he could close the door and shut out the cold.

Luis entered the house. Carlos shoved Whitey and followed him in. From one of the back rooms there was the glow of lighted candles. The flickering light came into this room and showed some people sleeping on the floor. There was no furniture except for a chair that was used for a table. On the chair Whitey saw an empty wine bottle and some unused candles and the melted wax from previous candles.

They went into the next room and there were more people sleeping on the floor. Several of them had blankets and the others were covered with assorted burlap bags and old carpets. A few were covered with newspaper. Whitey saw there were a lot of children sleeping close together, their arms flung over one another, their legs drawn up close to their bellies. He saw a very short, very fat woman sleeping flat on her back. Her mouth was open and she was snoring loudly. With one arm she held a sleeping infant, and her other arm provided a pillow for a two-year-old. There were several mothers holding their children while they slept. It was not a large room, but there were many sleepers on the floor. He saw it was really crowded in here, and as he walked behind Luis he stepped carefully to avoid treading on them. Luis and Carlos walked with less care, ignoring the fretful mutterings as their feet made contact with chins and shoulders and outstretched arms.

Then there was a stairway with some of the steps missing,

and other steps sagging as he climbed behind Luis, with Carlos following. On the steps and along the walls there were a great many roaches and bugs, moving slowly and contentedly in the dim light coming down from the second floor.

The light on the second floor was from a single candle placed on a window sill. Also, some light was showing through cracks in a door at the far end of the hall. They went down the hall and Luis opened the door. Several men were standing in the room and talking quietly in Spanish. A few men were seated on wooden boxes arranged along the walls. In the center of the room there was a pile of baseball bats, broken bottles, lengths of lead pipe, and a varied assortment of bread knives, butcher knives, switchblades, and meat cleavers. As the men talked they gestured toward the collection of weapons. It appeared they were having a problem with the weapons. They were deeply concerned with the problem, but when they saw Whitey they stopped talking. They stared questioningly at Luis and Carlos.

It went on like that and there was no sound in the room. Then one of the men moved slowly toward Luis and said something in Spanish. The man was pointing to Whitey and wanting to know who he was and what he was doing here. Luis began to talk rapidly, addressing the man as Gerardo. It was obvious he had much respect for the man, because he kept saying "Gerardo" in the way that overly humble people who talk to doctors keep saying "Doctor," starting or ending each phrase with "Doctor." While Luis talked, Gerardo wore a detached gaze that gave the impression that he wasn't listening. And when Luis was finished, Gerardo didn't bother to comment. He was looking at the pile-up of weapons on the floor. He said in English, "Is not enough meat cleavers. Little knives no good. We need more meat cleavers."

"I get some," Luis said.

"You?" Gerardo looked directly at Luis. "You go out and find meat cleavers?"

"Sure," Luis said eagerly. "I do it now, Gerardo. I go right now. You say O.K., Gerardo?"

Gerardo said very quietly, "I send you out for meat cleavers, maybe you bring back something else. Maybe you bring another gringo."

There was a laugh from Carlos. The other Puerto Ricans laughed also. They did it hesitantly at first, and then it really struck them funny and there was much laughter in the room.

"Shut up," Gerardo said to them. And instantly they stopped laughing. But Carlos couldn't check it completely and he was grinning open-mouthed. Gerardo looked at Carlos and said, "Is not funny."

Carlos got rid of the grin.

"Is for sure not funny," Gerardo said. Again he was looking at Luis. "Is more sad, I think. Is very sad my men they always make mistakes."

"I –" Luis was swallowing hard. "Leesen, Gerardo –"

"You keep quiet now," Gerardo said. "You do smart thing, you keep quiet."

Luis swallowed very hard and looked down at the floor.

Gerardo turned to Whitey and said, "They bring you here, they make mistake."

"Not me" Carlos said quickly. "Eet wasn't my idea. I tell Luis we have this man in alley, we kill him there. Luis he say no."

"Bad mistake," Gerardo went on, as though Carlos weren't there. "Very bad." He nodded slowly and solemnly. The single bulb that dangled on a wire from the ceiling was directly over his head and the glow was focused on him, highlighting his features. He was an exceptionally good-looking man in his middle thirties. His build was lean and nicely balanced and he stood about five-nine. He featured a thick crop of heavily greased straight combed black hair, and every hair was in place.

140

It was evident he gave much attention to his scalp. Also, his eyebrows were neatly trimmed, and his face looked cleaner than the other faces.

But that was the only difference. His clothing was just as tattered and shabby as the rags they wore. He was wearing a very old overcoat that looked about ready to come apart. At one time it had been camel's hair but now it was only a weary jumble of loose yellow threads. He saw Whitey looking at the overcoat and he said, "Is nice? You like it?"

"Yes" Whitey said. "It's a very nice coat."

"Is very expensive," Gerardo said. "Is genuine camel's hair."

Whitey nodded. He started to say something, and then, whatever it was, he lost track of it, and he stood there looking blankly at Gerardo's overcoat.

Gerardo frowned slightly. "Why you do this? Why you look at the coat?"

Whitey didn't say anything. He wondered why he was staring at the camel's-hair coat. He tried to look away but the coat wouldn't let him turn his head. He told himself it was just a piece of castoff clothing that the Puerto Rican had lifted from a rubbish can. That's all it is, he insisted to himself.

He went on staring at it.

Gerardo took a step toward him. "Here," Gerardo said quietly, "I give you a better look."

The camel's-hair coat was very close to his eyes and he blinked hard.

"What is it?" Gerardo asked. "What this thing with coat?"

"I don't know," Whitey said. He was telling the truth. He really didn't know why he was doing it, staring at the ragged garment as though it had some meaning, some importance. Of course there was a reason, there had to be a reason. Well, he thought, maybe it'll come, but right now you're nowhere near it. Just then Carlos laughed again.

Gerardo looked at Carlos and said, "*Qué hay?* What is funny now?"

Carlos was laughing loudly and pointing to Whitey "He likes coat. He wants you to take it off and geeve it to him."

"You think so?" Gerardo murmured. "You think that is what he wants?"

"Sure." Carlos was shaking with laughter. "Thees is crazy man here. In alley he sees we come to kill him, he pay no mind to that. He ask if we got cigarette. Now we bring him here to kill him and he wants your overcoat."

The other Puerto Ricans were grinning.

Gerardo had a calculating look on his face. He turned to Whitey and his eyes drilled into Whitey's eyes. He said, "Maybe Carlos is wrong. Maybe you not crazy like he thinks."

Whitey stared at the loose threads of the camel's-hair overcoat.

He heard Gerardo saying, "In school, long ago, I study the numbers. *La matemática.* They teach me one and one it equals two. And two and two it equals four. And four and four – you see? I learn to add the numbers. Is what I'm doing now."

Carlos had stopped laughing. His face was solemn and he said emphatically, "Four and four is ten."

"No" Gerardo said. He wasn't smiling. "Is not ten. Is eight. Is always eight."

Carlos shrugged. "No matter to me."

"That is right," Gerardo said. "No matter to you, because you no can add the numbers. So you stay away from numbers, you leave that to me. I do all thinking here, all adding up the score."

Yes," Carlos agreed quickly. "Yes, Gerardo."

Gerardo looked at Luis. "And you? What you say?"

Luis blinked a few times. Then he nodded slowly.

"Not enough," Gerardo murmured. "Say it with the mouth."

142

"You do all thinking," Luis said. "You the boss."

"Always," Gerardo said. "Always the boss."

"Yes," Luis nodded again. "Sure. Always. You top man, Gerardo. You the leader."

"And good leader, too," Gerardo said. "I no make mistakes. But my men, they make mistakes sometimes. They no do like I say." He turned to Whitey and his tone was mild and conversational. "My men, they sometimes give me a headache. They make me sick sometimes. Is no easy job to be leader of these men."

Carlos opened his mouth to say something.

"Close it," Gerardo said. "Keep it closed." And then he looked at the other Puerto Ricans. "Keep quiet, everybody. No move around. Just stand and listen."

They stood quietly, stiffly, fully attentive.

Gerardo said, "I tell you now what I tell you many times before. This house is secret place. Is headquarters. Is what is called center of operations. So then is understood we no take chances they find us here. They find us here, they wipe us out. We finished."

"We fight them," one of the Puerto Ricans said. "We fight until we die."

"You like to die?" Gerardo asked quietly. "You think it is a happy business?"

"I think we should stop waiting," the man said. "Let them find us here. Let them come. Is better that way. We have showdown battle and get it ended once and for all."

"You are brave man, Chávez."

The man stood there with his spine erect and his head held high and he was gazing upward like someone paying allegiance to a banner.

"Yes," Gerardo said. "You are very brave. You are also very stupid."

The man winced. His chin sagged.

"You are a goddamn fool, Chávez. You need examination of the brain. We no make fight to die. We fight to win, to teach gringos a lesson they no forget. To make them understand we no get pushed around, we no get kicked in face. They treat us like animals, we strike back like animals. But not like clumsy jackass with nothing inside the head. Instead, we hide and wait, we sharpen our teeth, we make our plans very careful. When time is right, we jump on them, we make big riot and they run away."

"They no run away tonight," the man said. He looked sullen.

"Tonight was bad luck," Gerardo told him. "We make good plans but they get break when cops come."

The man's face remained sullen. "Other times was bad luck too. Always something happens."

"You saying it is my fault?" Gerardo asked mildly.

The man didn't reply.

"Say it, Chávez. You can say it. Go on, say it."

Chávez took a deep breath. He was a medium-sized but strongly built man in his middle forties. His eyes aimed past Gerardo and he said quietly, "I no like these riots in street. Is no way for men to fight. Is not respectable."

"Respectable?" Gerardo murmured. He allowed himself the slightest trace of a smile. "What you mean, Chávez?"

Chávez looked directly at Gerardo and said, "I am respectable man. Very poor in the pockets but not lacking in good manners, clean life. I no drink too much or use dope or —"

"So," Gerardo cut in. The smile was fading. "So what are you trying to say?"

"I am not a bum in the streets," Chávez said. "I am working man with family. I come here from San Juan with my wife and seven children. Much trouble finding job, getting place to live. Is here a bad neighborhood with roughnecks, hoodlums,

144

thugs. For reason we not know, they hate Puerto Ricans, they make trouble. So then we do the same. We come out on River Street and give them plenty bad business, much commotion. The police they come and we run back here to hiding place. But I no like to hide. Why should I hide? Better I should make announcement, I should give hoodlums my address, say to them, 'Now you know where I live, you want to get me you know where to come, I wait for you, I fight you with all my strength.'"

"And then," Gerardo murmured, "they come in a mob. They break down the door and—"

"They no break it down. I open it for them."

"And they walk in. They smash your head. Maybe they kill you."

"At least I die fighting in house where I live. I die respectable."

Gerardo was silent for some moments. He gazed at the faces of the other Puerto Ricans. Some of them were nodding in solemn agreement with Chávez. These were the older men. The younger ones were frowning thoughtfully. And a few, both young and old, had nothing in their eyes. They hadn't been affected by what Chávez had said; they were waiting for Gerardo to react so they could mirror his reaction.

Finally Gerardo said, "I tell you something, Chávez. Maybe you die respectable this minute. Maybe I kill you."

Chávez stood stiffly. Again he was staring past Gerardo. He didn't say anything.

"Yes" Gerardo said. "Maybe I do it. Is my privilege, you know. I am leader here. Like general of army. Like captain of ship. I have full right to stop rebellion."

"I no make rebellion," Chávez said. "I only make statement."

Gerardo smiled again. It was a twisted smile. He said, "Sometimes is very expensive to make statements."

And then he took the bread knife from Carlos' hand. He ran his finger along the blade.

Chávez looked at the knife. In his eyes there was more sadness than worry. The sadness deepened his voice as he said, "You would do this, Gerardo? You would put me in the grave?"

"I am thinking about it," Gerardo said. He went on running his finger along the blade. "I am thinking maybe you are not useful now. Like broken wheel. Keeps other wheels from moving."

Chávez took a very deep breath and held it. He stood there waiting to be stabbed.

Gerardo stabbed him. It was more slash than stab, and the knife went in fairly deep, going into the shoulder and ripping down along the arm to the elbow. Then Gerardo stepped back and the knife slashed wide with the blade cutting a deep gash across the forehead of Chávez. *"Ay, Jesús,"* Chávez moaned, and Gerardo cut him again, slicing his cheek, the blood spurting from a slanting gash that started under the cheekbone and ended at the mouth.

Chávez fell to his knees. He had one hand pressed against his carved cheek and with his other hand he was trying to stop the flow of blood from his forehead and his upper arm. His hand made a rapid blurry motion going from forehead to shoulder and back to forehead. He was getting a lot of blood all over himself and there was much blood on the floor.

Gerardo was looking at Carlos and saying, "This is good knife, you know? I think I will keep it."

"Sure." Carlos nodded eagerly. "You keep it, boss. Is present from me."

"Thank you," Gerardo said politely. He wiped the dripping blade on his sleeve. And then, gesturing with the blade to indicate the bleeding man, "Take him out of here. Take him downstairs, give him some water. Make bandages."

146

A few of the older men came forward and lifted Chávez from the floor. And as they stood him upright he fainted. They carried him out of the room.

Gerardo looked at the blood on the floor. "Statements," he said. "My famous fighters, all they do is make statements and mistakes."

The Puerto Ricans were quiet. Some of them were staring at the knife in Gerardo's hand. Most of them were trying not to look at the knife.

Gerardo studied their faces. He said, "Do I hear further talk? Is anyone else like to make statements?"

The men kept their mouths shut tightly.

"All right, then," Gerardo said. "So now we finished with making statements. Now I deal with man who make mistake."

He turned his head slowly and looked directly at Luis. Luis opened his mouth just a little. Then his face was like that of a child forcing down some castor oil. He swallowed very hard.

"I say it now like I say it many times before," Gerardo said. "I say this is important secret place and you no bring gringos here. There is chance gringo gets away. And then what?"

Luis swallowed hard again. He put his hands in his trousers pockets and took them out and put them in again.

Gerardo pointed at Whitey and said to Luis, "You see this man? You see what he has on his face?"

"On his face?" Luis mumbled, his lips twitching nervously.

"Yes," Gerardo said. "On his face."

"Is just a face," Luis said. He managed a slight shrug. "Like any other face."

Gerardo nodded slowly. "Yes, very true. Like any face that has eyes and mouth. You see what is? You understand what I mean?"

Luis blinked several times. He shook his head vaguely.

"All right, I tell you," Gerardo said. "With the eyes he see. With the mouth he talks."

147

"But—"

"You hear what I say, Luis? With the mouth he talks."

Carlos let out a murmuring laugh and said, "This gringo no talk. We make sure he no get away."

Moving quickly, Carlos reached toward the pile of weapons on the floor and selected a meat cleaver.

Gerardo smiled. "And now you fix him?"

"Sure," Carlos said. "I fix thees bastard so he no talk."

Carlos raised the meat cleaver above his shoulder started walking slowly toward Whitey.

-Nine-

"No," Gerardo said. He motioned Carlos to stay away from Whitey.

"But why?" Carlos frowned puzzledly. "Is easy to do it. Is very simple job."

"And then?" Gerardo murmured.

Carlos shrugged. "Get rid of body."

"How? Where?"

Carlos shrugged again. "Dig hole. Bury him. Or maybe throw him in river. No trouble."

"Plenty trouble," Gerardo said. "No place to dig outside this house. Ground too hard. Big stones. Too much cement. Is softer ground on empty lot. But empty lot too far away."

"Not so far, Gerardo," Carlos was very anxious to get started with the meat cleaver. "We carry body there in a few minutes."

"In a few minutes much can happen," Gerardo said. "Is many police in this area. Maybe they see we carry something. They get curious, you know? The police, they are very curious people."

"Maybe—" Carlos was stumped for a moment. He tried again, saying, "Maybe is better the river. Is much closer the river."

"Is not close enough," Gerardo said. "The river is three blocks away."

Carlos looked disappointed. Then all at once his eyes lit up and he said eagerly, "Listen, Gerardo. I have answer to problem. We kill him and keep him here."

"Here? In this house?"

"Sure," Carlos said. "We put him in closet. We put him under bed. Plenty of places to put him."

Gerardo was thoughtful for a moment. Then he shook his head.

"But why not?" Carlos asked.

"Dead body make smell," Gerardo said. "Is enough stink in this house without more stink."

"It no have stink," Carlos persisted. "We steal perfume from dime store. We—"

"Oh, shut up," Gerardo said wearily. "You sometimes talk like damn fool." And then, slowly and emphatically, "Is no good to kill him here. Is much risk. Would not be risk if we had plumbing. Easy that way. Down the drain. In pieces cut him up and put it down the drain. But we no have plumbing. I think of that when I tell you many times, you kill a gringo, you do it in gringo section of Hellhole."

Carlos slowly lowered the meat cleaver. He tossed it onto the pile of weapons in the center of the floor.

During the conversation between Gerardo and Carlos, it had been difficult for Whitey to breathe. For the past several moments he'd been holding his breath. Now he let it out and it came out fast.

But he knew the relief was only temporary. He was watching Gerardo's face and focusing on Gerardo's eyes. He saw what was in Gerardo's eyes and again he had trouble breathing. His chest felt tight and it seemed his lungs were out of commission.

Gerardo turned to Luis and said, "You see what bad mistake you have made? You bring him here and now we have big problem."

Luis wet his lips. He didn't say anything. He was looking at the knife in Gerardo's hand.

"Big serious problem," Gerardo said. "And all because you no listen to what I say. I think maybe I teach you something, Luis. I teach you to listen."

Gerardo took a step toward Luis. He'd been holding the knife loosely and now his fingers tightened on the handle.

"Gerardo – " Luis was barely able to produce sound. His eyes widened as he saw the blade coming closer. And then in a frenzy of trying to prevent himself from getting cut, he gasped, "No problem, Gerardo." His arm trembled as he pointed to Whitey. "No problem with this man. This man friend."

"Friend?" Gerardo was in the midst of taking another step toward Luis. He stopped and murmured, "You make joke, Luis? This gringo here, you call him a friend?"

"Is many gringos no hate Puerto Ricans," Luis said.

Gerardo smiled. He folded his arms. "So," he said with thin sarcasm. "So now we hear speech. Go ahead, Luis. Make speech."

"This man," Luis began, speaking slowly and carefully, working hard to choose the right words, "he is very good friend of Puerto Ricans. He do us big favor tonight. In station house he play trick on cops and is much excitement and we make escape. Me and Carlos and other Puerto Ricans run out the door. We make good getaway. And so you see, Gerardo. If not for this man, we still there in station house and then we go to prison."

Gerardo turned slowly and looked at Whitey. "Is true?"

Whitey nodded.

"You were arrested in riot?" Gerardo asked.

"No," Whitey said. "I wasn't mixed up in the riot. I ain't been in any of these riots."

"Why were you arrested?"

"They said I — " He thought about the dead policeman. It occurred to him that maybe he had a chance now. There was no friendship between these men and the Thirty-seventh District. It was possible that Gerardo would be favorably impressed with a cop-killer. "Well, I might as well tell you. I killed a policeman."

"You did what?"

"He killed a cop," Luis said. "You hear what he tells you? He no fight the Puerto Ricans. Only thing he do is kill a cop."

"Be quiet," Gerardo told Luis. "I let this man talk for himself." He went on looking at Whitey. "Tell me, now. About this cop. When you kill him?"

"Tonight," Whitey said.

"Where?"

"In an alley."

"What alley?" Gerardo's eyes were getting narrow. "I am adding the numbers again, mister. I am listening to you very careful. Be sure you give me the right numbers so is adding up so everything fits. Maybe it winds up you get a break, after all. If this is all true what you say, is possible you live to be old man. If not true, is gonna be very bad. I no like to be played for fool. I take you for a walk somewhere and you die slow. Is not pleasant to die slow. Sometimes it hurts so much you go crazy before you die."

"I get the idea," Whitey said. He told himself to stay as close to the truth as possible. "It was an alley not far from here."

"In this neighborhood? In Hellhole?"

"That's right."

"Give me location," Gerardo said. "I want location of alley."

"I can't remember exactly."

"You can't?" Gerardo murmured. "I think you can. A man kills someone, he remembers the exact location."

"I ain't familiar with this neighborhood," Whitey said. "I don't live around here. There's so many alleys — "

"All right, we'll forget the alley. We'll come back to it later. So now we talk about the cop. What happens with the cop? How you kill him?"

"I hit him on the head."

Gerardo was quiet for a long moment. Then, scarcely moving his lips, "With what?"

With what? Whitey asked himself. In his mind he saw the dying policeman, the wet red seeping through the scalp, and shiny streams of it flowing down the cop's face. Well, it needed something heavy to crack a skull that badly, so maybe the weapon was a brick, or a hammer, or then again it could have been a baseball bat.

"Baseball bat," Whitey said.

Gerardo looked at the collection of knives and lead pipes and baseball bats resting in a heap in the center of the floor. "Now tell me," he said. "Where you get the baseball bat?"

"I found it in the alley," Whitey said. He waited for Gerardo to ask another question. Gerardo was smiling at him. There was something in the smile that told him to keep talking. Or maybe it wasn't that kind of smile. Maybe he'd loused it up already and further talk was useless. He gazed past Gerardo's smiling lips and begged himself to keep talking, to make it clear and brief and fully logical. He said, "The cop was chasing me. I tried to rob a store and the job went haywire and this cop was chasing me down the alley. So then I tripped and fell and he closed in on me. I looked for something to hit him with and I saw the baseball bat. It was busted, it was broken off at the handle. I got a grip on it and when he grabbed for me I let him have it and it cracked his head wide open. Before I could get

153

away there were other cops moving in. They put cuffs on me and took me to the station house."

He told himself it sounded all right. He wondered if Gerardo thought it sounded all right.

He heard Gerardo saying, "You tell me more about this cop. What he look like?"

"He had gray hair," Whitey said. "Well, anyway, it was mostly gray. He was sort of beefy, and he looked around forty-five or so. Or maybe older. It was hard to tell, there was so much blood on his face."

"All right," Gerardo interrupted. "Is enough about the cop. So now we come back to alley where it happen. You give me location of alley."

"I told you, I can't remember."

"Is important that you remember. Is very important."

"Well —" Whitey frowned and bit his lip. He wasn't trying to remember the location of the alley. He told himself he damn well knew the location. And it would be nice if he could also know what Gerardo was getting at. He was trying very hard to figure what Gerardo had in mind.

"Come on," Gerardo said. "Is no good this stalling. I no like stalling."

"The alley..." He hesitated. He wondered why he hesitated.

"Come on," Gerardo said. "Quick now. Where this alley is?"

"Near River Street." And then, as he said it, he had the feeling it was an error to be truthful about the location.

But Gerardo seemed satisfied. Gerardo was nodding slowly and saying, "We getting closer now. Is very good." Turned and looked at the other Puerto Ricans. He gave them a pleasant smile and held it for some moments while he went on nodding. Finally, still looking at the Puerto Ricans, he said to Whitey, "Now tell me, mister. This alley, it is east or west of River?"

"East," Whitey said. But to himself, without sound: What

154

goes on here? What the hell is he building? Maybe you should have said west instead of east. Well, you can fix that if you want to. You can still give him a false location. Trouble is, you don't know what to give him. Hell, you're sure having a bad time tonight. And all because you had to see her again. All right, let's not start with that. You've had enough of that. What you hafta do now is think in terms of staying alive. Maybe if you use your brains you can save your ass. All right, then, what's it gonna be? You gonna switch the location of the alley? Come on, make up your mind, the man's waiting. I think the best thing is to play it straight with the geography. He wants the exact location of the alley and you better give him what he wants. But why does he want it? Oh, well, the hell with it, you'll hafta' take your chances and give it to him.

Gerardo was saying, "How far, mister? How far east of River Street?"

"One block," he said. "Make it the middle of the block. It's a very narrow alley and it's off a little side street."

Gerardo started to laugh. It wasn't much of a sound, it was almost no sound at all.

"Yes," Gerardo said. And then he laughed just a bit louder. "Is very funny, you know?"

"What's funny?" Whitey murmured.

"Is same alley," Gerardo laughed. "Same policeman."

"What?" Whitey said. He blinked several times "What are you talking about?"

Gerardo didn't answer. Now he was laughing loudly. The other Puerto Ricans had no idea why he was laughing and they looked at one another. A few were frowning puzzledly. And some were trying to get with it, grinning and looking foolish and uncertain. The ones who were fanatically loyal to Gerardo were imitating his laughter. Carlos was laughing the loudest and holding his sides and choking on his forced guffaws as he wondered what all this comedy was about.

Suddenly Gerardo stopped laughing. Then all the laughing stopped and they waited for Gerardo to speak. He was in no hurry to speak, and for some moments all he did was run his finger along the edge of the bread knife in his hand.

Whitey looked at the knife. He looked at the tattered and scraggly fabric of Gerardo's camel's-hair overcoat. He thought: It's funny about the coat. And the knife is funny, too. Yes, everything here is very funny. It's just as funny as rain coming down on a graveyard.

Then Gerardo was saying, "You tell good story, mister. Very much truth in it. But not truth enough. Not hardly truth enough."

Whitey took a deep breath. He held it.

"You no kill policeman," Gerardo said.

Oh, Whitey said without sound. Oh, God. God Almighty.

"Because," Gerardo said very slowly, "I know who kill policeman. Name of killer is Gerardo."

– Ten –

Then it was quiet in the room and it was a thick quiet that came in layers, falling on Whitey and giving him the feeling that he was being smothered by it.

He heard Gerardo saying, "You want to say something?"

He shook his head.

"Is very sensible," Gerardo said. "You say nothing because there is nothing you can say."

"Gerardo – " It was Carlos. "You really kill the cop?"

Gerardo nodded. His tone was matter-of-fact as he said, "It was during the riot. He grabbed me from the back. He not see what I hold in my hand. I think it was a hammer. Maybe a monkey-wrench. I no remember for sure. Only thing I remember is how I hit him. I hit him on head real hard."

"Good," Carlos said. "I no like cops. Is with cops like cowboys in movie picture say about Indians. Best policeman is dead policeman."

"This one was stupid policeman," Gerardo said.

"All policemen, they are stupid," Carlos said.

"No," Gerardo murmured. "Not all."

"They are stupid like jackass," Carlos insisted.

Gerardo looked at him and said, "Your mouth, it is always busy. Why you have such a busy mouth?"

"I only say —"

"You say nothing. " Gerardo spoke very quietly. "You talk and talk and what comes out is nothing."

"All right," Carlos said. "All right. All right."

Gerardo looked at the other Puerto Ricans. "Listen careful now. Is what I'm saying very important. I go out now with gringo. I take him for a walk. I come back in fifteen, twenty minutes, maybe half an hour. You wait here. You no go outside for any reason. You stay inside so outside it's quiet, so me and gringo we go for nice walk. You understand?"

They nodded.

Gerardo looked at Whitey. "Come on, mister. We go now. You walk in front of me."

Whitey moved slowly toward the door. One of the Puerto Ricans opened the door. Gerardo stepped in close behind Whitey and said, "I give you advice, mister. You try to run, I throw the knife. With throwing a knife I am first-rank expert. You don't believe it, you try me out."

"I believe it," Whitey said.

They were approaching the doorway and Carlos came up to Gerardo and said, "Look, boss, I have idea. I think is best you throw him in river. No trace."

Gerardo smiled at Carlos. "Is that your idea?"

Carlos nodded vigorously.

"And you think it is good idea?"

"Sure," Carlos said. "Is best to throw him in river with something heavy tied to feet so he stays down. And then they no find him."

"But I want them to find him," Gerardo said.

"What?" Carlos said. "What you mean?"

Gerardo smiled widely now. He was very much amused at Carlos. He said, "Is much luck for me when they find him. Is much luck for all of us."

Carlos frowned. "I do not understand."

"Because you are an idiot," Gerardo said affectionately. He turned to the other Puerto Ricans. "You see what is my plan? You know why I want them to find him?"

They stared blankly at Gerardo.

"Well, then," Gerardo said, "I explain, and maybe you learn something and you see how I use the brains." He paused to make it impressive, and went on: "The police, they are wanting this man here they think is cop-killer. And while they look for him they no close the case. So in mean time is possible they get information somewhere and they find out cop-killer is Gerardo."

"Is bad if that happen," someone said.

"But it will not happen," Gerardo said. "I make sure it will not happen. They will find dead body of cop-killer and then everything is all right. Case is closed."

"*Bueno,*" someone said with admiration. "*Muy bueno.*"

"You clever, boss," another one said. "You real clever."

"For sure," Carlos said loudly. "Is nobody clever like Gerardo."

Some of the men were grinning to show their fondness and praise and worship for the leader. Gerardo winked at them and they winked back. But there were others who looked at one another with solemn disapproval of what was happening. Luis was looking at Whitey and his eyes were dismal, saying without sound, Is not fair, is goddamn shame.

"Is time to go," Gerardo said to Whitey. He gave him a gentle shove toward the doorway. Whitey walked out of the room and Gerardo stayed close behind him going down the hall to the stairs.

They went down the stairs and through the rooms where

the women and children and older people were sleeping on the floor. Gerardo opened the front door and they walked out together, Gerardo now moving close at his side so that their shoulders touched.

"Slow and easy, now," Gerardo said softly. "Is just a couple friends going out for a walk. So we walk nice and slow and peaceful. O.K.?"

Whitey didn't answer. He was looking down at Gerardo's right arm. There was nothing in Gerardo's hand, and he thought: Where's he got the knife? But then he took a closer look and he saw the tip of the shiny blade projecting from the ragged sleeve of the camel's hair overcoat.

They walked slowly through the labyrinth of winding alleys. It was very cold and the wind rushing down the alleys was a mean, wet wind that yowled like something alive and going berserk. He wanted to pull up the collar of his coat but he didn't want to move his arms because maybe Gerardo would get the wrong idea. He kept his hands in his pockets and wished he could pull up the collar of his coat. He told himself it was too damn cold out here. Yeah, he said dryly to himself, you're in a fine position to worry about the weather. Where you're going, there ain't gonna be no weather.

But it would be nice if he could have a drink. One final drink. Anything at all, just so it had some sock in it. Maybe a shot of that goathead, that stuff manufactured by Jones Jarvis. That would taste real good right now. Well, no matter what it was, it would taste good. Even if it was antifreeze, it would taste good. He'd heard of them drinking antifreeze and going blind or getting a fast ride to the morgue, but if some of it was offered to him now, he'd grab it. Sure he'd grab it, and drink it, and what would he have to lose? At least he'd get that one last jolt before the curtain came down.

Goddamn, he said to himself, you're sure a sucker for liquid refreshment. But you ain't alone in that, you sure got plenty of company there. I wonder whaT-bones and Phillips are doing. They still sitting on the pavement in front of that flophouse? They sure were thirsty. That empty bottle wasn't easy to look at. Well, maybe they put their heads together and figured something out, and got their hands on another bottle. That would be good news. Maybe someone dropped a dollar bill in the street and they picked it up. Yeah, sure. Fat chance. Like the chance you got now. All right, don't start that routine. That ain't gonna help. Well, as far as that's concerned, nothing's gonna help.

Now they were away from the alleys and moving across the flat wide area on which were heaps of scrap metal. They were going toward the lumberyard and they were at the edge of the yard when Gerardo stopped and looked at him.

He thought: Well, here it is. It happens now.

But nothing happened just then. Gerardo was frowning slightly and saying aloud to himself, "No, this not the place. We go farther."

"Yeah," Whitey said. "The farther, the better."

"Shut up," Gerardo said. "I do some thinking. I choose the right spot."

"Let's go to City Hall."

"I said shut up."

"Why should I?" Whitey asked. He wondered why he was doing this. He grinned at Gerardo and said, "Come on, let's walk to City Hall. You can do it there. If you want them to find my body, they're sure to find it in City Hall."

"Goddamn you," Gerardo said. "You gonna shut up?"

"Go to hell," Whitey said. He told himself it was a silly thing to say. But he liked the sound of it. He knew he was grinning widely and he heard himself saying, "Go to hell, Gerardo."

"So?" Gerardo murmured thoughtfully. "So is gonna be like this?"

Whitey shrugged. He sent the grin past Gerardo and he

said to the empty air, "How's about a drink? I could sure use a drink."

"What? What you say?"

"A drink." He went on grinning past Gerardo. "I need a drink."

Gerardo mixed a frown with a thin smile. "I think maybe Carlos was right. Maybe you really crazy."

"Let's go somewhere and get a drink."

"All right," Gerardo said, humoring him. "I take you somewhere and we have nice party."

"With girls?"

"Sure. Plenty girls. Very pretty. Real angels."

Then Gerardo nudged him and they were walking again. They came out of the lumberyard and onto the vacant lot. They moved along the edge of the lot and he kept saying he needed a drink but now Gerardo didn't answer. Gerardo was studying the terrain and not liking it. So then they continued along the north boundary of the lot, then went down along the west boundary and past the south boundary, entering a long alley that had no paving and consisted mostly of loose stones and thick mud.

He remembered walking through this alley with Carlos and Luis, and he knew the next thing would be the narrow cobblestoned street. He recalled seeing a lamppost where the alley met the street, and even now he could see the dim glow far down there. He thought: That's where it's gonna happen. He'll give it to you there, right there under that lamppost.

Now Gerardo was walking behind him. He told himself this was a very long alley. He wished it were longer. He saw the glow of the street light coming closer. And then it was very close and he saw the glow reflected on the cobblestones of the narrow street.

Thirty seconds, he estimated. We'll be there in thirty seconds and then it's all over.

Or make it twenty seconds. Or fifteen. So right about now you can start counting them off and predict your future. You know just how long you've got to live. Fifteen seconds... fourteen...thirteen...You oughta be a fortune teller, you're really good at this. Eleven...ten...nine...eight...We're almost there, just a few more steps, a few more seconds. Five...four... three...

They were coming out of the alley.

"All right," Gerardo said, "Stop here."

He stopped. He was under the glow of the street light, standing there on the cobblestones with his back to Gerardo. In his brain he could see the knife emerging from the sleeve of the camel's hair overcoat, and Gerardo's fingers getting a grip on the handle.

He heard himself saying, "You can't do it here."

"No?" Gerardo murmured. "Why not?"

He turned very slowly and faced Gerardo and said, "You can't do it anyplace. You just can't do it, that's all."

Gerardo was holding the knife with the blade pointed at Whitey's stomach. He was waiting for Whitey to take a step backward or sideways.

Whitey didn't move. He said, "That's a heavy overcoat you're wearing. Another thing, it's too big for you. It's much too big."

"You think it makes me clumsy? Slows me down?"

"No," Whitey said. "That ain't what I'm thinking. It's just that I'm wondering about the coat. It ain't no cheap article."

Gerardo smiled but it was an uncertain smile and his voice quivered slightly as he said, "Why you talk about coat now? You talking just to gain time?"

"It's camel's-hair," Whitey said. "Genuine camel's-hair."

"So?" Gerardo was trying to see inside Whitey's head. "So what is connection here? What is business with camel's-hair?"

163

Whitey didn't say anything. He was looking at the over-coat.

Gerardo blinked several times. He was impatient to get busy with the knife, but this matter of the overcoat made him very curious and somewhat worried. He was remembering the way Whitey had stared at the overcoat when they were in the room upstairs. He wondered why this little white-haired bum was able to stall him, to give him a feeling of indecision and confusion. He knew it showed in his eyes and he tried to get it out of his eyes but it stayed there.

And Whitey saw it. Whitey said, "Let's talk about the coat. Where'd you get it?"

"Is make any difference?" Gerardo worked the words through his teeth, his lips stiff.

"Someone give it to you?" Whitey asked.

"Yes." It was a hissing sound. "Yes. So what?"

"Tell me something," Whitey said conversationally. "Who gave it to you?"

For an instant Gerardo's eyes were wide and he was staring past Whitey. In the next instant Whitey kicked him in the groin.

Gerardo let out a choked scream and as he fell backward he was trying to double up. Whitey came in close and kicked him again.

The knife fell out of Gerardo's hand. It hit the cobblestones and bounced and hit again and came down in some stagnant milky water in the gutter. Gerardo was on his knees, trying to hurl himself at the knife, but all he could do was crawl. Whitey moved in between Gerardo and the milky water, made a grab at the knife, and almost had it when Gerardo snatched blindly at his ankle, found him, held him, gripped him hard, and pulled him down. Then very quickly, forgetting the pain in the groin, Gerardo threw a clenched right hand at Whitey's face and caught him on the jaw and Whitey fell over on his side. He told himself he'd been hit very hard and he wondered if he could get up. As he tried to get up, he saw Gerardo crawling again, making another try for the knife.

He managed to get up. He leaped at Gerardo and his shoulder made contact with Gerardo's ribs. They went down together and rolled over and kept rolling with Gerardo's hands going for his throat. He butted Gerardo in the face and broke Gerardo's nose. Gerardo went on grabbing for his throat and now they were rolling over and over in the milky water. It was slimy, greasy water and now it became streaked with red dripping from Gerardo's smashed nose. Whitey told himself this party was getting very sloppy. He was on his back now and he felt Gerardo's fingers closing on his throat. He reached up and took a handful of Gerardo's hair and started to rip the hair from Gerardo's scalp. Gerardo gasped and groaned and let go of his throat. He held onto the handful of hair and kept on pulling and some blood streamed down Gerardo's forehead. But Gerardo was still on top of him and again going for his throat and he knew the important thing was to get out from under. He wondered if he had the strength to roll them over again, told himself to stop wondering and start working, and then he let go of Gerardo's hair and heaved very hard. They went over and for a moment he was on top of Gerardo but they kept rolling and then Gerardo was on top of him. He heaved again and they went on rolling and suddenly Gerardo pulled free and stood up. Gerardo aimed a kick at his face and missed and caught him in the chest. Gerardo circled him and aimed another kick. He rolled away and got to his knees and then got to his feet and now Gerardo came at him with fists.

He slipped away from a roundhouse right hand trying for his head, ducked to avoid a short left hook, stepped back and then came inside another left hook and shot a short right to Gerardo's belly. Gerardo was past feeling it and wouldn't give ground and countered mechanically with another left hook that caught Whitey on the temple and staggered him. Gerardo moved in, completely mechanical now, measuring him very carefully with a right hand, then throwing the right, shooting it in a straight streaking path going from the shoulder. It hit Whitey's chin and it was like falling a few hundred feet and landing on the chin, or something like that, or maybe like getting smashed on the chin with a crowbar. Well, he thought as he went down, it was a cute session while you were in it but you're not in it now. He really made good with that one.

Whitey was down and flat on his back and his eyes were closed. He tried to open his eyes and they wouldn't open. He could feel Gerardo coming toward him. He knew Gerardo was taking his own sweet time, there was no need to hurry things now. Damn it, he said to himself, you're paralyzed, you're really paralyzed, and all he's gotta do is move in and finish the job. Maybe he's finished it already and you're way out there off the rim of the world. It sure feels that way, it feels like the world is someplace else and you're nowhere. Or maybe you're somewhere in between, I mean in between the dark and the light, not really out of it altogether, because you know you're still breathing. And your brain's working, so you know you're still conscious. Well, that's something, anyway. All right, what's the good of that? It's only for a short time. How short? Or how long? What's he waiting for? What the hell is he waiting for?

Just then Whitey was able to open his eyes. He saw Gerardo standing a few feet away and looking down at him. Or rather, Gerardo was looking at the arm stretched sideways with the hand in the milky water and resting on the handle of the knife.

Whitey's fingers closed around the handle. He thought: The bastard wasn't taking any chances, he thought you were trying to suck him in, pretending you were out cold. Pretending, hell. You had no idea the knife was there, right there under your palm. Well, it's there, all right. You have it now and he knows

166

you have it and he can't decide what to do. If he decides to move in, it's gonna be lousy for you, because you're in no shape for more action. You won't be doing much with the knife, you can hardly move your arm. I sure hope he don't move in. Look at his face. He's trying to make up his mind. Look at his eyes popping out, staring at the knife. Well, come on, Gerardo, hurry up and decide, it's gotta be one thing or the other. But I wish you'd decide to take a walk. I'd really appreciate that.

Gerardo opened his mouth just a little and showed his teeth. He took a hesitant step toward Whitey.

Whitey tightened his grip on the knife handle. He was half sitting, braced on his elbows. He grinned at Gerardo and said, "Come on. Come on. Whatcha waiting for?"

It was a difficult problem for Gerardo. He was wondering if he had enough strength left to take the knife away from Whitey. He had serious doubts about that because there was a lot of pain in his groin and his head was throbbing and his arms were very tired. He felt sick and weak and he was terribly unhappy about his smashed nose. But he was anxious to get at that knife. He told himself to give it a try. He took another step forward.

Whitey sat up straighter, not knowing how he was able to do it. And then somehow he managed to get to his feet.

Gerardo turned and ran.

–Eleven–

Whitey stood there with the knife in his hand. He watched Gerardo running away from him, the ragged camel's-hair coat flapping in the wind. He saw Gerardo crossing the cobblestoned street and aiming at the alley on the other side. There was something acutely purposeful in the way Gerardo headed toward the alley. Whitey saw him stumble and fall and get up and go lunging at the alley.

As Gerardo darted into the alley, it occurred to Whitey that he ought to cross the street and take a look. He was wondering why the Puerto Rican had selected that alley. It didn't make sense for Gerardo to go in that direction; it was the opposite direction from where he ought to be going. It stood to reason that Gerardo should be running north, toward home, or east, toward the river, for an all-out getaway. And there he was, running south.

There he was, running down the alley. Whitey stood at the alley entrance and watched the camel's hair coat showing yellow down there in the darkness. In the thick black of half past three in the morning, the camel's-hair coat was a distinct yellow, almost luminous. Whitey frowned and thought: That coat. And now this alley. I wonder if—

He wasn't sure what he was wondering. Whatever it was, his brain lost track of it, like a hand groping vainly in thick fog, not knowing what it was groping for, but knowing there was something.

Whitey entered the alley. He walked slowly, staying close to the back-yard fences, telling himself that he didn't want to be seen. He was focusing on the moving yellow of the camel's-hair coat some forty yards away.

Then the distance was about fifty yards, but he could still see it clearly. He saw Gerardo coming to a stop, fumbling with a fence gate and not able to get it open, and then climbing over the fence.

Whitey walked faster now, but quietly, sort of Indian fashion, coming down on his toes, his body crouched. He saw the camel's-hair coat going across the back yard and then up on the kitchen doorstep.

And then Gerardo was banging on the door.

"Open it," Gerardo yelled. "Hurry!"

Whitey came to a stop. He crouched very low, peering through the gaps between the fence posts. He watched Gerardo banging both fists against the back door.

"Is me," the Puerto Rican yelled. "Is me — Gerardo."

And his fists hit the door harder. He was looking down the alley to see if he was being followed.

Whitey moved forward very quietly and carefully. He knew Gerardo hadn't seen him. He told himself to keep it this way, quiet and careful, slow and easy, don't let anything happen to spoil it. And now, as he came closer to the house, he could feel a tightness inside himself. He was gripped with a sense of expectancy that pushed aside the throbbing in his jaw where Gerardo's right hand had landed.

He heard Gerardo banging on the door and wailing, "For crissake, hurry! Let me in!"

And then, very near the house, he took another look through the fence posts. The kitchen light was on and he saw Gerardo waiting for the door to open.

The door opened and Gerardo went in very fast, barging past the man who stood in the doorway. In the instant before the door closed, Whitey got a clear frontal view of the man's face.

It was the man who'd given away a very old and tattered camel's-hair coat. There was nothing generous in the giving, because the coat had been worn out seven years ago, when Whitey had seen it in the railroad station, unbuttoned and falling loosely from the heavy shoulders of Sharkey.

All right, Whitey said to himself. So what's the connection?

Or maybe it's nothing, he thought. Maybe it's just one of them situations where Gerardo does odd jobs around the house, like taking care of the furnace, hauling out the ashes. So it's a very cold November and he ain't got no overcoat and Sharkey gives him the camel's hair.

But no. You know there's more to it than that. Your chum Gerardo hit that back door like he belonged in that house, not like a handy man who works there part time, more like a member of the family, or let's make it just a bit deeper than that. Let's make it he's maybe a member of the organization.

What organization? What are you building here with thinking about an organization? And another thing, what's it matter to you what it is? It ain't none of your affair.

It ain't?

The hell it ain't. You're on the wanted list for killing a cop, you might as well remember that. You damn well better remember that. And while you're at it, remember the Captain, and what he'll be inclined to do when he lays his hands on you.

Of course, the man he really wants is Gerardo, but he doesn't know that. The thing is, you know it. You know how the cop died and what did it and who did it. You heard Gerardo tell it from his own mouth. So there's your cop-killer and he's in that 'house and you got plenty reason to be gandering that house.

But it's sorta weird, you know? It's weird because she's in there and —

All right, forget that. Or at least try to think you can forget it. What you hafta do now is concentrate on Gerardo. You gotta figure some way to get him out of that house, to get him up the steps and through the front door of the Thirty-seventh District, to have him say to the Captain what he said to you.

Yeah, that's gonna be easy to manage. Very easy. Like trying to tear down a brick wall with your bare hands. Or your front teeth. Or your head.

Your head. Start using it. Start adding up the numbers. Like our boy Gerardo says, *la matemática*, two and two is four and so forth, except in this case it's more on the order of algebra, where you got some unknown quantities. All right, you never took much algebra, so it's gotta be mostly guesswork, or maybe like the science guys who get their answers with the slow but sure procedure of try this and try that and keep on trying until it fits together. I think you got enough brains for that. Anyway, hope so. But it ain't no cinch to use the brains right now. That wallop he fetched you on the jaw was no patty-cake handout, it's got you sorta blocked upstairs, your skull feels like it's all jammed up with putty. Well, anyway, let's try. Let's see if we can do some thinking here.

Well, begin with Gerardo. Or no, that's doing it assbackwards. It's you that's gotta talk to the Captain, and when you tell him the deal you can't begin with Gerardo, because sure as hell that ain't where it begins. So where does it begin?

The race riots?

No, you can't start with that. In regard to that, you know from nothing. Or wait a minute here. Wait just a minute. It's the race riots that's got the Captain all screwed up and blowing his top. If you could give him something on the riots, it would help your case, maybe. At least it would quiet him down so's he'd give you a chance to get your point across.

All right, then, figure it. What is it with these race riots? What started the fuss? My God, now we're exploring in the field of racial aggravations, some-kind-of-ology, and you ain't geared for that, that just ain't your department. But hold it right there. Don't let it get away. Thing to do is take it from another angle. Like in case it ain't only a matter of race, it's more than gangs of riled-up local citizens fighting riled-up Puerto Ricans, it's maybe a situation where the race hate is secondary, where something else is the important issue.

Something else. Like what? Like— Easy, now, don't stretch it too far, you gotta know what you're aiming at. Better take it on a short-range basis and— But no, goddamnit, it's strictly from long range, it's from way out there, way back. It's from seven years ago.

It's from that night you sat with her in the taproom and she was talking about Sharkey and she said, "He's been mooching around and looking for an angle" and went on to tell about certain projects that didn't pay off, and then she said, "Maybe one of these days he'll find that angle he's looking for."

All right, all right, I think you got something here. Stay with it now.

Keep remembering. That night, that taproom, and you sat there with her in that booth, you looked at her face and you thought—

Well, the hell with that you thought. The hell with what you felt. That ain't what you're remembering now. You gotta stay with this race-riot business, the big question you gotta answer to pull yourself out of this jam you're in, this cop-killing rap.

172

So don't go off the track. Only things you gotta remember are the words that came out of her mouth, the statements she made about Sharkey. Like when she said that Sharkey was certain he'd someday get the bright idea that would haul in the heavy cash. The way she'd put it, "He says it's around somewhere, all he's gotta do is find it."

Find it where?

Find it here? In the Hellhole?

Look. Let's understand something. I think you're on the track and it figures to be the right track, but just about here is where it stops. I mean, it stops here because your brain just can't take it any farther. Only way to keep it going is with the eyes, the ears. You get the point? You see what the next move is?

Wanna take the chance?

All right. But it's a lead-pipe cinch you're asking for grief. The way you gotta do it is the hard way, there just ain't no other way. It's gonna be getting information from Sharkey, with Sharkey not knowing he's giving it out. So first it's this fence, and then it's the back yard, and finally it's the house.

Well, let's get started. What's the delay? Why you standing here? And why you grinning? How come it all of a sudden hits you comical? It ain't the least bit comical, unless you're thinking of Chop and Bertha and when they had you in the woods, what they did to you, the way they made it plain, no two ways about it, really giving it to you to get you convinced.

But here we are again. And they didn't convince you after all.

–Twelve–

He climbed over the fence and moved slowly, very quietly, across the back yard. He was focusing on the cellar window that had no glass in it.

The opening was stingy and he had to worm his way through. He went in legs first, his feet probing for support as he arched his back, his hands clutching the upper side of the window, his torso squirming, pushing past the splintered frame. Then, as he went through and down, his feet found a narrow shelf. From there it was just a short drop to the cellar floor.

There was no light in the cellar. He took a few steps and bumped into the side of a coal bin. A few more steps and his knees came up against the pile of coal. He groped in his pockets, searching for a match. There were no matches and he wondered how he could get past the coal without making noise. It was a lot of coal, and if he tried to crawl over it, the chunks would give way and there'd be considerable noise. The important thing now was quiet. It had to be handled with a maximum of quiet.

He backed away from the pile of coal, then moved parallel

174

with it, got past the wooden wall of the bin, inched his way forward, and hit another obstruction. It felt like an ash can. He touched it and it was metal and he knew it was an ash can. And then another ash can. And still another. He decided the best way to get past the row of ash cans was to get down on all fours and do it by inches.

Crawling, using his forehead to feel what was in front of him, he kept bumping very lightly against the ash cans. He was moving sideways and then there were no more ash cans and again he went forward, still crawling. He kept on that way, going toward the middle of the cellar, gradually feeling the heat coming from the furnace, and then seeing the thin ribbon of bright orange glow that showed through a crack in the furnace door. He crawled toward it, thinking: Maybe we'll find something to light up and use for a torch.

Coming closer to the furnace, he reached out, felt for the handle of the furnace door, found it, and worked it slowly and very carefully. With very little noise the furnace door came open. The orange glow flowed out and showed him the floor surrounding the furnace. He saw a used safety match and got his fingers on it, put it in the furnace to get it lit, and thought: Well, now we can find the stairs.

The flaming match showed something that postponed the stairs.

It was a neatly laid-out row of brand-new baseball bats. And knives, all sorts of knives. In the instant that he sighted it, he thought of the similar but sloppier collection he'd seen in the Puerto Rican meeting place. Then, frowning, staring at the bats and knives, he noticed something else. It was a stack of small wooden boxes, say a dozen of them. The ones on top displayed labels and he came closer, peering past the flare of the match, and saw the printed words: "Handle with care—.38 caliber."

For another instant he looked at the cartridge boxes. And

then he saw the glint of metal near the boxes, the glinting barrels and butts of several brand-new revolvers.

Well, now, he said without sound. Well, now.

The burning match was dying fast and he held it higher to find the stairway. The glow showed the stairway off to the right and he checked the distance and then blew out the match. Now he was on his feet and moving lightly toward the stairway, telling himself to do as it said on the cartridge boxes, to handle these stairs with care.

Sure enough, it was a very old flight of stairs, and when he hit the first step it creaked. He crouched low, using his hands on the higher steps, going up monkey style and distributing his weight between the steps to lessen the creaking.

He was halfway up the steps when the mouse came running down.

Or rather, it came falling down, it must have been blind or sick, or maybe one of them lunatic mice that just can't do things in a sensible way. Its tiny furry shape hit him full in the face and instinctively it fought for a hold with its legs. He locked his lips to hold back the startled yell and heard the mouse giving its own outcry of shock. It squeaked as loud as it could, decided this was not the place for it to be, and leaped off.

Whitey shook his head slowly and thought: That almost did it.

He rested there a few moments, trying to forget the feeling of the mouse dancing on his face. He said to himself: Let's disregard these minor issues, you got more stairs to climb, keep climbing.

So then it was the next step going up. And the next. And as he climbed it was like the very slow and precise action of thread passing through the eye of a needle. His head was down and he was watching the barely visible edges of the steps, gray-black against the blackness. Then gradually the steps were tinged with a faint amber glow and he knew it was light coming from the first floor. He raised his head and saw the yellow seeping through the crack in the door at the top of the stairs. The door was maybe five steps ahead. He tightened his mouth just a little, and thought: Careful, now, don't get excited, please don't get excited.

A moment passed. It was a very long moment and he felt it pressing hard on him as he negotiated the next step. The feeling of anxiety was a set of clamps getting him in the belly and squeezing like some practical joker carrying the joke too far.

Or maybe he was the joker, and not a very good one, at that. A first-rate joker never took himself seriously and it was everything for laughs. For instance, that on-and-off comedian who worked from the Thirty-seventh District, that detective lieutenant, that Pertnoy. Now, if it was Pertnoy going up these stairs, it would be a breeze, nothing to it, the man would be grinning and having himself a grand time. On the other hand, if it was Lieutenant Whatsisname, the fashion plate, name starts with D or T – oh, yes, Taggert – well, if it was Taggert climbing up these cellar steps, he'd be strictly business, absolutely a machine, except maybe it would bother him that his clothes were getting dirty. He's sure a sucker for the haberdashers and the tailors, that Taggert. And for barbershops, too. Guess it's always the same routine when he sits himself in the chair. You can hear him saying, "The works, Dominic." But why's it gotta be Dominic? Not all barbers are Italians. Like with Poles, not all coal miners are Poles. You know, Phillips was a coal miner, and Phillips is – As if it makes any difference what he is. As if race has anything to do with it. Yeah, go try and tell that to the Puerto Ricans. People call them Puerto Ricans and right away they're branded like with an iron and given a low road to travel, the lousiest places to live, like that house where you saw them jam-packed sleeping on a cold floor. But you saw some damn fine quality in that house. That Chávez. He was really something, that Chávez.

And Luis, too. Luis almost got himself slashed bloody going to bat for you.

Say, come to think of it, you have been having yourself a time tonight, you've come across some real personalities. Take, for example, that Jones Jarvis. If conditions were different it could be Admiral Jarvis, U.S.N. And you know he could do the job, you know damn well he could do it. So it figures it's mostly a matter of conditions. Sure it is. Take Captain Kinnard and put him in charge of a nursery, he'd be like melted butter and them kids would run all over him. But how do you know that? Well, you just know it, that's all. It's that way with some people; you take one look at them and later when you think about it, it hits you and you know. Or sometimes you get hit right away. You ought to know about that, when it comes to that you're an old campaigner. That first time you saw her, the way it hit you. And the way it's been coming back tonight, hitting you, hitting you. All right, for Christ's sake, cut it out. But I wonder if Firpo is still alive and sometimes at night he wakes up and remembers the way Dempsey hit him.

He went up another step and it brought him to the top of the stairs. He stood against the door and his hand drifted to the knob. His fingers tested the give of the knob and at first it wouldn't give, not soundlessly, anyway. He tried it again and felt it turning. A little more, and still more, and then there was the faint noise, more feathery than metallic, of the latch coming free. And now very carefully, working it by fractions of inches, he opened the door.

It showed him the lit-up kitchen. There was no one in the kitchen. But he could hear voices coming from the next room, and there was the clinking of glasses on a wooden table.

He had the door opened not quite two inches. There was the scraping of a chair and then someone was coming into the kitchen. He gave a slight pull on the door to make it appear closed. For some moments there was activity in the kitchen, the sound of a running faucet, glass tinkling against the sink. He heard Chop shouting from the next room, "Not from the sink! There's cold water in the icebox." And in the kitchen the icebox was being opened and he heard Bertha's voice saying, "The bottle's empty." A pause, and then from the next room it was Sharkey's voice: "We got any beer?" and Bertha replying, "It's all gone," and Chop again, "There's some in the cellar."

Whitey closed his eyes. Without sound he said: Goddamn it.

He heard Chop yelling, "We got some quart bottles down there. Go down and bring up a few."

Then Bertha's footsteps were coming toward the door.

He thought: Some people have it nice, they can travel anywhere they wanna go. But you, you can't travel anywhere, you can't go down the steps, and when the door opens you can't get behind it because it don't open in, it opens out. You're gonna be right here when it opens, right here at the top of the stairs where there ain't no room to move around, so this looks to be the windup.

Then he realized the footsteps had stopped. He heard Bertha shouting, "Go get the beer yourself. I ain't no waitress."

Chop yelled, "What is it, a big deal?"

"Get it yourself. Run your own errands."

"You goddamn lazy – "

"Aw, go break a leg."

"Lazy elephant, she won't even – "

"Make it both legs," Bertha yapped at Chop. "I'm tired of you giving me orders. All day long I'm running up and down the steps. This morning you were – "

"I was sick this morning."

"You're gonna be sick tonight if you don't lay off me."

Whitey heard Bertha's footsteps going out of the kitchen. In the next room the argument continued between Bertha and Chop and finally Sharkey cut in with "All right, the hell with the beer. We'll drink what we got here."

There was more tinkling of glasses. And then he heard them talking but now their voices were low and he couldn't make out what they were saying. Again he worked on the door and got it open a few inches. Then a few more inches, and he was straining to hear, gradually getting it.

Sharkey was saying, "Go on, Gerardo. Have another drink."

"I no need—"

"Sure you do." Sharkey's voice was soft and soothing. "We'll make this the bracer."

There was the sound of liquor splashing into a glass. Whatever it was, there was a lot of it going into the glass.

"Drink it down," Sharkey said. "Go on, Gerardo, get it all down."

"But I—"

And then loudly, from Bertha, "You hear what Sharkey says? You do what he says."

"Is too much whisky," Gerardo complained. "I no—"

"Yes, you will," Bertha shouted. "You'll drink it or I hold your nose and force it down."

"Why you do me like this?" Gerardo whined.

"Like what?" It was Chop and he was laughing dryly. "You're lucky, Gerardo. You're lucky Bertha ain't giving you lumps."

"I got lumps already," Gerardo said. Then, drinking the whisky, he gasped, went on drinking it, gasped again. There was the sound of the glass coming down on the table, and Gerardo saying, "Enough lumps I get tonight. Look at lumps. Look at my nose."

"It looks busted," Sharkey said.

"All smashed up," the Puerto Rican wailed. "Was perfect nose and now look at it."

"Finish what's in the glass," Bertha said.

180

"But I can't — "

"Drink it all up," she said. "Drink it up, Gerardo."

"Please — "

"You'll drink it if I hold your nose," Bertha said. "And then you'll really have a nose to worry about."

Then again there was the sound of the glass, the gurgling and gulping as Gerardo forced it down, and the bitter rasping, the gasping.

"Very good," Bertha said. "Not a drop in the glass. But you got some on your chin. I'll wipe it off."

Whitey heard the sound of a backhand crack across the mouth, then louder with the open palm, then very loud with the backhand again. He heard a chair toppling, and a thud, and he knew that Gerardo was on the floor.

He heard Gerardo whimpering, sobbing, "I no understand."

"It's instruction," Bertha said. "You're getting instruction, Gerardo. You gotta learn to do what Sharkey says."

"My mouth!"

Whitey visualized Gerardo's mouth. He knew it was a sad-looking mouth right now. It had received the full force of Bertha's tree-trunk arm, with over three hundred pounds of hard-packed beef behind Bertha's oversized hand. Whitey said to himself: You know how it feels, you had a taste of it, a big taste, and —

He heard Bertha saying, "It's like baseball, Gerardo. You catch on? It's like baseball and Sharkey's the manager and you gotta do what he says."

And Chop said, "It ain't sand-lot ball, Gerardo. It's big-league action and you gotta watch the signals very careful. When you're safe on third you don't take any chances. You don't try for home plate unless you get the signal."

"I come here because — "

"Because you got scared," Bertha said. "You're not supposed to get scared." And then, to Sharkey, "Should I give our boy more instruction?"

There was no reply from Sharkey.

Whitey heard the terribly loud sound of another open-handed wallop, then the thud as Gerardo went back against a wall, bounced away, fell forward toward the table to get it again from Bertha's hand, and again, and then really getting it and starting to cry like a baby.

Poor bastard, Whitey thought. He heard the noise of Gerardo getting it and yowling now with the pain of it. He felt sort of sorry for Gerardo, and yet he was thinking: If Chávez could see it, if Luis could see it, they'd find it interesting, very interesting.

Just then, through the sound of the blows, through Gerardo's yowls and pleas, he heard the voice of Celia.

He heard Celia saying, "What are you doing, Bertha? What are you doing to him?"

"What's — " Bertha grunted, her arm swinging, her hand making contact with the battered, swollen face. "What's it look like?"

Celia's voice was calm. "You keep that up and he won't have a face."

"But he'll have brains," Bertha said. Then another grunt, another wallop, an animal scream from Gerardo, and Bertha saying, "You see what I'm doing? I'm putting brains in his head."

Gerardo was crying out, blubbering, talking in Spanish.

"You calling me names?" Bertha asked. "You cursing me?"

Sharkey said, "All right, Bertha. Leave him alone."

"Was he cursing me? I'd like to know if he was cursing me."

"He wasn't cursing you," Sharkey said. "Let go of him. Let him sit down. I wanna talk to him."

"You think he'll hear you?" It was Celia. "Look at his ears."

182

And again the dry laugh from Chop, and Chop saying, "The left one ain't so bad."

"But look at him," Celia said. "Look at his face. God Almighty. Give him some water. Give him something."

"I think—" It was Gerardo and he'd stopped crying. He spoke quietly and solemnly. "I think I die now."

"You won't die," Bertha said. "You'll sit there and listen to Sharkey."

"Wait," Sharkey said. "Give him a napkin. He's dripping blood all over the table."

Bertha said, "Where we keep the napkins?"

"I no want napkin," Gerardo said. "I want I should bleed more. I want I should die."

Whitey heard the sound of a cabinet drawer being opened. After that the sounds were minor and he knew they were taking time to stop the flow of blood from Gerardo's face. He wondered how long it would take to get Gerardo out of the fog. It was more or less evident that Sharkey wanted Gerardo's full attention. Whitey hoped it wouldn't take too long to bring Gerardo back to clear thinking. It was getting somewhat difficult, standing here and not making a sound. It was definitely uncomfortable because there wasn't much space here at the top of the cellar stairs. He told himself to quit complaining, all he had to do was stand still and listen. And yet it wasn't easy. He wanted to move around, make some noise, do something, anything, and it sure as hell wasn't easy to stand here like some Buffalo Bill in a wax museum.

He heard Gerardo talking dully, dazedly, in Spanish.

And Chop was saying, "Hey, this ain't so good. He's in bad shape. His eyes—"

"I'll bring him out of it," Bertha said. "Here. Let me—"

"You keep away from him," Sharkey said quietly. "You've done enough already."

"All I wanna do is—"

"No," Sharkey said. "Stay away from him. Stay the hell away from him."

"Whatsa matter?" Bertha asked. "Whatcha getting peeved about?"

"Oh, he ain't peeved." It was Celia again. "He likes the way you work. Don't you, Sharkey? Go on, Sharkey, tell her. Tell her how much you admire her work."

Bertha's voice said, "You still here?"

"Yes," Celia said slowly and distinctly, "I'm still here."

"I wonder why," Bertha said.

"Me too." Celia said it very slowly. "I always wonder about that."

"You got a problem, honey," Bertha said. "You oughta do something about it."

"No." And then a long pause. "There ain't nothing I can do about it."

"Oh, don't say that." Bertha's voice was gentle but sour, soft yet sneering, and dripping with sarcasm. "You can always take a walk, you know."

"Can I? Let's hear what Sharkey says. How about it, Sharkey? Can I take a walk?"

"Drop it," Sharkey said.

Bertha said, "She's asking a question, Sharkey. She wants to know if she can take a walk."

"I said drop it." Sharkey's voice was low and tight. "The two of you, drop it."

"I guess he don't want me to go for a walk," Celia said.

"Yeah," Bertha said. "That's the way it figures."

"Well, anyway, I asked him. You satisfied, Bertha?"

"Sure, honey. I'm always satisfied. I feel very satisfied right now."

"That's nice," Celia said.

"And how is it with you?" Bertha asked, with each word aimed like a jab. "Are you satisfied?"

184

"I hafta go to the bathroom," Celia said.

Bertha spoke to Sharkey. "You hear what she says? She has to go to the bathroom. She got your permission?"

"I better make a run for the bathroom," Celia said. "I don't wanna throw up in here."

Whitey heard Celia's footsteps running out of the adjoining room. He heard Sharkey muttering to Bertha, "What's the matter with you? Why don't you leave her alone?"

"She started it," Bertha said.

"You'd do me a favor if you'd leave her alone."

"But she's always starting, Sharkey. She's always making remarks."

Gerardo was still mumbling in Spanish. And Chop was saying, "Maybe if we give him smelling salts — "

Bertha said, "I don't like when she makes remarks. I don't like it and I don't hafta take it."

"Then do like I do. Let her talk. Don't listen to her."

"You kidding? Come off it, Sharkey. You know you're always tuned in. You take in everything she says."

"It goes in one ear and — "

"And stays inside," Bertha said. "Deep inside. I watch your face sometimes when she says them things to you, little things, but it's like little knives, and I see you getting cut. Real deep."

Chop again: "We got any smelling salts?"

"Like earlier tonight," Bertha went on, "she makes with the routine about maybe if you'd see a specialist — "

"All right," Sharkey interrupted quickly. "Let it fade, Bertha. I don't wanna hear no more about it."

But Bertha had it going and she couldn't stop it and she said, "Not a heart specialist, either. Not a brain specialist. She meant something else. I know what she meant. It's bedroom trouble. You can't give her nothing in the bedroom. Only thing you do in the bed is sleep."

Then it was quiet. Whitey waited for Sharkey to say some-

185

thing. But the quiet went on. It was a dismal quiet, like the stillness of a stagnant pool. He could almost feel the staleness of it, as though the adjoining room were a sickroom and the air was thick with decay.

Finally Chop said, "I think we got smelling salts in the –"

"He don't need smelling salts," Sharkey said quietly. "He's coming around."

"Sure he is," Bertha said. "How you doing, Gerardo?"

"Very nice." Gerardo spoke as though he had glue in his mouth. "I am doing very nice."

"Want a cigarette?" Bertha asked.

"All right," Gerardo said. "I smoke a cigarette. Then everything is fine. Cigarette fixes everything."

Whitey heard the sound of a match being struck. He heard Gerardo saying, "Is question I have, maybe you can answer. How can I smoke when there is no mouth?"

"You can smoke," Bertha said. "Go on, smoke. And quit singing the blues. It ain't as bad as you make it."

"How you know? Is not your face banged up. Is mine. You no can say how it feels."

Whitey heard Chop laughing and saying, "That's right, Gerardo. Tell her."

"I no tell her anything. I say more, she hit me again."

Sharkey said, "That's using your head, Gerardo. I think you're getting with it now."

"Not hardly," Bertha said. "If you're gonna talk to him, Sharkey, you'll hafta make it later. He ain't ready to listen."

"I listen," Gerardo said. "I just sit here and listen. What else for me to do?"

"You see, Sharkey?" she said. "He just ain't ready yet. Look at him. He can't pay attention to you. He's too burned up at me."

"No," Gerardo said. "I no burn up at you, Bertha. I just afraid of you, that's all."

186

"You are?" Bertha sounded pleased. "Well, now, that's good. That's the way it should be."

But then Sharkey was saying, "You think so, Bertha? I don't think so. I don't want it that way."

"Why not?" Bertha asked. "He's gotta be made to understand —"

"Sure, I know," Sharkey cut in softly. "But I don't want him all scared and nervous and upset. He's got important work to do. Ain't that right, Gerardo?"

There was no reply from Gerardo.

"Come on, Gerardo. Get with it." The voice of Sharkey was velvety, soothing, very gentle. "Look at me. And listen. Will you do that? Will you listen careful?"

Whitey stood motionless at the top of the cellar stairs with his head bent forward slightly in the three-inch gap of opened door between stairway and kitchen. Without sound he was saying to Sharkey: All right, Mac, we'll listen very careful. We ain't gonna miss a word.

-Thirteen-

He heard the velvety voice of Sharkey saying, "First thing, Gerardo, I wanna get it across again, like when I told you this was a big-time operation and every move hadda be handled with style. With making sure it's perfect timing. And above all, keeping cool. You remember, I said the important thing is to keep cool."

"I try very hard to — "

"It ain't a matter of trying, Gerardo. I didn't tell you to try. I said keep cool, period."

"Yes. Keep cool. Yes. But — "

"Another thing I made clear, the schedule. I said we gotta stick to the schedule. I meant stick to it no matter what happens. So let's have a look at what you did. You messed up the schedule and almost messed up everything."

"Sometime comes bad luck. If comes bad luck is maybe not my fault."

"You weren't due here until tomorrow night. You know what's fixed for tomorrow night and how we got it figured. It's the big move. The big left hook. We're hoping it's the knockout punch so then we go out and celebrate. You listening, Gerardo? I'm talking about tomorrow night."

"I understand about tomorrow night. But – "

"But nothing." And now Sharkey sounded as though he were trying hard to keep his voice down, keep it gentle and very patient. He said, "Look, Gerardo. See if you can get this. It ain't no ordinary action, it's a full-dress show, and we're in it deep. In this kind of job there's no such thing as excuses."

"Is maybe excuse when – "

"No, Gerardo. Believe me. There's no excuse at all for what you did tonight. Making all that noise outside. Running in here like a wild man. All that commotion. What if the cops were around?"

"Was no police."

"But suppose there was? Suppose they got curious and came in to ask questions? And then they're taking a look around. They're looking in the cellar. They're seeing what's down there – "

"Sharkey, please. Tonight was emergency. I no have time to think."

"Think? I never told you to think. All I told you was what to do. And what not to do."

"Yes. You right, Sharkey. Is very stupid what I do tonight. But you no give me chance to explain about emergency. Was bad emergency. Was – "

"I don't care what it was. I'm not interested. I asked you if it was heat and you said no, so that checks it off. As long as it wasn't heat, it ain't important, and we're not gonna worry about it. Only thing worries me is this caper you pulled. I wanna be sure it won't happen again."

"But sometimes is coming an emergency and – "

"God give me strength." Then a long pause. And then, almost pleadingly, "Listen, Gerardo, you gotta understand we can't

189

afford these mistakes. There's too much on the table to let it slip off. To lose it now, when we're so close to getting it."

"Get what?" Gerardo asked. "You never tell me what we get."

"Sure I told you. I made a promise. I said like this, I said if it paid off you'd wind up with a fat wallet."

"How fat?" Gerardo sounded different now. He sounded as though he'd abruptly forgotten his bleeding swollen face and was thinking in practical terms. "How much money you give me?"

"Well, let's see now. It's all a matter of – "

"I tell you something," Gerardo cut in quickly. "This job I am doing for you, Sharkey, like you say, it is big-time business. Takes much time. Much trouble. And much risk. Is no easy work for me to do."

"Well, sure. We both know that. I told you in the beginning it wouldn't be easy."

"In beginning you tell me I will get much money. But you no say how much. And all these weeks I work for you, I wonder sometimes, I feel in my pockets and there is nothing. The nickels and dimes you give me, they go fast, Sharkey."

"How you fixed now? You need some cash? I'll give you – "

"Two bits? Four bits? No, Sharkey. Is no good this way."

"For Christ's sake – "

"Is no way to do business. I make big special job for you and you pay me off in little bits."

Sharkey took a deep breath. " Look, you don't get the drift. This small change ain't your pay envelope. It's just to keep you going until the loot comes in."

"How much loot? I like to hear numbers."

"If I told you how much, you wouldn't believe me."

"Take chance. Tell me anyway."

"I can tell you like this. It's gonna be important money. Heavy cash."

190

"Is nice to think about," Gerardo said. "But tonight for supper I eat one piece stale bread and two bananas."

"You hear him, Sharkey?" It was Bertha. "You got labor trouble."

"Keep quiet," Sharkey told her. Then again he was talking to Gerardo. "If things go right tomorrow night, you'll soon be living like a prince. It's gonna be real gold rolling in, in wagonloads, and you're due for a thick slice. I wasn't just talking when I said you'd be a partner."

"Partner." Gerardo said it very slowly, rolling the "r's," biting hard on the "t." And then with a grunt, saying it aloud to himself, "Fine partner."

"I know what's wrong here." It was Bertha again. "I didn't hit him hard enough."

"Will you please keep quiet?" Sharkey said. Then, to the Puerto Rican, "All right, let's have it. What's the major complaint?"

"You say I am partner," Gerardo said. "Now I ask you something. Partner in what?"

"In what? You kidding? You know what. I told you — "

"You told me what my job is. But you no make clear what business we are in."

There was no reply from Sharkey.

And Gerardo went on: "You say we make much money but you no say how. I think is maybe good idea you put all cards on table. Is better partnership that way."

Then quiet again. Nothing from Sharkey. It went on like that for some moments. And then there was the sound of Sharkey's footsteps pacing the floor.

Whitey listened to the footsteps going back and forth. He thought: It's like on the radio when you tune in late and you only hear part of the game, and some of these announcers, they won't tell you the score, it drives you bughouse waiting to hear the score.

Just then he heard Gerardo saying, "Is not fair, Sharkey. Why you no tell me? Maybe you think I will know too much? I will open my mouth?"

"You might." It was Bertha.

"And if I did, I would be a fool," Gerardo said. "Would be like putting knife in my own throat."

"You know it too?" Bertha said

"Yes, I know it," Gerardo replied solemnly. And then, sort of sad and hurt, "Another thing I know. From very beginning I play straight game with you people. I do what Sharkey tells me to do. I follow orders, no matter what. Five weeks ago – "

"Skip it" Sharkey said. "I know what orders I gave you. I know you carried them out. You don't need to remind me."

"Is maybe better if I remind you " And then, saying it slowly, distinctly, "Five weeks ago you tell me to start race riot."

Well, now, Whitey said without sound. That's interesting. That's very interesting.

And he heard Gerardo saying, "So I do what you tell me. On River Street I see an American girl and I follow her. Then I jump on her, I beat her up, I take off her dress. She runs away screaming and then Americans they come and chase me. I get way from them, I tell Puerto Ricans that Americans chase me for no reason. Just like you tell me to do, I make loud speech that Americans hate Puerto Ricans and give us rough time and we must fight back.

"So then it starts. I get Carlos and some others and we go to River Street and make noise, break windows, throw bottles and bricks at gringos. Is nice riot that night. And later that week is another riot, bigger crowd, many people getting hurt. And then more riots with some getting killed, and each time is me who leads the Puerto Ricans into fight, is me who takes chance with my life. Is me who – "

"All right, all right," Sharkey said, and he sounded impatient. "I know what chances you took. It ain't as if I'm forgetting. I'm not fluffing you off."

"Of course not." Gerardo gave a little dry laugh. "You are in no position to fluff me off. You need me tomorrow night when we have biggest riot. With guns."

Sharkey's voice was somewhat tight. "You trying to make a point?"

"What you think?"

Sharkey didn't answer.

And Gerardo said, "You smart man, Sharkey. Very smart. I learn much from you. So now I am smart too."

"Don't get too smart." It was Bertha again.

Gerardo gave another dry laugh. "I get just smart enough to know is my turn now, my turn to deal the cards."

"You're talking too much," Bertha said.

"Let him talk," Sharkey murmured tightly. "I like to hear him talk."

"No," Gerardo said. "Is you who do the talking, Sharkey. Is time for you to make the explaining. Is like this: You tell me reason for riots. Deep inside reason. All details. Is best you tell me everything."

"And if I don't?"

"Then is nothing happen tomorrow night. No riot."

Chop said, "Well, I'll be a — "

Bertha breathed, "If this ain't the limit!"

And Chop again: "He's got you, Sharkey. He's got you over a barrel."

"Yeah, it looks that way," Sharkey said mildly. There was a shrug in his voice. And then he laughed lightly and good-naturedly and said, "All right, Gerardo. Here's the setup."

Then Sharkey was explaining it. He spoke matter-of-factly and there were no pauses, no stumbling over the phrases. It was medium-slow tempo, it came out easily, and Whitey thought: This ain't no made-up story, he's giving Gerardo the true picture.

It was a picture of the Hellhole. Sharkey said the Hellhole

was the goal he'd been seeking for a long time. He said the Hellhole was the only territory not covered by the big operators and sure as hell they'd missed a juicy bet when they'd overlooked this neighborhood. As it stood now, it was jam-packed with independent hustlers and scufflers who were always getting in each other's way, with the law always on their tails and giving them a bad time. What the Hellhole needed was the establishment of a system, an organization, and for sure it needed a controlling hand.

Sharkey said he intended to take over the Hellhole. The way he had it figured, he'd soon be in charge of all activities — the gambling joints, the numbers banks, the sale of bootleg whisky and weed and capsules, and of course the whore houses. It would all be handled from one desk, one filing cabinet, and it would follow the general pattern of big-time merchandising.

The most important angle was the law. The layout he had in mind would require an arrangement with the law, a definite mutual benefit agreement wherein the law would work closely with the organization. In return for a slice of the profits, the law would guarantee full co-operation; there would be no trouble, no raids, no squad cars cruising around and scaring away the customers. He said he'd already arranged for that, he'd made with a certain party who was now a detective lieutenant and campaigning for promotion.

"This certain party," Sharkey said, "he wants to wear a captain's badge. He wants to be captain of the Thirty-seventh District."

It was quiet for a moment.

Then Sharkey said, "The captain they got now is due to be tossed out. It figures he's gonna be tossed because he's losing his grip on the neighborhood. He's going crazy trying to stop these race riots."

More quiet. And Whitey could feel it sinking in.

He heard Sharkey saying, "You get the drift?"

Yeah, Whitey said without sound. Yeah, we're getting it.

"I played around with a hundred ideas before I hit on the riots," Sharkey said. "I hadda give him something that he couldn't handle."

"Bueno," Gerardo murmured. "I begin to understand. Is seeming like good setup."

"Yes. I think it's pretty good," Sharkey said. "I don't see how it can miss. This party I'm dealing with is next in line for the captaincy. Each time there's a riot he comes closer to getting it. As soon as he gets it, we're in business."

"*Magnifico,*" Gerardo said. And he laughed lightly and admiringly. "Is everything fits in place. Your man takes over Thirty-seventh and this gives you green light and you take over Hellhole."

"That's it," Sharkey said. "But remember, the light ain't green yet. I'm hoping it turns green tomorrow night."

"It will," Gerardo said eagerly. "You count on me, Sharkey. I guarantee big riot."

"It's gotta be more than that. It's gotta be a shooting war. If it happens the way I want it to happen, they'll blow their tops in City Hall, they'll throw him out of that station house and put my man in. I get the wire they been playing with the idea these past couple weeks, so all it needs now is a final explosion."

"I produce," Gerardo said. "I come through for you."

"And for yourself, too. Once we get started, you'll be drawing a heavy salary. You do a good job tomorrow night and you'll wind up with a penthouse."

After that the talk became technical and it concerned the use of a pushcart. Gerardo was saying it would be best to use a pushcart for the transfer of the guns and ammunition to the Puerto Rican section. He said they had plenty of baseball bats and knives but they could use some meat cleavers. Sharkey asked how many meat cleavers and Gerardo estimated ten would be enough. Sharkey wondered aloud if the pushcart would be all right. Maybe they ought to do it the way they'd done it before, hiring a horse and wagon and covering the weapons with rags and papers. Gerardo said that the last time he'd had some trouble with the horse and he'd feel more secure with a pushcart. Sharkey said O.K., it would be a pushcart, and Gerardo could come for it early tomorrow night.

They went on talking but now Whitey didn't hear. He was making his way very carefully and quietly down the cellar steps.

-Fourteen-

Now it was easier in the cellar and he didn't need to crawl. Some moonlight came in through the opened window and he went toward it, passing the furnace and the ash cans, telling himself to take his time getting past the coal bin. He was getting near the window and it would be a damn shame if he hit the coal pile now and they heard it upstairs. It would certainly be a damn shame, and yet he wasn't thinking about himself. He was thinking about the neighborhood and what it was in for tomorrow night. But maybe he could stop it from happening. Well, he hoped so. He'd give it a try. He had to make good on the try, he couldn't let it happen.

He thought: Maybe what you oughta do is forget the window right now and do something about them guns and cartridge boxes. If you could hide them someplace -but no, that would take too long, and where the hell could you hide them, anyway? And another thing, there's a chance you'd make noise and you better forget about the guns. But you can't forget what the guns can do. Like your friend Sharkey says, he wants real hell on River Street, and like Gerardo said, he means to produce. That Gerardo. He's one for the books, all right. What kind of books? Maybe the history books. Yes, in a way it's on the order of history. That is, if you wanna start drawing parallels. I guess a lot of history is made by the sell-out artists, like Benedict Arnold and so forth. But he'd get worse than Arnold got if them Puerto Ricans found out what he was doing. For instance, if Chávez found out. Or if Luis found out. They'd give it to him, all right, they'd give it to him slow. Maybe for an entire day. Maybe a couple of days. Maybe they'd keep him alive for a week like it used to be in olden times when they'd cut off the fingers one by one and then start on the toes and — Or maybe with fire, like it says in the history books. There you go again with the history books. Say, what's all this with history?

Well, it sorta follows a pattern, I guess. Whaddya mean, you guess? Who are you to guess? Who are you to think about history? You better get your mind on that window. You better hurry up and climb through and get outta here.

Wait now, not so fast. Remember, no noise. Do it careful. Nice and easy, watch your step, you'll hafta feel for a foothold to reach that window.

Benedict Arnold Gerardo. And what would you call Sharkey? What name in history applies to Sharkey? Well, there was more than one expert in that particular field. I mean the field of going for the big loot by getting some suckers to start a war. In Africa it was the English always doing business with some tribal chief and everything nice and friendly until they had it fixed the way they wanted and then good-by chief. So sooner or later it's good-by Gerardo, with Chop and Bertha taking him out for a stroll or a ride. Well, they all get it sooner or later, if that helps your feelings any. But it doesn't. Because your feelings got nothing to do with this. You're strictly from Western Union, all you're doing here is delivering a message.

You're taking it to the Thirty-seventh District and hoping they'll do something with it.

Yeah. You're hoping. As if there's the slightest possible chance you can sell all this to the Captain.

Let's say there's one chance in a thousand.

And on the other side of it there's every chance you'll get your brains knocked out, your face mashed in, your name checked off the list marked "wanted" and placed on that other list of "cases closed" or something on that order.

Of course, there's the water front. There's them ships. They'll be sailing a long ways off from here. Why, you sonofabitch, you. If you don't drop that line of thought —

All right, all right, it's dropped. We're on our way to the station house. Our merry way. Crazy, like the man says. One chance in a thousand. And that makes it comical. Well, so it's comical. But even so, it seems right. Somehow it seems right.

He was climbing through the window.

Then he was in the back yard and climbing over the fence. He went down the narrow alley, came to the cobblestoned street, and turned west. He walked four blocks west to Clayton and saw the one-story brick structure with the frosted-glass lamps on either side of the entrance. The lamps were like eyes coming closer. And the entrance with its opened doors was like an open mouth all set to swallow him. He moved slowly toward the station house, and he thought: You could walk right past it and go back to Skid Row, where there ain't no worries at all.

But Skid Row was a long ways off. It was just a few blocks away and yet it was a long ways off. It was a land of boozed-up dreams where nothing mattered, where nothing special happened, like on the moon. There was no use trying for the moon and it was the same no-dice with Skid Row. Both places were off limits and the boundary line was the station house.

He went up the stone steps, went past the frosted-glass

lamps, then through the opened doorway and into the roll room, where the benches were empty except for a wino sleeping flat on his back. A blue-shirted attendant was sweeping the floor. On the wall the clock showed four-twenty. From the corridor on the other side of the room there was twangy chatter coming in from car radios.

He crossed the roll room to the corridor, and walked down the corridor past the door marked "House Sergeant" and the door marked "Detectives" and toward the door marked "Captain" He opened the door and entered the office and saw Captain Kinnard sitting at a desk, bent over with his head on his folded arms. On the desk there was a whisky bottle, three quarters full. On the floor beside the desk there was another bottle and it was empty.

Whitey coughed to get the attention of the Captain.

The Captain raised his head and looked. Then he shut his eyes tightly. He opened his eyes and took another look. His mouth opened and closed, then opened very wide as he leaped up from the desk, hurling himself across the room with his fist shooting from the shoulder and smashing against Whitey's jaw. Whitey went sailing through the opened doorway and landed sitting down in the corridor.

The door marked "Detectives" had opened and Lieutenants Pertnoy and Taggert were standing in the corridor. They were staring at the Captain and the Captain was pointing at the small white-haired man sitting on the floor.

"Look at this," the Captain said. "Look what we got here."

"Well, now," Lieutenant Taggert said.

"Who brought him in?" Pertnoy asked.

The Captain had no answer. All he had was a tightly clamped mouth and a mixture of flame and ice in his eyes as he moved toward Whitey. He aimed a kick at Whitey's ribs. Whitey didn't move, and the heavy shoe made contact with Whitey's side. As Whitey fell over on his face, the Captain kicked him again. The Captain was making noises like an animal and stepping back to ready another kick.

Whitey looked up at Captain Kinnard and said, "How's it feel?"

The Captain blinked. He took another step backward.

"Does it hurt?" Whitey asked.

The Captain blinked again. His mouth was open but he couldn't say anything.

"I hope it don't hurt too much," Whitey said.

Taggert looked at Pertnoy and said, "I know what this one needs. A straitjacket. Listen to him talking to himself."

"No," Whitey said. He sat up slowly. "I'm talking to the Captain."

"Really?" Taggert murmured. His expression was clinical, and he leaned over with his hands on his knees, like a nerve specialist talking to a patient. "I think you got it twisted. You didn't kick him. He kicked you."

Whitey smiled dimly. "That the way you see it? I don't see it that way. I think he kicked himself."

Taggert straightened and frowned at Pertnoy. The Captain was staring at Whitey. For a few moments it was very quiet in the corridor. The only sound was the muffled noise coming from the roll room, where the wino was snoring and the attendant was sweeping the floor.

Whitey was aiming the smile at nothing in particular and saying, "You ready, Captain?"

"Ready for what?" The Captain's voice was choked.

"For the news," Whitey said. "For the morning extra edition."

"You're the morning extra," the Captain said. He was trying not to tremble as he looked at Whitey. "I got the headline right in front of me."

You ain't just kidding, Whitey said without sound, and he thought: He's got the headline standing there where it's one of these lieutenants who's hungry for a captain's badge and itching for the big loot that comes in when Sharkey makes this station house the branch office of Sharkey and Company. So it's either Pertnoy or Taggert. But which one? You can't flip your finger and say eeny, meeny, miney, mo. It's gotta be arithmetic. It's two minus one equals one. That's what's gotta be done here, it's strictly a matter of subtraction. But how do we go about it?

He sat there on the corridor floor and heard the Captain saying, "Get up."

He looked at the Captain's big fists and told himself he was in no hurry to get up.

"Get up, killer," the Captain said. "Get up so I can knock you down again."

Whitey's eyes moved up from the Captain's fists to focus on the Captain's face. It was the color of milk. Poor sick bastard, Whitey thought, and he wanted to perform some brotherly act like giving the Captain a soft pillow for his splitting head. But sometimes, he knew, you gotta knock them out before you can help them. Like when they're going under, in deep water and sure as hell this one is going under. What you'll hafta do is hit him with a left hook, give it to him dead center between the eyes. So don't wait, don't think about it, just give it to him.

"You're dying," Whitey said to the Captain. "You're a dying man."

The Captain closed his eyes and kept them closed for a long moment.

"And nobody cares," Whitey said, knowing it was a very hard left hook, seeing the Captain reeling with the impact, although actually the Captain was motionless.

Whitey hooked him again. "You're all alone," Whitey said. "You ain't got a friend in the world, not even that whisky bottle I saw on your desk. It can't give you no lift because you're too far down."

The Captain's eyes were wide open and staring past Whitey, past Taggert and Pertnoy, aiming all the way down the corridor, going on across the roll room and out the door, going on and on and away from everything.

It's working, Whitey thought. I think it's working.

But then he couldn't be too sure because now the Captain looked at him again. There was a moment of knowing it was touch and go, it was gonna be this or that, and the Captain would either lunge at him and rip him apart or take hold of the other prisoner who wore a blue shirt and a captain's badge.

The Captain turned away from Whitey and walked with his head down, his arms limp at his sides as he entered his office.

–Fifteen–

Whitey remained sitting on the corridor floor. He looked up at the two detectives and saw they were watching the opened doorway of the Captain's office. No sound was coming from the office and it went on like that for the better part of a minute. Then there was the sound of glass on wood, the whisky bottle on the desktop, the bottle lifted and lowered and lifted again, the glass bottom tapping on the wood as the drinker played with the bottle and fought with it, fighting against the idea of another drink.

The glass hit hard on the wood and Whitey heard the ice-cold voice of the Captain: "All right, I'm ready for him now. Bring him in."

Whitey stood up. Followed closely by the two detectives, he moved toward the office. In the doorway he turned and looked at the two detectives. He saw the light-brown pompadour and clean-shaven face of Taggert, saw Taggert's carefully knotted tie and expensively tailored Oxford-gray suit and the semiglossy black Scotch-grain shoes. He thought: This tells you exactly nothing. And his eyes went to Pertnoy, taking

204

in the flat-brushed pale-blond hair, the gray sort-of-poolroom complexion, the slim physique attired in flannel that needed pressing. Then up again to Pertnoy's face to check the notion that this man was on the cute side, cute with a cue stick or a deck of cards. But it was just a notion so far.

He heard the Captain telling him to sit down. The Captain spoke flatly, pointing to a chair at the side of the desk. Whitey seated himself, his arms crossed in his lap, his eyes looking directly at the Captain.

"Start talking," the Captain said.

Whitey told himself to forget there were others in the room. The two detectives were standing near the desk and he knew they were there, but now he had to talk as though they weren't there, and he said, "Nobody brought me in. I came in on my own two feet."

"Your conscience?" the Captain said. And he managed a trace of a smile.

"No," Whitey said. "It ain't conscience. It's information."

"I don't think so," the Captain murmured. "I think you're gonna tell me a fairy tale. Or something from Ripley."

"Ripley always backed it up," Whitey said.

"Can you?"

"I think so. It depends."

"On what?"

"On you, Captain." And then, making it a gamble, "It depends on how much brains you got left."

Captain Kinnard started to lose the smile. His lips strained to hold it, managed to hold it, and then went farther than that and made it wider, almost a pleasant smile. He nodded slowly as though admitting that the prisoner had made a point. He said, "I think there's still some tools upstairs. Keep talking."

"Here's item one. I didn't kill the policeman."

The Captain didn't say anything.

"Item two. I know who did it."

And he waited for the Captain to say something. The Captain remained silent and went on smiling at him.

He returned the smile and said, "You ready for item three?"

The Captain nodded again.

"Item three is the clincher," Whitey said. "The riots." The Captain shivered as though he'd been pushed into icy water. He sat there with his hands sliding across the desktop, searching for the edge so he could grip it.

Whitey said, "The riots are a put-up job."

For some moments the only sound was three men breathing. The Captain wasn't breathing.

Then Whitey said, "It's an organization. The man who killed the cop is working for them. They're racket people and they wanna take over the neighborhood."

Another pause. Whitey told himself it was all timing now and he had to get it timed just right.

He said, "They can't take over while you're in this station house. They're trying to get you out."

And another pause. And the Captain saying, "Go on, mister. I'm listening."

"They have it figured you can't be bought, you can't be bumped, they ain't in no position to put pills in your coffee. So they're doing it the slow way. Slow but sure. And when it comes, it'll come from City Hall. They know you're slated to go if you can't stop these race riots."

The Captain looked down at his hands. His hands gripped the edge of the desk. He said very quietly, "Where'd you get this?"

"I can take you there," Whitey said.

"And then what? What can you show me? Can you show me something that proves what you're saying?"

Whitey nodded. "It's in the cellar," he said. "They got a big show arranged for tomorrow night. The way they got it planned, it's gonna be the biggest of all. This time they're

206

looking for the payoff, and if you look in the cellar you'll see they're not playing. They got guns stacked there."

The Captain raised his head and for a long moment he gazed at Whitey. Then, getting up very slowly, he said, "All right, let's you and me go for a ride."

Whitey didn't move.

"Come on," the Captain said.

But Whitey sat there, knowing he had to swing it now, it had to be complete or it wasn't any good. He looked at the two detective lieutenants and wished he could see inside their heads so he could point his finger at one instead of two. His finger was indicating both of them and he was saying, "I want these men to come along." The Captain was halfway to the door. He stopped and looked at Whitey and said, "Why?"

"For my protection," Whitey said. He smiled at Captain Kinnard. "For yours, too."

"How come?"

"Just in case you blow your top again."

"You think I'm that bad off?"

"Yes," Whitey said. "I'm scared to be alone with you."

But his eyes were saying something different, begging the Captain to understand, to add some number and arrive at a total.

The Captain looked at the two detective lieutenants. For some moments the Captain didn't say anything. And then, his voice toneless, "All right, we'll make it a foursome."

Whitey got up from the chair.

The four of them walked out of the room.

On the instrument panel of the black-and-orange squad car the clock showed four-forty. The speedometer showed twenty miles per hour. The Captain was driving and he had to drive slowly because they were on River Street and this section of the street was hard on tires. There were a lot of bumps and deep chuckholes. From curb to curb the street was littered with overturned ash cans, fruit boxes, and broken glass, the tokens of the action that had taken place earlier tonight, The car's headlights put a bright polish on the asphalt ribboned with bloodstains.

Whitey sat beside the Captain. In the rear-view mirror he saw the two detectives in the back seat. Pertnoy was smoking a cigarette and Taggert was leaning back comfortably with his arms folded.

"Where do I turn?" the Captain asked.

"Next block. You go left," Whitey said.

They hit one of the ash cans and it made a clatter as it rolled toward the curb. Whitey focused on the rear-view mirror and saw that Pertnoy was finished with the cigarette, and now he was busy with something else. Whatever it was, it sounded metallic. Then it made an efficient clicking sound and Whitey knew it was a revolver and Pertnoy was loading it. The rear-view mirror showed a vague smile on Pertnoy's face.

Whitey turned and looked directly at Pertnoy. The detective went on smiling and inserting rounds in the revolver. He saw Whitey looking at him and he widened the smile just a little and said, "You ever get hit with one of these?"

"No," Whitey said.

"It don't shoot water," Pertnoy said.

"I guess not." Whitey returned Pertnoy's smile. Then it occurred to him that he was paying too much attention to Pertnoy. He got rid of the smile and looked at Taggert and said, "You better load up, too."

"Mine's loaded already," Taggert said.

"Naturally," Pertnoy murmured.

Taggert looked at Pertnoy. "What do you mean, naturally?"

Pertnoy pointed to Taggert and said to Whitey, "He's a former boy scout. He's always prepared."

208

"And you're always funny," Taggert said. "You're always very funny."

"Cut it out," the Captain told them.

"You ought to be in vaudeville," Taggert said to Pertnoy. "You'd be a big hit."

"I don't think so," Pertnoy said. "I don't care much for the spotlight."

"Meaning what?" Taggert's voice was stiff.

"Meaning nothing," Pertnoy said mildly. "Unless it means something to you. Does it mean something to you?"

"No," Taggert said. "Why should it?"

Pertnoy shrugged. He didn't say anything. The squad car had turned left and it was moving very slowly on the narrow street. The street was extremely narrow and on both sides the tires scraped the curbs. The car bumped lightly on the cobblestones. Whitey was still facing the back seat and he saw Pertnoy replacing the loaded revolver in the shoulder holster. He was doing it very slowly and carefully, smiling while he did it. Taggert was watching him. There was no expression on Taggert's face. But it seemed he was aching to say something to Pertnoy. His mouth opened and closed and opened again.

And then, not looking at Taggert, but letting the smile drift sideways toward him, Pertnoy said, "Go on, say it. I don't mind if you say it."

"I don't like working with you," Taggert said. "I never liked working with you."

"When they feel that way," Pertnoy said aloud to himself, "they oughta quit."

"I been thinking," Taggert said. "I have a definite desire to punch you in the mouth."

"Now look," the Captain said. "I won't have this." He was trying to concentrate on the wheel and the accelerator. The car was creeping along at five miles per hour and every few moments the front tires got jammed against the curbs and the

Captain had to put it in reverse and straighten the wheels. Now it was quiet in the back seat but the quiet was colder and deeper than the talking and the Captain said to them, "I said stop it and I mean stop it. And you." He spoke to Whitey. "You face front. You wanna look at something, look at the windshield."

Whitey turned and faced the windshield and his eyes were aimed at the rear-view mirror. He saw Pertnoy lighting another cigarette. Taggert was sitting up straight and rigid, breathing somewhat heavily and looking at Pertnoy.

"Because I know," Taggert blurted, and it was like someone throwing up curdled milk. "You think I don't know, but I do. I got it from good authority you're a long ways off center."

"Really?" Pertnoy sipped lightly at the cigarette.

"Yes really. The comedy is just a front. Actually you're nothing but a freak."

"Is that what they call it?" Pertnoy murmured.

"Yes. Because that's what it is. You're a freak, Pertnoy. You hear what I'm saying? You're just a freak."

"All right, if you want it that way," Pertnoy said.

"You men gonna stop it?" the Captain shot at them.

"This one isn't a man," Taggert said. "This one belongs in a sideshow. I'm told he likes to be locked in dark closets. Once a week he gives a local whore ten dollars to tie his wrists and bind his eyes and put him in the closet for an hour."

"An hour and a half," Pertnoy corrected.

"You hear that?" Taggert said it very loudly, as though he stood on a platform facing a large audience. "He ain't even ashamed."

"What goes on here?" the Captain wanted to know. "What kind of talk is this?"

Whitey pointed toward the windshield. "Down there, Captain. You park near that street lamp."

Pertnoy was saying, "In the final analysis we're all in the same boat. We're all ashamed of something."

"That's right, get witty again," Taggert said. "Cover it up with a gag."

"No gag, Taggert. It's fundamental truth. With me it's because I do the kind of work that makes a lot of people unhappy. Some of them don't deserve it and that puts things off balance. So once a week I let her put me in the closet and maybe that gets it balanced. At any rate, it helps to — "

"You're a liar," Taggert interrupted. "That ain't the reason. The reason is pleasure. That's the only way you can get your pleasure."

"And you?" Pertnoy purred. "What's your weakness?"

"I — "

"You'll answer him later," the Captain said. He was switching off the ignition and pulling up on the brake. They were parked near the street lamp and the Captain opened the door on Whitey's side and told Whitey to climb out. The Captain followed close behind him and then the two detectives joined them, the four of them walking now toward the street lamp, walking abreast on the cobblestones until they reached the alley.

Whitey pointed to the alley entrance on the right and they started down the alley with Whitey and the Captain in front, Whitey looking at the houses and telling himself he'd recognize the house when they came to it. He saw a flashlight in the Captain's hand but it wasn't lighted; there was enough moonlight here to let them see where they were going.

They were walking slowly in close formation, his shoulders rubbing against the Captain's shoulders and the footsteps of the two detectives very close on his heels. There was no talk. But one of the detectives was beginning to breathe somewhat heavily. Whitey could hear it, and he thought: I'd like to turn and look at them and see which one it is, that heavy breathing puts the finger on him, he's worried plenty right now and every step we take he gets worried more. Well, we'll soon be there. We're getting there, all right. What's he gonna do when we get there? What can he do? Well, that's his problem. It's quite a problem. Maybe he'll make a run for it before we arrive. But no, he wouldn't do that. He knows he can't run from bullets. He knows. But there's your house, Captain, there it is with the cellar window with no glass in it, saying, Everybody welcome, come on in and get warm.

He touched the Captain's arm and pointed to the house. Then he turned and looked at the two detectives. Whichever one of them had been breathing heavily, he had stopped now; they both breathed at the normal rate and their eyes showed nothing. They were watching the Captain, who was working on the rusty latch of the fence gate.

The Captain worked on it very carefully and it made hardly any noise as he pulled it free. The gate swung open and the four of them walked across the back yard.

And then they stood at the cellar window and the Captain was looking at Whitey. "The guns," the Captain said. "Where are they stashed?"

"On the floor. Near the furnace."

The Captain turned to the two detectives. "This won't take long," he said. "All it needs is a look."

"You going in alone?" It was Pertnoy.

The Captain nodded very slowly.

"Be careful," Pertnoy said.

The Captain turned and faced the cellar window. He crouched low and began to climb through. He had a hard time getting through. At first it seemed that his thick body was too wide for the window frame. He twisted and squirmed and got one shoulder through, then squirmed some more and got stuck and they watched him reaching up above his head, trying to get a hold on something for leverage. He found it and went on squirming his way in. Altogether it took him more than a minute to get in. They could hear him moving around in there and they saw the reflected glow of his flashlight pouring out in tiny splashes of bright yellow. It went on that way for some moments and then there was no light at all, and Whitey knew that the Captain was on the other side of the coal bin.

He heard Pertnoy saying, "How do you feel?"

"Me?" He faced Pertnoy. "I feel all right."

"You're not worried?"

"No," Whitey said.

"And you?" Pertnoy said to Taggert.

Taggert didn't say anything. His lips were clamped tightly and he was staring at the cellar window.

Pertnoy said, "You look plenty worried, Lieutenant."

"Leave me alone," Taggert said. He sounded as though he were talking to himself.

"You wanna spill it?" Pertnoy murmured.

Taggert glanced at Pertnoy and then at Whitey. He blinked a few times and let out a cough and followed it with a louder cough.

"You trying something?" Pertnoy asked gently, some what sadly. Then, with a gesture toward the house, "You'll need more noise than that to tip them off."

Whitey looked at the face of Detective Lieutenant Taggert. The eyes were glazed and it seemed the skin was stretched to the cracking point. He wondered if Taggert was really cracking up and in the next moment he was sure of it because he saw Taggert going for the shoulder holster.

"Oh, for Christ's sake," Pertnoy said wearily.

Taggert had the revolver in his hand and it was pointed at Pertnoy's chest.

"You freak bastard, " Taggert said, and Whitey knew it was sick talk, it was persecution stuff, the way they talk to the attendants and the visitors when they're very sick. "I won't let you laugh at me."

"I only laugh when it's funny," Pertnoy said. There was real pity in his voice.

But it didn't reach Taggert. It seemed that nothing could reach Taggert now. He began to sob like a child, and what came out of his mouth was a kindergarten complaint. "You – you're always picking on me. Just – just because I get my shaves in barbershops. And get my suits custom-made. And wear expensive shoes. What's – what's wrong with that?"

Pertnoy didn't reply. It was as though he realized he couldn't make contact with Taggert.

"And," Taggert choked on it, "that mirror I put up on the wall. In the office. That tickled you, didn't it? You had a lot of fun with that mirror. You thought it was so comical I like to look at myself."

"You need that mirror now" Pertnoy said. His voice was like a dash of cold water, trying to bring Taggert out of it. "You ought to see yourself now."

"I – " Taggert blinked several times. He turned his head slowly and looked at the house. He said very quietly, "How'd you know I was in with them?"

"Just a notion I had," Pertnoy said. "I guess it was growing on me. A lot of little things, but I couldn't put them together. You listening?"

Taggert nodded solemnly. He came a step closer to Pertnoy and he had the gun just a few inches away from Pertnoy's chest.

Pertnoy wasn't looking at the gun. He was saying, "In the car, when we were driving here. When you called me a pervert. As if you just had to get it out. As if you'd been holding it back for a long time and you had that one last chance to get it out."

"But it didn't hurt you." Taggert was sobbing again. "It didn't even move you."

Pertnoy shrugged. He looked at Whitey and shrugged again.

"I wonder – " Taggert blubbered. "I wonder if this can move you," and he pulled the trigger.

-Sixteen-

Pertnoy went down with a bullet in his lung and before he hit the ground another bullet went into his abdomen. Taggert walked toward him to shoot him again and Whitey came in from the side and made a grab for Taggert's wrist. Taggert turned and shot at Whitey and missed. Then Taggert aimed again at Whitey but just then a bullet came from the cellar window and went into Taggert's shoulder.

Whitey had thrown himself to the ground, and as he rolled over he caught a glimpse of the cellar window. He saw Captain Kinnard pointing the gun at Taggert. He heard the Captain saying, "Here I am, Taggert. Right here."

But as the Captain said it, a light was switched on in the cellar, and someone was shooting at the Captain. Then the Captain wasn't there at the window and Whitey heard a lot of shooting going on in the cellar. He told himself to forget the cellar and concentrate on Taggert. As he turned his head, he saw Taggert clutching the injured shoulder with the arm hanging limply, the hand straining to hold onto the gun. Taggert was backing away from Pertnoy, who had pulled himself up to a sitting position and taken out his revolver. Pertnoy was biting hard on his lip, biting so hard that blood came seeping out. It was bright blood and it mixed with the frothy blood that welled up from his throat and gushed out of his mouth. The front of Pertnoy's jacket was covered with blood pouring down from the wound in his chest, and from his punctured middle the blood spurted and streamed over his trousers. But the revolver in Pertnoy's hand was fairly steady and he had it aimed at Taggert. Whitey saw Taggert lifting the bad arm and aiming at Pertnoy's stomach. He heard Pertnoy saying, "This is silly."

Taggert shot first, but before the bullet went in, Pertnoy was able to pull the trigger. A red-black hole showed on Taggert's forehead and he was instantly dead. Pertnoy was sitting there and then sagging sideways, finally resting face down.

Whitey moved toward Pertnoy to see if he could do something for him. He knew it was a stupid thought, there really wasn't anything he could do. As he knelt beside Pertnoy, he heard the sound of the back door. He turned and saw them coming out. It was Chop and Bertha and Gerardo. They came out running. Whitey saw a gun in Chop's hand. Chop took a shot at Whitey and the bullet went into Pertnoy's face. Whitey reached for Pertnoy's revolver, telling himself he'd never handled one before, and wondering what he could do with it. He saw Chop taking aim at him and he decided the only thing to do with a gun was pull the trigger. He pulled it and the bullet went past Chop and past Bertha and hit Gerardo in the thigh. He pulled it again and saw Chop dropping the gun and hopping around, holding onto his hand.

Bertha went for the gun and Whitey shot at her and missed and caught Gerardo in the knee. Gerardo was sitting with his legs crossed and he was screeching. Chop was running back into the house. Bertha stood there frowning down at Chop's gun on the ground. Then she frowned at Whitey, and then at the gun again. She was trying to make up her mind. Whitey aimed at her immense bulk and said, "You move and you're dead."

She looked at him and said quietly, "You mean you'd hit a lady?"

He didn't know how to answer that. He saw her walking toward him. He told himself it was a female and he didn't like the idea of hurting a female. He said to himself: How stupid can you get? She walked in closer and he knew it would be very stupid if he didn't shoot her. Of course, both of them were acting stupid. The only thing that wasn't stupid was the gun. It felt solid and capable in his hand and he told himself to use it. Now Bertha was in very close and he begged himself to shoot her. He shot at her and missed and knew he'd missed purposely.

"Sucker," she said, and swung her right arm with all her weight behind it. Her big fist put the impact of more than three hundred pounds against his jaw. A few stars came down and flared in his eyes and through his eyes and then he was out of it.

In the station house the clock on the roll-room wall showed ten minutes past five. The roll room was crowded with policemen. The wino who'd been sleeping on the bench was still asleep. On the same bench Whitey sat leaning back with his head against the wall. He had an ice bag pressed to his jaw. He told himself the cops were very considerate to let him use the ice bag. It sure helped. But a drink would help more. He wished he had a drink in front of him.

"How you doing?"

He looked up. It was Captain Kinnard.

"I guess I'll make it," Whitey said. He took the ice bag away from his swollen jaw. He touched his jaw and winced slightly. Then he shrugged and placed the ice bag on the bench beside him.

"You wanna go now?" the Captain asked.

"Is it all right?"

The Captain nodded. "You're clear. We got a confession from your friend Gerardo."

Whitey stood up. For some moments he was quiet. And then, not looking at the Captain, "Only Gerardo?"

"The others got away."

"What?"

"I said they got away. They had a car and they got away."

"Oh," Whitey said. He was staring at the floor.

"What's the matter?" the Captain said.

He shook his head slowly. "Nothing."

"Well, anyway," the Captain said, "we put them out of business. There won't be no more riots, that's for sure."

Whitey wasn't listening. He was thinking about her. In his mind he could see the gray-green eyes and the lighter-than-bronze hair, and he said to himself: You didn't even get a chance to talk to her. And if you'd had the chance? What then? What could be said? Not a damn thing more than hello again and good-bye again. Because she'd never leave Sharkey. She can't leave Sharkey. If she tries to leave him, he puts the hook on her and drags her back. She knows she can't skip out on him. So that's the way it is. She's hooked, that's all. Maybe she wants to be hooked, whether she knows it or not. After all, that's the only life she knows, and without it she's nowhere. Like you're nowhere without a drink. And sure as hell you need one now. All right, stop carrying on. At least you had another look at her. You had that, anyway. So you ought to be satisfied. All right, you're satisfied. You feel great. But where can I get a drink?

He heard the Captain saying, "You look knocked out. If you want to, you can sleep here."

"No," he said. "But I could use a bracer. I'm kinda thirsty."

The Captain nodded toward the corridor. "Go in my office. It's on the desk. Take it with you."

Whitey smiled. "Thanks, Captain."

"No," the Captain said. He didn't smile. "I'm saying thanks. Thanks a million, mister."

Whitey walked across the roll room and down the corridor and into the Captain's office. It was there on the desk, the whisky bottle three quarters full. He picked it up and held it under his coat as he walked out the side door of the station house.

It was very cold outside and he walked fast to get some circulation in his legs. After a while he stopped and uncapped the bottle and drank, and a few minutes later he drank again. It felt fine going down. On River Street, headed north toward Skid Row, he stopped and took a big drink. Then he looked at the bottle. It was about half filled. He wondered where he could find Bones and Phillips. They ought to be somewhere around.

Then he was on Skid Row and he found them in the all-night eatery across the street from the flophouse. They were seated at the counter near the window. Of course, they weren't eating anything; the hash house never handed out free meals. They were just sitting there at the counter.

Whitey tapped on the window. Bones and Phillips looked up. They came hurrying out of the hash house and Phillips said loudly, "We been worried to death. Where the hell you been?"

"I took a walk," Whitey said.

"He took a walk," Bones told Phillips. "He keeps us sitting up all night and he says he just took a walk."

"Look at his face," Phillips said. "He's all banged up."

Whitey shrugged and didn't say anything. Bones came in close to Whitey and sniffed a few times. Then Bones looked sideways at Phillips and said quietly, "I'll be a sonofabitch, he scored for the booze."

Whitey smiled and reached under his coat and took out the bottle.

The three of them walked across the street. They sat down

on the pavement with their backs against the wall of the flophouse. The pavement was terribly cold and the wet wind from the river came blasting into their faces. But it didn't bother them. They sat there passing the bottle around, and there was nothing that could bother them, nothing at all.

THE END

-Black Pudding-

They spotted him on Race Street between Ninth and Tenth. It was Chinatown in the tenderloin of Philadelphia and he stood gazing into the window of the Wong Ho restaurant and wishing he had the cash to buy himself some egg-foo-yung. The menu in the window priced egg-foo-yung at eighty cents an order and he had exactly thirty-one cents in his pocket. He shrugged and started to turn away from the window and just then he heard them coming.

It was their footsteps that told him who they were. There was the squeaky sound of Oscar's brand-new shoes. And the clumping noise of Coley's heavy feet. It was nine years since he'd heard their footsteps but he remembered that Oscar had a weakness for new shoes and Coley always walked heavily.

He faced them. They were smiling at him, their features somewhat greenish under the green neon glow that drifted through after-midnight blackness. He saw the weasel eyes and buzzard nose of little Oscar. He transferred his gaze to the thick lips and puffed-out cheeks of tall, obese Coley.

"Hello, Ken." It was Oscar's purring voice, Oscar's lips scarcely moving.

"Hello," he said to both of them. He blinked a few times. Now the shock was coming. He could feel the waves of shock surging toward him.

"We been looking for you," Coley said. He flipped his thick thumb over his shoulder to indicate the black Olds 88 parked across the street. "We've driven that car clear across the country."

Ken blinked again. The shock had hit him and now it was past and he was blinking from worry. He knew why they'd been looking for him and he was very worried.

He said quietly, "How'd you know I was in Philly?"

"Grapevine," Oscar said. "It's strictly coast-to-coast. It starts from San Quentin and we get tipped-off in Los Angeles. It's a letter telling the Boss you been paroled. That's three weeks ago. Then we get letters from Denver and Omaha and a wire from Chicago. And then a phone call from Detroit. We wait to see how far east you'll travel. Finally we get the call from Philly, and the man tells us you're on the bum around Skid Row."

Ken shrugged. He tried to sound casual as he said, "Three thousand miles is a long trip. You must have been anxious to see me."

Oscar nodded. "Very anxious." He sort of floated closer to Ken. And Coley also moved in. It was slow and quiet and it didn't seem like menace but they were crowding him and finally they had him backed up against the restaurant window.

He said to himself, *They've got you, they've found you and they've got you and you're finished.*

He shrugged again. "You can't do it here."

"Can't we?" Oscar purred.

"It's a crowded street," Ken said. He turned his head to look at the lazy parade of tenderloin citizens on both sides of the street. He saw the bums and the beggars, the winos and the ginheads, the yellow faces of middle-aged opium smokers and the grey faces of two-bit scufflers and hustlers.

"Don't look at them," Oscar said. "They can't help you. Even if they could, they wouldn't."

Ken's smile was sad and resigned. "You're so right," he said. His shoulders drooped and his head went down and he saw Oscar reaching into a jacket pocket and taking out the silver-handled tool that had a button on it to release a five-inch blade. He knew there would be no further talk, only action, and it would happen within the next split-second.

In that tiny fraction of time, some gears clanged to shift from low to high in Ken's brain. His senses and reflexes, dulled from nine years in prison, were suddenly keen and acutely technical and there was no emotion on his face as he moved. He moved very fast, his arms crossing to shape an X, the left hand flat and rigid and banging against Oscar's wrist, the right hand a fist that caught Coley in the mouth. It sent the two of them staggering backward arid gave him the space he wanted and he darted through the gap, sprinting east on Race Street toward Ninth.

As he turned the corrider to head north on Ninth, he glanced backward and saw them getting into the Olds. He took a deep breath and continued running up Ninth. He ran straight ahead for approximately fifteen yards and then turned again to make a dash down a narrow alley. In the middle of the alley he hopped a fence, ran across a backyard, hopped another fence, then a few more backyards with more fence-hopping, and then the opened window of a tenement cellar. He lunged at the window, went in head-first, groped for a handhold, couldn't find any, and plunged through eight feet of blackness onto a pile of empty boxes and tin cans. He landed on his side, his thigh taking most of the impact, so that it didn't hurt too much. He rolled over and hit the floor and Jay there flat on his belly. From a few feet away a pair of green eyes stared at him and he stared back, and then he grinned as though to say, *Don't be afraid, pussy, stay here and keep me company, it's a tough life and an evil world and us alleycats got to stick together.*

But the cat wasn't trusting any living soul. It let out a soft meow and scampered away. Ken sighed and his grin faded arid he felt the pressure of the blackness and the quiet and the loneliness. His mind reached slowly for the road going backward nine years...

It was Los Angeles, and they were a small outfit operating from a first-floor apartment near Figueroa and Jefferson. Their business was armed robbery arid their work-area included Beverly Hills and Bel-Air and the wealthy residential districts of Pasadena. They concentrated on expensive jewelry and wouldn't touch any job that offered less than a ten-grand haul.

There were five of them, Ken and Oscar and Coley and Ken's wife and the Boss. The name of the Boss was Riker and he was very kind to Ken until the face and body of Ken's wife became a need and then a craving and finally an obsession. It showed in Riker's eyes whenever he looked at her. She was a platinum blonde dazzler, a former burlesque dancer named Hilda. She'd been married to Ken for seven months when Riker reached the point where he couldn't stand it any longer and during a Job in Bel-air he banged Ken's skull with the butt end of a revolver. When the police arrived, Ken was unconscious on the floor and later in the hospital they asked him questions but he wouldn't answer. In the courtroom he sat with his head bandaged and they asked him more questions and he wouldn't answer. They gave him five-to-twenty and during his first month in San Quentin he learned from his lawyer that Hilda had obtained a Reno divorce and was married to Riker. He went more or less insane and couldn't be handled and they put him in solitary.

Later they had him in the infirmary, chained to the bed, and they tried some psychology. They told him he'd regain his emotional health if he'd talk and name some names. He laughed at them. Whenever they coaxed him to talk, he laughed in their faces and presently they'd shrug and walk away.

His first few years in Quentin were spent either in solitary or the infirmary, or under special guard. Then, gradually, he quieted down. He became very quiet and in the laundry-room he worked very hard and was extremely cooperative. During the fifth year he was up for parole and they asked him about the Bel-Air job and he replied quite reasonably that he couldn't remember, he was afraid to remember, he wanted to forget all about it and arrange a new life for himself. They told him he'd talk or he'd do the limit. He said he was sorry but he couldn't give them the information they wanted. He explained that he was trying to get straight with himself and be clean inside and he wouldn't feel clean if he earned his freedom that way.

So then it was nine years and they were convinced he'd finally paid his debt to the people of California. They gave him a suit of clothes and a ten-dollar bill and told him he was a free man.

In a Sacramento hash-house he worked as a dishwasher lust long enough to earn the bus-fare for a trip across the country. He was thinking in terms of the town where he'd been born and raised, telling himself he'd made a wrong start in Philadelphia and the thing to do was go back there and start again and make it right this time, really legitimate. The parole board okayed the job he'd been promised. That was a healthy thought and it made the bus-trip very enjoyable. But the nicest thing about the bus was its fast engine that took him away from California, far away from certain faces he didn't want to see.

Yet now, as he rested on the floor of the tenement cellar, he could see the faces again. The faces were worried and frightened and he saw them in his brain and heard their trembling voices. He heard Riker saying, "They've released him from Quentin. We'll have to do something." And Hilda saying, "What can we do?" And Riker replying, "We'll get him before he gets us."

He sat up, colliding with an empty tin can that rolled across the floor and made a clatter. For some moments there was quiet and then he heard a shuffling sound and a voice saying, "Who's there?"

It was a female voice, sort of a cracked whisper. It had a touch of asthma in it, some alcohol, and something else that had no connection with health or happiness.

Ken didn't say anything. He hoped she'd go away. Maybe she'd figure it was a rat that had knocked over the tin can and she wouldn't bother to investigate.

But he heard the shuffling footsteps approaching through the blackness. He focused directly ahead and saw the silhouette coming toward him. She was on the slender side, neatly constructed. It was a very interesting silhouette. Her height was approximately five-five and he estimated her weight in the neighborhood of one-ten. He sat up straighter. He was very anxious to get a look at her face.

She came closer and there was the scratchy sound of a match against a matchbook. The match flared and he saw her face. She had medium-brown eyes that matched the color of her hair, and her nose and lips were nicely sculptured, somewhat delicate but blending prettily with the shape of her head. He told himself she was a very pretty girl. But just then he saw the scar.

It was a wide jagged scar that started high on her forehead and crawled down the side of her face and ended less than an inch above her upper lip. The color of it was a livid purple with lateral streaks of pink and white. It was a terrible scar, really hideous.

She saw that he was wincing, but it didn't seem to bother her. The lit match stayed lit and she was sizing him up. She saw a man of medium height and weight, about thirty-six years old, with yellow hair that needed cutting, a face that needed shaving, and sad lonely grey eyes that needed someone's smile.

She tried to smile for him. But only one side of her mouth could manage it. On the other side the scar was like a hook that pulled at her flesh and caused a grimace that was more anguish than physical pain. He told himself it was a damn shame. Such a pretty girl. And so young. She couldn't be more than twenty-five. Well, some people had all the luck. All the rotten luck.

The match was burned halfway down when she reached into the pocket of a tattered dress and took out a candle. She went through the process of lighting the candle and melting the base of it. The softened wax adhered to the cement floor of the cellar and she sat down facing him and said quietly, "All right, let's have it. What's the pitch?"

He pointed backward to the opened window to indicate the November night. He said, "It's chilly out there. I came in to get warm."

She leaned forward just a little to peer at his eyes. Then, shaking her head slowly, she murmured, "No sale."

He shrugged. He didn't say anything.

"Come on," she urged gently. "Let's try it again."

"All right." He grinned at her. And then it came out easily. "I'm hiding."

"From the Law?"

"No," he said. "From trouble."

He started to tell her about it. He couldn't understand why he was telling her. It didn't make sense that he should be spilling the story to someone he'd just met in a dark cellar, someone out of nowhere. But she was company and he needed company. He went on telling her.

It took more than an hour. He was providing all the details of events stretched across nine years. The candlelight showed her sitting there, not moving, her eyes riveted to his face as he spoke in low tones, Sometimes there were pauses, some of them long, some very long, but she never interrupted, she waited patiently while he groped for the words to make the meaning clear.

Finally he said, "—It's a cinch they won't stop, they'll get me sooner or later."

"If they find you," she said,

"They'll find me."

"Not here."

He stared at the flickering candle. "They'll spend money to get information. There's more than one big mouth in this neighborhood, And the biggest mouths of all belong to the landlords."

"There's no landlord here," she told him. "There's no tenants except me and you."

"Nobody upstairs?"

"Only mice and rats and roaches. It's a condemned house and City Hall calls it a firetrap and from the first floor up the windows are boarded. You can't get up because there's no stairs. One of these days the City'll tear down this dump but I'll worry about that when it happens."

He looked at her. "You live here in the cellar?"

She nodded. "It's a good place to play solitaire."

He smiled and murmured, "Some people like to be alone."

"I don't like it," she said. Then, with a shrug, she pointed to the scar on her face. "What man would live with me?"

He stopped smiling. He didn't say anything.

She said, "It's a long drop when you're tossed out of a third-story window. Most folks are lucky and they land on their feet or their fanny. I came down head first, cracked my collar-bone and got a fractured skull, and split my face wide open."

He took a closer look at the livid scar. For some moments he was quiet and then he frowned thoughtfully and said, "Maybe it won't be there for long. It's not as deep as I thought it was. If you had it treated—"

230

"No," she said. "The hell with it."

"You wouldn't need much cash," he urged quietly. "You could go to a clinic. They're doing fancy tricks with plastic surgery these days."

"Yeah, I know." Her voice was toneless. She wasn't looking at him. "The point is, I want the scar to stay there. It keeps me away from men. I've had too many problems with men and now, whenever they see my face, they turn their heads the other way. And that's fine with me. That's just how I want it."

He frowned again. This time it was a deeper frown and it wasn't just thoughtful. He said, "Who threw you out of the window?"

"My husband." She laughed without sound. "My wonderful husband."

"Where is he now?"

"In the cemetery," she said. She shrugged again, and her tone was matter-of-fact. "It happened while I was in the hospital. I think he got to the point where he couldn't stand to live with himself. Or maybe he just did it for kicks, I don't know. Anyway, he got hold of a meat-cleaver and chopped his own throat. When they found him, he damn near didn't have a head."

"Well, that's one way of ending a marriage."

Again she uttered the soundless laugh. "It was a fine marriage while it lasted. I was drunk most of the time. I had to get drunk to take what he dished out. He had some weird notions about wedding vows."

"He went with other women?"

"No," she said. "He made me go with other men."

For some moments it was quiet.

And then she went on, "We lived here in this neighborhood. It's a perfect neighborhood for that sort of deal. He had me out on the street looking for customers and bringing the money home to him, and when I came in with excuses instead of cash

231

he'd throw me on the floor and kick me. I'd beg him to stop and he'd laugh and go on kicking me. Some nights I have bad dreams and he's kicking me. So then I need the sweet dreams, and that's when I reach for the pipe."

"The pipe?"

"Opium," she said. She said it with fondness and affection. "Opium." There was tenderness in her eyes. "That's my new husband."

He nodded understandingly.

She said, "I get it from a Chinaman on Ninth Street. He's a user himself and he's more than eighty years old and still in there pitching, so I guess with him it's like anything else, it's all a matter of how you use it." Her voice dropped off just a little and her eyes were dull and sort of dismal as she added, "I wish I didn't need so much of it. It takes most of my weekly salary."

"What kind of work you do?"

"I scrub floors," she said. "In night-clubs and dance-halls. All day long I scrub the floors to make them clean and shiny for the night-time customers. Some nights I sit here and think of the pretty girls dancing on them polished floors. The pretty girls with flowers in their hair and no scars on their faces—" She broke it off abruptly, her hand making a brushing gesture as though to disparage the self-pity. She stood up and said, "I gotta go out to do some shopping. You wanna wait here till I come back?"

Without waiting for his answer, she moved across the cellar toward a battered door leading to the backyard. As she opened the door, she turned and looked at him. "Make yourself comfortable," she said. "There's a mattress in the next room. It aln't the Ritz Carlton exactly, but it's better than nothing."

He was asking himself whether he should stay there.

He heard her saying, "Incidentally, my name is Tillie."

She stood there waiting,

"Kenneth," he said. "Kenneth Rockland."

But that wasn't what she was waiting for. Several moments passed, and then somehow he knew what she wanted him to say.

He said, "I'll be here when you come back."

"Good." The candlelight showed her crooked grin, a grimace on the scarred face. But what he saw was a gentle smile. It seemed to drift toward him like a soothing caress. And then he heard her saying, "Maybe I'll come back with some news. You told me it was two men. There's a chance I can check on them if you'll tell me what they look like."

He shook his head. "You better stay out of it. You might get hurt."

"Nothing can hurt me," she said. She pointed her finger at the wreckage of her face. Her tone was almost pleading as she said, "Come on, tell me what they look like."

He shrugged. He gave a brief description of Oscar and Coley. And the Olds 88.

"Check," Tillie said. "I don't have 20-20 but I'll keep them open and see what's happening."

She turned and walked out and the door closed. Ken lifted himself from the floor and picked up the candle. He walked across the cement floor and the candle showed him a small space off to one side, a former coal-bin arranged with a mattress against the wall, a splintered chair and a splintered bureau and a table stacked with books. There was a candleholder on the table and he set the candle on it and then he had a look at the books.

It was an odd mixture of literature. There were books dealing with idyllic romance, strictly from fluttering hearts and soft moonlight and violins. And there were books that probed much deeper, explaining the scientific side of sex, with drawings and photos to show what it was all about. There was one book in particular that looked as though she'd been concentrating on it. The pages were considerably thumbed and

233

she'd used a pencil to underline certain paragraphs. The title was, "The Sex Problem of the Single Woman."

He shook his head slowly. He thought, *It's a damn shame...*

And then, for some unaccountable reason, he thought of Hilda. She flowed into his mind with a rustling of silk that sheathed the exquisite contours of her slender torso and legs. Her platinum blonde hair was glimmering and her longlashed green eyes were beckoning to say, Come on, take my hand and we'll go down Memory Lane.

He shut his eyes tiiorhtly. He wondered why he was thinking about her. A long time ago he'd managed to get her out of his mind and he couldn't understand what brought her back again. He begged himself to get rid of the thought, but now It was more than a thought, it was the white-hot memory of tasting that mouth and possessing that elegant body. Without sound he said, *Goddamn her.*

And suddenly he realized why he was thinking of Hilda. It was like a curtain lifted to reveal the hidden channels of his brain. He was comparing Hilda's physical perfection with the scarred face of Tillie. His eyes were open and he gazed down at the mattress on the floor and for a moment he saw Hilda naked on the mattress. She smiled teasingly and then she shook her head and said, *Nothing doing.* So then she vanished and in the next moment it was Tillie on the mattress but somehow he didn't feel bitter or disappointed; he had the feeling that the perfection was all on Tillie's side.

He took off his shoes and lowered himself to the mattress. He yawned a few times and then he fell asleep.

A voice said, "Kenneth—"

He was instantly awake. He looked up and saw Tillie. He smiled at her and said, "What time is it?"

"Half-past five." She had a paperback in her hand and she

234

was taking things out of the bag and putting them on the table. There was some dried fish and a package of tea leaves and some cold fried noodles. She reached deeper into the bag and took out a bottle containing colorless liquid.

"Rice wine," she said. She set the bottle on the table. Then again she reached into the bag and her hand came out holding a cardboard box.

"Opium?" he murmured.

She nodded. "I got some cigarettes, too." She took a pack of Luckles from her pocket, opened the pack and extended it to him.

He sat up and put a cigarette in his mouth and used the candle to light it. He said, "You going to smoke the opium?"

"No, I'll smoke what you're smoking."

He put another cigarette in his mouth and lit it and handed it to her.

She took a few drags and then she said quietly, "I didn't want to wake you up, but I thought you'd want to hear the news."

He blinked a few times. "What news?"

"I saw them," she said.

He blinked again. "Where?"

"On Tenth Street." She took more smoke into her mouth and let it come out of her nose. "It was a couple hours ago, after I come out of the Chinaman's."

He sat up straighter. "You been watching them for two hours?"

"Watching them? I been with them. They took me for a ride."

He stared at her. His mouth was open but no sound came out.

Tillie grinned. "They didn't know I was in the car."

He took a deep breath. "How'd you manage it?"

She shrugged. "It was easy. I saw them sitting in the car and then they got out and I followed them. They were taking a stroll

235

around the block and peeping into alleys and finally I heard the little one saying they might as well powder and come back tomorrow. The big one said they should keep on searching the neighborhood. They got into an argument and I had a feeling the little one would win. So I walked back to the car. The door was open and I climbed in the back and got flat on the floor. About five minutes later they're up front and the car starts and we're riding."

His eyes were narrow. "Where?"

Downtown, she said. "It wasn't much of a ride. It only took a few minutes. They parked in front of a house on Spruce near Eleventh. I watched them go in. Then I got out of the car—"

"And walked back here?"

"Not right away," she said. "First I cased the house."

Silly Tillie, he thought. *If they'd seen her they'd have dragged her in and killed her.*

She said, "It's one of them little old-fashioned houses. There's a vacant lot on one side and on the other side there's an alley. I went down the alley and came up on the back porch and peeped through the window. They were in the kitchen, the four of them."

He made no sound, but his lips shaped the word. "Four?" And then, with sound, "Who were the other two?"

"A man and a woman."

He stiffened. He tried to get up from the mattress and couldn't move. His eyes aimed past Tillie as he said tightly, "Describe them."

"The man was about five-ten and sort of beefy. I figure about two hundred. He looked about forty or so. Had a suntan and wore expensive clothes. Brown wavy hair and brown eyes and—"

"That's Riker," he murmured.

He managed to lift himself from the mattress. His voice was a whisper as he said, "Now let's have the woman."

"She was something," Tillie said. "She was really something."

"Blonde?" And with both hands he made a gesture begging Tillie to speed the reply.

"Platinum blonde," Tillie said. "With the kind of a face that makes men sweat in the wintertime. That kind of a face, and a shape that goes along with it. She was wearing—"

"Pearls," he said. "She always had a weakness for pearls."

Tillie didn't say anything.

He moved past Tillie. He stood facing the dark wall of the cellar and seeing the yellow-black play of candlelight and shadow on the cracked plaster. "Hilda," he said. "Hilda."

It was quiet for some moments. He told himself it was wintertime and he wondered if he was sweating,

Then very slowly he turned and looked at Tillie. She was sitting oil the edge of the mattress and drinking from the bottle of rice-wine. She took it in short, measured gulps, taking it down slowly to get the full effect of it. When the bottle was half-empty she raised her head and grinned at him and said, "Have some?"

He nodded. She handed him the bottle and he drank. The Chinese wine was mostly fire and it burned all the way going down and when it hit his belly it was electric-hot. But the climate it sent to his brain was cool and mild and the mildness showed in his eyes. His voice was quiet and relaxed as he said, "I thought Oscar and Coley made the trip alone. It didn't figure that Riker and Hilda would come with them. But now it adds. I can see the way it adds."

"It's a long ride from Los Angeles," Tillie said.

"They didn't mind. They enjoyed the ride."

"The scenery?"

"No," he said. "They weren't looking at the scenery. They were thinking of the setup here in Philly. With Oscar putting the blade in me and then the funeral and Riker seeing me in the coffin and telling himself his worries were over."

237

"And Hilda?"

"The same," he said. "She's been worried just as much as Riker. Maybe more."

Tillie nodded slowly. "From the story you told me, she's got more reason to worry."

He laughed lightly. He liked the sound of it and went on with it. He said, through the easy laughter, "They really don't need to worry. They're making it a big thing and it's nothing at all. I forgot all about them a long time ago. But they couldn't forget about me."

Tillie had her head inclined and she seemed to be studying the sound of his laughter. Some moments passed and then she said quietly, "You don't like black pudding?"

He didn't get the drift of that. He stopped laughing and his eyes were asking what she meant.

"There's an old saying," she said. "Revenge is black pudding."

He laughed again.

"Don't pull away from it," Tillie said. "Just listen to it. Let it hit you and sink in. Revenge is black pudding."

He went on laughing, shaking his head and saying, "I'm not in the market."

"You sure?"

"Positive," he said. Then, with a grin, "Only pudding I like is vanilla."

"The black tastes better," Tillie said. "I've had some, and I know. I had it when they told me what he did to himself with the meatcleaver."

He winced slightly. He saw Tillie getting up from the mattress and moving toward him. He heard her saying, "That black pudding has a wonderful flavor. You ought to try a spoonful."

"No," he said. "No, Tillie."

She came closer. She spoke very slowly and there was a

238

slight hissing in her voice. "They put you in prison for nine years. They cheated you and robbed you and tortured you."

"That's all past," he said. "That's from yesterday."

"It's from now." She stood very close to him. "They're itching to hit you again and see you dead. They won't stop until you're dead. That puts a poison label on them. And there's only one way to deal with poison. Get rid of it."

"No," he said. "I'll let it stay the way it is."

"You can't," Tillie said. "It's a choice you have to make. Either you'll drink bitter poison or you'll taste that sweet black pudding."

He grinned again. "There's a third choice."

"Like what?"

"This." And he pointed to the bottle of rice-wine. "I like the taste of this. Let's stay with it until it's empty."

"That won't solve the problem," Tillie said.

"The hell with the problem." His grin was wide. It was very wide and he didn't realize that it was forced.

"You fool," Tillie said.

He had the bottle raised and he was taking a drink.

"You poor fool," she said. Then she shrugged and turned away from him and lowered herself to the mattress.

The forced grin stayed on his face as he went on drinking. Now he was drinking slowly because the rice-wine dulled the action in his brain and he had difficulty lifting the bottle to his mouth. Gradually he became aware of a change taking place in the air of the cellar; it was thicker, sort of smoky. His eyes tried to focus and there was too much wine in him and he couldn't see straight. But then the smoke came up in front of his eyes and into his eyes. He looked down and saw the white clay pipe in Tillie's hand. She was sitting on the mattress with her legs crossed, Buddha-like, puffing at the opium, taking it in very slowly, the smoke coming out past the corners of her lips.

The grin faded from his face. And somehow the alcohol-mist

was drifting away from his brain. He thought, *She smokes it because she's been kicked around.* But there was no pity in his eyes, just the level took of clear thinking. He said to himself, *There's only two kinds of people in this world, the ones who get kicked around and the ones who do the kicking.*

He lowered the bottle to the table. He turned and took a few steps going away and then heard Tillie saying, "Moving out?"

"No," he said. "Just taking a walk."

"Where?"

"Spruce Street," he said.

"Good," she said. "I'll go with you."

He shook his head. He faced her and saw that she'd put the pipe aside. She was getting up from the mattress. He went on shaking his head and saying, "It can't be played that way. I gotta do this alone."

She moved toward him. "Maybe it's good-bye."

"If it is," he said, "there's only one way to say it."

His eyes told her to come closer. He put his arms around her and held her with a tenderness and a feeling of not wanting to let her go. He kissed her. He knew she felt the meaning of the kiss, she was returning it and as her breath went into him it was sweet and pure and somehow like nectar.

Then, very gently, she pulled away from him. She said, "Go now. It's still dark outside. It'll be another hour before the sun comes out."

He grinned. It was a soft grin that wasn't forced. "This job won't take more than an hour," he said. "Whichever way it goes, it'll be a matter of minutes. Either I'll get them or they'll get me."

He turned away and walked across the cellar toward the splintered door. Tillie stood there watching him as he opened the door and went out.

It was less than three minutes later and they had him. He was walking south on Ninth, between Race Street and Arch, and the black Olds 88 was cruising on Arch and he didn't see them but they saw him, with Oscar grinning at Coley and saying, "There's our boy."

Oscar drove the car past the intersection and parked it on the north side of Arch about twenty feet away from the corner. They got out and walked toward the corner and stayed close to the brick wall of the corner building. They listened to the approaching footsteps and grinned at each other and a few moments later he arrived on the corner and they grabbed him.

He felt Coley's thick arm wrapped tight around his throat, pulling his head back. He saw the glimmer of the five-inch blade in Oscar's hand. He told himself to think fast and he thought very fast and managed to say, "You'll be the losers. I made a connection."

Oscar hesitated. He blinked puzzledly. "What connection?"

He smiled at Oscar. Then he waited for Coley to loosen the armhold on his throat. Coley loosened it, then lowered it to his chest, using both arms to clamp him and prevent him from moving.

He made no attempt to move. He went on smiling at Oscar, and saying, "An important connection. It's important enough to louse you up."

"Prove it," Oscar said.

"You're traced." He narrowed the smile just a little. "If anything happens to me, they know where to get you."

"He's faking," Coley said. Then urgently, "Go on, Oscar, give him the knife."

"Not yet," Oscar murmured. He was studying Ken's eyes and his own eyes were somewhat worried. He said to Ken, "Who did the tracing?"

"I'll tell that to Riker."

Oscar laughed without sound. "Riker's in Los Angeles."

"No he isn't," Ken said. "He's here in Philly."

Oscar stopped laughing. The worry deepened in his eyes. He stared past Ken, focusing on Coley.

"He's here with Hilda," Ken said.

"It's just a guess," Coley said. "It's gotta be a guess." He tightened his bear-hug on Ken. "Do it, Oscar. Don't let him stall you. Put the   knife in him."

Oscar looked at Ken and said, "You making this a quiz game?"

Ken shrugged. "It's more like stud poker."

"Maybe," Oscar admitted. "But you're not the dealer."

Ken shrugged again. He didn't say anything.

Oscar said, "You're not the dealer and all you can do is hope for the right card."

"I got it already," Ken said. "It fills an inside straight."

Oscar bit the edge of his lip. "All   right, I'll take a look." He had the knife aiming at Ken's chest, and then he lowered it and moved in closer and the tip of the blade was touching Ken's belly. "Let's see your hole-card, sonny. All you gotta do is name the street and the house."

"Spruce Street," Ken said. "Near Eleventh."

Oscar's face became pale. Again he was staring at Coley.

Ken said, "It's an old house,   detached. On one side there's a vacant lot and oil the other side there's an alley."

It was quiet for some moments and then Oscar was talking aloud to himself, saying, "He knows, he really knows."

"What's the move?" Coley asked. He sounded somewhat unhappy.

"We gotta think," Oscar said. "This makes it complicated and we gotta think it through very careful."

Coley muttered a four-letter word. He said, "We ain't getting paid to do our own thinking. Riker gave us orders to find him and bump him."

"We can't bump him now," Oscar said. "Not under these

242

conditions. The way it stacks up, it's Riker's play. We'll have to take him to Riker."

"Riker won't like that," Coley said.

Oscar didn't reply. Again lie was biting his lip and it went on that way for some moments and then he made a gesture toward the parked car. He told Coley to take the wheel and said he'd sit in the back with Rockland. As he opened the rear door he had the blade touching Ken's side, gently urging Ken to get in first. Coley was up front behind the wheel and then Oscar and Ken occupied the rear seat and the knife in Oscar's hand was aimed at Ken's abdomen.

The engine started and the Olds 88 moved east on Arch and went past Eighth and turned south on Seventh. There was no talk in the car as they passed Market and Chestnut and Walnut. They had a red light on Locust but Coley ignored it and went through at forty-five.

"Slow down," Oscar said.

Coley was hunched low over the wheel and the speedometer went up to fifty and Oscar yelled, "For Christ's sake, slow down. You wanna be stopped by a red car?"

"There's one now," Ken said, and he pointed toward the side window that showed only the front of a grocery store. But Oscar thought it might really be a side-street with a police car approaching, and the thought was in his brain for a tiny fraction of a second. In that segment of time he turned his head to have a look. Ken's hand moved automatically to grab Oscar's wrist and twist hard. The knife fell away from Oscar's fingers and Ken's other hand caught it. Oscar let out a screech and Ken put the knife in Oscar's throat and had it in there deep just under the ear, pulled it out and put it in again. The car was skidding to a stop as Ken stabbed Oscar a third time to finish him. Coley was screaming curses and trying to hurl himself sideways and backward toward the rear seat and Ken showed him the knife and it didn't stop him. Ken ducked as Coley came vaulting over the top of the front seat, the knife slashing upward to catch Coley in the belly, slashing sideways to rip from navel to kidney, then across again to the other kidney, then up to the ribs to hit bone with Coley gurgling and trying to sob, doubled over with his knees on the floor and his chin on the edge of the back seat, his arms flung over the sprawled corpse of Oscar.

"I'm dying," Coley gurgled. "I'm—" That was his final sound. His eyes opened very wide and his head snapped sideways and he was through for this night and all nights.

Ken opened the rear door and got out. He had the knife in his pocket as he walked with medium-fast stride going south on Seventh to Spruce. Then he turned west on Spruce and walked just a bit faster. Every now and then he glanced backward to see if there were any red cars but all he saw was the empty street and some alley cats mooching around under the street lamps.

In the blackness above the rooftops the bright yellow face of the City Hall clock showed ten minutes past six. He estimated the sky would be dark for another half-hour. It wasn't much time, but it was time enough for what he intended to do. He told himself he wouldn't enjoy the action, and yet somehow his mouth was watering, almost like anticipating a tasty dish. Something on the order of pudding, and the color of it was black.

He quickened his pace just a little, crossed Eighth Street and Ninth, and walked faster as he passed Tenth. There were no lit windows on Spruce Street but as lie neared Eleventh the moonlight blended with the glow of a street lamp and showed him the vacant lot. He gazed across the empty space to the wall of the old-fashioned house.

Then he was on the vacant lot and moving slowly and quietly toward the rear of the house. He worked his way to the sagging steps of the back porch, saw a light in the kitchen window, climbed two steps and three and four and then he was on the porch and peering through the window and seeing Hilda.

244

She was alone in the kitchen, sitting at a white-topped table and smoking a cigarette. There was a cup and saucer on the table, the saucer littered with coffee-stained cigarette butts. As he watched, she got up from the table and went to the stove to lift a percolator off the fire and pour another cup of coffee.

She moved with a slow weaving of her shoulders and a flow of her hips that was more drifting, than walking. He thought, *She still has it, that certain way of moving around, using that body like a long-stemmed lily in a quiet breeze. That's what got you the first time you laid eyes on her. The way she moves. And one time very long ago you said to her, "To set me on fire, all you have to do is walk across a room." You couldn't believe you were actually married to that hothouse-prize, that platinum blonde hair like melted eighteen-karat, that face, she still has it, that body, she still has it. It's been nine years, and she still has it.*

She was wearing bottle-green velvet that set off the pale green of her eyes. The dress was cut low, went in tight around her very narrow waist and stayed tight going down all the way past her knees. She featured pearls around her throat and in her ears and on her wrists. He thought, *You gave her pearls for her birthday and Christmas and you wanted to give her more for the first wedding anniversary. But they don't sell pearls in San Quentin. All they sell is plans for getting out. Like lessons in how to crawl through a pipe, or how to conceal certain tools, or how to disguise the voice. The lessons never paid off, but maybe now's the time to use what you learned. Let's try Coley's voice.*

His knuckles rapped the kitchen door, and his mouth opened to let out Coley's thick, low-pitched voice saying, "It's me and Oscar."

He stood there counting off the seconds. It was four seconds and then the door opened. It opened wide and Hilda's mouth opened wider. Then she had her hand to her mouth and she was stepping backward.

245

"Hello, Hilda." He came into the kitchen and closed the door behind him.

She took another backward step. She shook her head and spoke through the trembling fingers that pressed against her lips. "It isn't—"

"Yes," he said. "It is."

Her hand fell away from her mouth. The moment was too much for her and it seemed she was going to collapse. But somehow she managed to stay on her feet. Then her eyes were shut tightly and she went on shaking her head.

"Look at me," he said. "Take a good look."

She opened her eyes. She looked him up and down and up again. Then, very slowly, she summoned air into her lungs and he knew she was going to let out a scream. His hand moved fast to his coat pocket and he took out Oscar's knife and said quietly, "No noise, Hilda."

She stared at the knife. The air went out of her without sound. Her arms were limp at her sides. She spoke in a half-whisper, talking to herself. "I don't believe it. Just can't believe it—"

"Why not?" His tone was mild. "It figures, doesn't it? You came to Philly to look for me. And here I am."

For some moments she stayed limp. Then, gradually, her shoulders straightened. She seemed to be getting a grip on herself. Her eyes narrowed just a little, as she went on looking at the silver-handled switchblade in his hand. She said, "That's Oscar's knife—?"

He nodded.

"Where is Oscar?" she asked. "Where's Coley?"

"They're dead." He pressed the button on the handle and the blade flicked out. It glimmered red with Oscar's blood and Coley's blood. He said, "It's a damn shame. They wouldn't be dead if they'd let me alone."

Hilda didn't say anything. She gave a little shrug, as though to indicate there was nothing she could say. He told himself it didn't make sense to wait any longer and the thing to do was put the knife in her heart. He wondered if the knife was sharp enough to cut through ice.

He took a forward step, then stopped. He wondered what was holding him back. Maybe he was waiting for her to break, to fall on her knees and beg for mercy.

But she didn't kneel and she didn't plead. Her voice was matter-of-fact as she said, "I'm wondering if we can make a deal."

It caught him off balance. He frowned slightly. "What kind of deal?"

"Fair trade," she said. "You give me a break and I'll give you Riker."

He changed the frown to a dim smile. "I've got him anyway. It's a cinch he's upstairs sound asleep."

"That's fifty percent right," she said. "He's a very light sleeper. Especially lately, since he heard you were out of Quentin."

He widened the smile. "In Quentin I learned to walk on tip-toe. There won't be any noise."

"There's always noise when you break down a door."

The frown came back. "You playing it shrewd?"

"I'm playing it straight," she said. "He keeps the door locked. Another thing he keeps is a .38 under his pillow."

He slanted his head just a little. "You expect me to buy that?"

"You don't have to buy it. I'm giving it to you."

He began to see what she was getting at. He said, "All right, thanks for the freebee. Now tell me what you're selling."

"A key," she said. "The key to his room. He has one and I have one. I'll sell you mine at bargain rates. All I want is your promise."

He didn't say anything.

She shrugged and said, "It's a gamble on both sides. I'll take a chance that you'll keep your word and let me stay alive, You'll be betting even-money that I'm telling the truth."

He smiled again. He saw she was looking past him, at the kitchen door. He said, "So the deal is, you give me the key to his room and I let you walk out that door."

"That's it." She was gazing hungrily at the door. Her lips scarcely moved as she murmured, "Fair enough?"

"No," he said. "It needs a tighter contract."

Her face was expressionless. She held her breath.

He let her hold it for awhile, and then he said, "Let's do it so there's no gamble. You get the key and I'll follow you upstairs. I'll be right in back of you when you walk into the room. I'll have the blade touching your spine."

She blinked a few times.

"Well?" he said.

She reached into a flap of the bottle-green velvet and took out a door-key. Then she turned slowly and started out of the kitchen. He moved in close behind her and followed the platinum blonde hair and elegant torso going through the small dining-room and the parlor and toward the dimly-lit stairway. He came up at her side as they climbed the stairs, the knifeblade scarcely an inch away from the shimmering velvet that covered her ribs.

They reached the top of the stairs and she pointed to the door of the front bedroom. He let the blade touch the velvet and his voice was a whisper saying, "Slow and quiet. Very quiet."

Then again he moved behind her. They walked slowly toward the bedroom door. The blade kissed the velvet and it told her to use the key with a minimum of sound. She put the key in the lock and there was no sound as she turned the key. There was only a slight clicking sound as the lock opened. Then no sound while she opened the door.

They entered the room and he saw Riker in the bed. He saw the brown wavy hair and there was some grey in it along the temples. In the suntanned face there were wrinkles and lines of dissipation and other lines that told of too much worry. Riker's eyes were shut tightly and it was the kind of slumber that rests the limbs but not the brain.

Ken thought, *He's aged a lot in nine years; it used to be mostly muscle and now it's mostly fat.*

Riker was, curled up, his knees close to his paunch. He had his shoes off but otherwise he was fully dressed. He wore a silk shirt and a hand-painted necktie, his Jacket was dark grey cashmere and his slacks were pale grey high-grade flannel. He had on a pair of argyle socks that must have set him back at least twenty dollars. On the wrist of his left hand there was a platinum watch to match the large star-emerald he wore on his little finger. On the third finger of his left hand he had a three-karat diamond. Ken was looking at the expensive clothes and the jewelry and thinking, *He travels first-class, he really rides the gravy train.*

It was a bitter thought and it bit deeper into Ken's brain. He said to himself, *Nine years ago this man of distinction pistol-whipped your skull and left you for dead. You've had nine years in Quentin and he's had the sunshine, the peaches-and-cream, the thousands of nights with the extra-lovely Mrs Riker while you slept alone in a cell —*

He looked at the extra-lovely Mrs Riker. She stood motionless at the side of the bed and he stood beside her with the switchblade aiming at her velvet-sheathed flesh. She was looking at the blade and waiting for him to aim it at Riker, to put it in the sleeping man and send it in deep.

But that wasn't the play. He smiled dimly to let her know he had something else in mind.

Riker's left hand dangled over the side of the bed and his right hand rested on the pillow. Ken kept the knife aimed at Hilda as he reached toward the pillow and then under the pillow. His fingers touched metal. It was the barrel of a revolver and he got a two-finger hold on it and eased it out from under the pillow. The butt came into his palm and his middle finger went through the trigger-guard and nestled against the back of the guard, not touching the trigger.

He closed the switchblade and put it in his pocket. He stepped back and away from the bed and said, "Now you can wake up your husband."

She was staring at the muzzle of the .38. It wasn't aiming at anything in particular.

"Wake him up," Ken murmured. "I want him to see his gun in my hand. I want him to know how I got it."

Hilda gasped and it became a sob and then a wall and it was a hook of sound that awakened Riker. At first he was looking at Hilda. Then he saw Ken and he sat up very slowly, as though he was something made of stone and ropes were pulling him up. His eyes were riveted to Ken's face and he hadn't yet noticed the .38. His hand crept down along the side of the pillow and then under the pillow.

There was no noise in the room as Riker's hand groped for the gun. Some moments passed and then there was sweat on Riker's forehead and under his lip and he went on searching for the gun and suddenly he seemed to realize it wasn't there. He focused on the weapon in Ken's hand and his body began to quiver. His lips scarcely moved as he said, "The gun—the gun—"

"It's yours," Ken said. "Mind if I borrow it?"

Riker went on staring at the revolver. Then very slowly his head turned and he was staring at Hilda. "You," he said. "You gave it to him."

"Not exactly," Ken said. "All she did was tell me where it was."

Riker shut his eyes very tightly, as though he was tied to a rack and it was pulling him apart.

Hilda's face was expressionless. She was looking at Ken and saying, "You promised to let me walk out—"

"I'm not stopping you," he said. Then, with a shrug and a dim smile, "I'm not stopping anyone from doing what they want to do." And he slipped the gun into his pocket.

Hilda started for the door. Riker was up from the bed and lunging at her, grabbing her wrist and hurling her across the room. Then Riker lunged again, and his hands reached for her throat as she tried to get up from the floor. Hilda began to make gurgling sounds but the noise was drowned in the torrent of insane screaming that came from Riker's lips. Riker choked her until she died. When Riker realized she was dead his screaming became louder and he went on choking her.

Ken stood there, watching it happen. He saw the corpse flapping like a rag-doll in the clutching hands of the screaming madman. He thought, *Well, they wanted each other, and now they got each other.*

He walked out of the room and down the hall and down the stairs. As he went out of the house he could still hear the screaming. On Spruce, walking toward Eleventh, he glanced back and saw a crowd gathering outside the house and then he heard the sound of approaching sirens. He waited there and saw the police-cars stopping in front of the house, the policemen rushing in with drawn guns. Some moments later he heard the shots and he knew that the screaming man was trying to make a getaway. There was more shooting and suddenly there was no sound at all. He knew they're be carrying two corpses out of the house.

He turned away from what was happening back there, walked along the curb toward the sewer-hole on the corner, took Riker's gun from his pocket and threw it into the sewer. In the instant that he did it, there was a warm sweet taste in his mouth. He smiled, knowing what it was. Again he could hear Tillie saying, "Revenge is black pudding."

Tillie, he thought. And the smile stayed on his face as he walked north on Eleventh. He was remembering the feeling he'd had when he'd kissed her. It was the feeling of wanting to take her out of that dark cellar, away from the loneliness and the opium. To carry her upward toward the world where they had such things as clinics, with plastic specialists who repaired scarred faces.

The feeling hit him again and he was anxious to be with Tillie and he walked faster.

Other Crime and Horror Classics available from Millipede Press